Nightfall

Dawn's End Book 1

Bonnie Ferrante

Nightfall (Dawn's End Book 1)

ISBN 978-0-9880530-9-0

Dedication

For my husband, Fred, who taught me to believe in

happily-ever-after.

Prologue

"Since the heart of Man is deceitful above all things, therefore for him that would truly know himself, . . . take notice . . . of his usual Dreams, there being scarce anything that more discovers the Secret bent of our minds and inclinations."

Thomas Tryon, *A Treatise of Dreams and Visions* (London, Second Ed. 1695), pp. 6-7, 57.

Chapter One—The Watcher

Like a tabby on a window sill, Nicole Newman stretched her lean body across the large gray boulder. The sun ignited the red highlights in her long, dark hair. She sighed and adjusted her hips. The pond lapped against the bulrushes, like a cat's tongue in a saucer of milk. A feline tongue. She held that image in her mind. It was oddly arousing. It had been so long since she had allowed herself to think such thoughts, but lately . . . .

Lately, her dreams were confusing, a jumble, but she often woke filled with yearning. Maybe it was time to let go of this self-imposed seclusion. However, the thought of dating again, getting to know a man—trusting, loving him— seemed overwhelming. Dreaming was so much easier than the real thing. So much easier than acting, doing, being. She felt like a mannequin tossed into a dark trunk, the lid shut and locked. Her sense of humor was suffocating along with her hopes.

Nicole had been coming here for a while, hoping to restart her engines. Spring was her favorite time of the year. She loved the way the pale, perfect tree buds unfurled, unblemished by insect or weather. The way the greens darkened from celery to forest-ranger green. She noted the growth of marsh marigolds, pitcher plants, and blue flags. She winced when the mosquitoes hatched and cheered the arrival of the dragonflies. No matter how long, how cold, or how brutal the winter had been, spring always returned. Out of darkness and death, life was reborn.

The colors and sounds around Nicole became muted. The smells of earth, pond plants, and wild creatures faded. Like a canoe carried downstream, Nicole floated into blissful, vulnerable sleep. The sunshine enveloped her like a lover's arms.

Beyond the cattails, beyond the swamp grass and brush, dark eyes studied her. The hidden eyes shifted, their owner moving upwind. He sniffed, smelling the scent of her feminine body below that of marsh and animal. He licked his lips. She was beautiful, far more beautiful than she realized. Soft, sensual, with a hidden core of strength. Wounded, but ready to heal. In his hands, could she awaken that strength and courage? Could he reignite the spark within?

It was not the first time his eyes had studied her. Today, his dark eyes edged closer, closer, closer than ever before. The dark one judged her potential to fulfill his needs, to react according to his purposes. He ignored spring blossoming around him. His mind was filled with thoughts of decay, ruin, and death, and the power within this beautiful woman.

Nicole did not seem aware that the forest held its own watcher. He was oblivious to the natural beauty around him, drawn instead to the delicate treasure stretched out on the rock. She had filled his mind for weeks, and now he was slowly seeping into hers as well.

The dark one nodded. He would enter her dreams, her mind, and her soul. He would bend her to his will.

She dreamed of a dark bird. The cormorant slid blackly toward her. He grew in size, his torso widening into the shape of a man's, wide-shouldered, slim-waisted, rippled with abdominal muscles. His powerful legs thickened and lengthened. His expanding shadow blanketed her. Nicole's breathing increased; she arched toward him. He stood over her, a dark angel, an incubus. Wings outstretched, his feathers mutated into hands. Nicole reached out to meet his fingers, then jerked back when his nails transformed into claws. She looked up as the light fell upon his face. His dark eyes summoned, commanded. His beak receded into lips. His smile revealed thin sharp fangs. He hissed.

Nicole snapped awake, trembling. She took deep, slow breaths, steadying herself. *Whoa, I have to cut back on the chocolate,* she thought. *It's making me have crazy dreams.*

The park seemed overly quiet. The shadows had lengthened. Water lapped like an eerie heartbeat. She swung her legs off the stone and stood. She had the feeling everyone had left the park, and, yet, there was an uncomfortable sense of . . . . It was time to leave. Nicole hurried toward her car.

The dark eyes blinked, fighting back disappointment. No matter. She would be back. Next time, he would have his chance. He had been planning for a long time. He had chosen her, and he was ready. She would come to him of her own free will.

Chapter Two—Contact

Nicole rinsed out the cup and wandered into the living room. It had been a long day at work. She felt tired and bored. She was sick of computers, carpet dust, artificial smiles, and the constant buzz of customers and their bizarre questions.

"Miss, do you think I could get this book with a different color cover?"

"Miss, I read this book, and I really don't like the ending. Could I exchange it for one I'll like?"

"I heard this book was really good, but do you have one just like it without so many words?"

At times, she was positive she was being punked, but, no, it was just another day in the life of a bookstore drone. Since "the breakup," Nicole had realized her life was Dull with a capital "D."

On the end table sat a framed photograph of her on graduation day. Nicole picked it up. Her blue eyes looked sad instead of proud. Her full lips wore a slight frown. Her face was pale, making the freckles all the more noticeable. She had not even wanted to go to her graduation, but her father insisted. They had already paid for the gown rental. Nicole thought her father would be more understanding, considering his own past.

Randy and Nicole had broken up less than two weeks before graduation. Thinking back, Nicole suspected she was still in a state of shock when the photograph was taken.

She had expected to be with Randy at graduation. She envisioned Randy with his arm around her, tall and lean, his mussed blonde hair falling in his steel-gray eyes, his smile wide. Sometimes she missed that smile. Sometimes she hated herself for being fooled by it. Sometimes she wanted to wipe it off his face with a street-wise bitch slap.

Randy had given her an engagement ring and then cheated on her, right under her nose. The girl, Andrea, lived a block away. Andrea was a cliché, empty-headed and large-breasted. Nicole wondered if Randy had stopped by to visit Andrea after dropping her off at home the night of their engagement.

Nicole was accepted at three universities, but she attended none. She had applied to business programs, at her parents' insistence, and she felt secretly relieved that the broken engagement gave her a reprieve. Although she was capable enough for business, it left her feeling unfulfilled.

Months passed as she became more and more withdrawn. A few guys from high school and the book store had asked her out. But she always found an excuse to say no. Even Carmen, her best friend since grade school, hardly ever called anymore. Below the heartbreak lay a whole lot of humiliation and self-loathing. How could she have been so gullible? To think she had given herself to that pig. For a while, she worried he might have passed an STD on to her, but, fortunately, only her heart had been damaged.

Just an Emotionally Transmitted Disease, she thought.

Nicole put down the photograph. She needed to get out. Moping wasn't doing any good. She didn't know what to do with herself. The only time her brain stopped buzzing with "what if's" was when she lost herself in a book. Adventure, mystery, science fiction, fantasy, and Shakespeare's plays were the only things she read now. Realistic fiction was just too . . . well . . . realistic. And romance, ugh! She'd rather stick a fork in her eye than read about love.

Dad was in Vancouver on business, trying to close some big sales deal. Her stepmother, Gloria, would be working late, piling on the billable hours. Nicole usually didn't leave a note when she went out anyway. She worked irregular shifts, and her stepmother and dad were seldom home. She was embarrassed to still be living with them. She had expected to have moved in with the love of her life by this point. Still, she was a long way from living in a rundown apartment with a dozen cats. It would take twelve cats right now to distract her. Or maybe just one. She had considered getting another cat after Whiskers had died, but Randy had objected. He had said, "Cats shed, scratch, and spray. A cat is more trouble than he's worth." She would have paid to watch one scratch and spray that two-timer right now. Talk about more trouble than he's worth.

Get a grip, she chided herself as she opened the refrigerator door. It was well-stocked with microwavable dinners, though she preferred to make fresh salads. Everyone in her family was coming and going at different times. She couldn't remember the last time the three of them had sat down together for a family meal.

She brushed her hair, slipped into jeans and a sweatshirt, and drove to the pond. She climbed onto her favorite rock and tried to daydream. She missed being with a man, going on dates, exchanging little gifts. But how could she miss a relationship that never really existed? It had obviously been a farce, at least on Randy's side. This last month, Randy's handsome face had been replaced in her daydreams by that of an indistinct dark man. He seemed like a character from one of her novels, but she couldn't quite place him.

Dark eyes watched Nicole. From the woods, dark hands moved aside the leaves. He had been checking for her throughout the day. Hoping for her return. The eyes narrowed when she climbed off the rock and kicked at the grass with the toe of her shoe. Was she about to leave? Time was running out. He would have to act now.

The dark watcher edged along the bush by the pond, keeping Nicole in sight.

Enjoy this beautiful day, Nicole muttered to herself, trying to be positive and "in the moment." She scanned the pond, watching the water fowl dip and dive, sparkling drops flinging from their wings.

I refuse, refuse, refuse to think about Randy anymore, thought Nicole. *I've been a hopeless fool. It's time to get on with something real. So, why do I keep dreaming about this imaginary dark man? Someone with the power to command my attention and make me forget the past. To take my thoughts away from what a mess I've made of things.* She raised her voice to shout theatrically into the pond's silence. "Why can't you be real?"

"But I am," came a husky reply.

Nicole jumped, stumbling back into the rock. That voice was close by.

"Who's there?" she called into the shadowed woods.

"He of whom you speak. Such as we are made of, such we be." The voice was deep and masculine.

"Damn," she muttered. "There's some kind of freak playing Shakespeare in the bush." She raised her voice. "Step out where I can see you."

"Not yet," he replied. "Soon."

Irritated, Nicole raised her voice. "What do you mean not yet? Who are you? Quit playing games."

"This is no game," he replied. "I just want to talk with you. To be sure you are ready."

"For . . . what?" Nicole edged away from the rock, toward the path, spooked by the hidden speaker, uncomfortable with the possible meanings of his remark.

"To help me," he replied.

Nicole tensed. Ready to run. But where? The voice seemed to be coming from a different part of the woods now.

She would not show her fear. Was this a homeless man looking for a place to crash or some crazy person looking for a savior? He sounded as though he expected her to go somewhere with him. She would have to set him straight right away. "I have no intention of going anywhere with you. Don't try to take me."

"Not unless you want to," he said. "But you will want to."

Nicole clenched her fists. This was creepy and getting creepier. The voice kept shifting from place to place, as though she were in an echo chamber.

"Dawn's End awaits you," said the man. "The place of your dreams."

"My dreams are none of your damn business." She tried to sound confident and tough.

"Your dreams *are* my business. I gave them to you, Nicole."

Nicole's breath hissed through her teeth as she edged further down the path. "How do you know my name?"

"Do not be so afraid. I know you the way you know me. Through the dreams. When you dream, I see and hear the images. I send you mine. I am the dark man. The one you have been dreaming of."

Nicole frowned. "That's not possible!"

"Everything is possible. A woman who reads the books you do should keep her mind more open to the realms of fantastical possibilities." His voice was scolding. "Come with me, and I will show you that more is possible than you expect."

"Get away from me! I'm not going anywhere with you!" Nicole took a few quick steps and then halted as the man moved quickly across the edge of the woods, passing through the fading light. His features were hidden, but a sense of familiarity surged through her at the sight of him.

"Please listen," he said. He spoke soothingly, as though calming a temperamental child.

"Stay where you are, or I'll scream murder," warned Nicole.

A blue jay soared overhead and then landed beside her, startling her with its unusual proximity. It jerkily looked her up and down and then flew away.

"She'll never come," said a sharp, little, female voice. "She wouldn't be any good anyway."

"Who's that?" said Nicole. "Is there someone with you? Is that a child?"

"It is Larina," answered the dark man. "She does not think I have made the right choice. I disagree. Please listen. You do know me. I contacted you in your dreams. I spoke to you through the dark bird. But you would not listen. You were lost in mourning." His voice was hypnotic.

"She'll never understand," said Larina. "She's damaged. Hopeless. Hasn't got a clue what to do with herself."

Nicole felt a surge of anger at the repetition of her own opinion of herself.

"Trust me, Nicole," said the man. "I can open all the doors you have shut on yourself. Do you not feel crushed in such a small, cold space of life?"

Nicole bit her lip. She suddenly felt emotionally naked and did not like the sensation. "I thought *you* wanted *my* help," she snapped.

"We can help each other. It is a quest."

"A quest!" He had obviously been taking note of the kind of books she read. Sometimes she brought them to the pond. Or perhaps this was someone from the book store. One of the guys she had turned down.

The voice continued. "It is what you have always dreamed of."

"Uh-huh," muttered Nicole as she scanned the bushes trying to get a fix on his location.

"I'm not going to harm you, if that's what you think." He sounded insulted. "I'm here to ask for your help. I'm not crazy, and neither are you."

Nicole nodded, her hands unclenched. His voice was soothing, inviting.

"Now is your chance. Break out of the rut you are in. Live a real adventure. Get away from everything, so you can figure out what you really want. This is an opportunity you will never have again. Do not hide from life."

"So, why are you hiding yourself?" asked Nicole.

"Because I am not a handsome man, and that seems to be the only kind of man you will have anything to do with."

"What? That's not true," insisted Nicole, even as she thought his words over.

"I cannot wait forever. I have little time. There are restrictions, pressures. You do not know. This door will not be open for long. This opportunity will disappear, and you will never know what you have let slip away."

Nicole took a step back toward the pond. "What door?"

"I'm telling you," said Larina. "She'll fold at the first challenge. She has no depth. She's flighty and shallow."

Nicole clenched her teeth.

The dark man replied, "I do not think so, and it is my choice to make. Nicole, you should know this quest will take you beyond your normal world."

Nicole thought of her empty life and snorted. She barely felt capable of handling her job at the bookstore, never mind anything beyond her "normal world." Disconnected and disengaged, she was just going through the motions. She hardly saw her friends anymore; she'd lost herself. She did not want to go back to her depressing house, with her cheerful stepmother flitting in and out like a hummingbird on speed, forever trying to interest Nicole in activities. The boredom was killing her. One day, they'd find her dead on the kitchen floor, just like the cormorant she had found in the

11

road and tried to save. It had flown into a hydro line, fallen into traffic, and been injured. Even with the generous support of a veterinarian, it had died after nine months of futile care.

She, too, would be dead. Dead from dullness and despair. Her normal world sucked. She had to do something. Maybe this was the answer.

"I'm not going to trust some stranger who hides in the bushes," said Nicole. "No matter how bored I am. Show yourself, or I won't take you seriously. I have questions, and I want straight answers. Who are you? Where did you come from? What do you want with me?"

"Fair enough," said the man. "I will show you myself tomorrow and answer your questions."

"Why tomorrow? Why not now?"

"I will give you time to think about my offer to join me in Dawn's End. If you return tomorrow, ready for a journey through the woods with Larina and myself, I will show you my face. Bring whatever materials you will need for a journey overland by foot. If I convince you to join me, we can start immediately. If not, then all you have lost is a little time packing."

"Where's Dawn's End?" Nicole asked. "Is that in the park?"

"I will take you there and back safely, if you choose."

Nicole paused. The water lapped softly, the setting sun turning the surface copper. Trees rustled in the twilight wind, whispering possibilities. Night slowly spread over the pond like a cool, gray blanket. She felt her resistance draining away.

A seagull called, pulling her back to awareness. This man's voice was mesmerizing. Who knew how many women he had lulled into a false sense of security before taking them who knew where? She had to leave before she did something stupid and dangerous.

Perhaps if she played along he would let her get to her car. She would keep him talking as she slowly made her way to safety.

"Why me?" she asked. "I'm not the kind of woman to be picked for a quest. I'm not strong or clever or beautiful."

"I believe you to be all three," he replied.

Nicole smiled. Bizarre, but she felt flattered. *His voice is so familiar. Maybe I can figure it out tonight and surprise him tomorrow. Tomorrow! I am crazy. Writing on the wall and chanting dire prophecies, crazy. This is the last place I'll be tomorrow.*

"So, how important is this quest?" she asked, edging down the path.

"The future of my entire world depends upon it." His voice was sorrowful.

"Is it dangerous?"

He gave no reply. Nicole paused on the gravel. She strove to sound believable. "I just can't go running off and leave everything at a moment's notice."

"Just what, exactly, would you be leaving?"

She thought of her job. Filling orders, shelving books, waiting on customers who didn't know the title of the book they were searching for, or the author. Her high-powered stepmother driving her crazy. Her father, returning from every work trip hoping she'd found Mr. Right. Friends. What friends?

"Okay," she admitted. "You're right. I don't have much to leave. But I have to sleep on it, take time to think over your request. And I have to see you, face to face. No skulking about in the bush after dark."

"If you come tomorrow at the same time, with a decision to help me, I will face you. If you say no, I will leave and never speak to you again."

She felt oddly dejected at these words. "Will you be with me throughout the quest?"

"Every moment," he replied, filling Nicole with an unsettling and unexpected flush of excitement.

"I'll see you tomorrow, then," said Nicole as she turned down the path to the parking lot. Her heart rate increased. Would he truly let her leave? She wished she had paid better attention when Randy made her watch all those Jackie Chan and Jet Li movies.

Gloria was still out when she returned. The only sound in the house was the sound of the kitchen clock. Ticking her life away one second at a time. Unless she escaped. She had nothing to lose by going with the dark man. Strangely, now that she had left the darkening park, he did not seem so threatening. Instead, he piqued her curiosity, even her interest. *But it's too big a risk*, she thought. *Going off in the bush with someone I've never even met, or seen. I probably need to see a therapist. A therapist and a cop.*

That night, she dreamt of the pond. The dark man stood on the opposite shore. A cormorant crossed between them.

Black and beautiful, it glided closer to the quartz rock. Nicole sat up. She recognized the bird and marveled at its dexterity. The sunlight pulsed over the surface of the pond, in a duet of light and dark. The cormorant dived, surfaced further off, and dived again, making almost no sound. Nicole stretched out on her back listening to the low buzz of insects and the intermittent squawks of water fowl.

Suddenly, her perspective changed. The dark-eyed watcher stood by Nicole's side. She saw his forehead furrow, yet the rest of his features were a blur. Now, she saw herself through his eyes. He studied her pale chin, and her small nose sprinkled with freckles and burned from too much spring sunshine. She was very thin, with a slight scar on her bottom lip. He could snap her as easily as a twig in his powerful grip. But that was not what he wanted. He reached for her. Waves of heat surged from his dark, muscular body as he crushed her against his strong, hairy chest. He ran a hand down her back, clutching her left buttock in his hand as his rough tongue twirled around her ear, down her throat to her shoulder, and onto her breast. She realized she was naked and flushed with desire.

Slowly, silently, he crouched. His tongue trailed toward her stomach, then lower. A shiver raced through her body. He spoke to her, but she could not understand the words, only the meaning. She smiled and nodded. He stood up, and she took his powerful hand.

All night, her dreams were filled with joy and excitement. The dark man dominated them all, protecting her and helping her strengthen. She woke refreshed and had to concentrate on altering her voice when she phoned in sick. Today, she would prepare for her journey.

Journey where? She hadn't asked anything about Dawn's End. She searched online maps but, although she found

Dawn's Pass, Dawn's Lane, Dawn's Trail, Dawn's Road, and Dawn's Way, Dawn's End was not listed. Strange? A non-existent dark man inviting her to a non-existent place. Maybe none of what she remembered from the pond the day before had actually happened. Maybe she had slipped into a crack between her fantasies and her monotonous world. Had she lost her grip on reality? So what if she had? At least she had woken up feeling excited about her day. She was going on a quest. It felt right. Like on the opening night of a play, she felt as though she had been rehearsing for this her whole life.

Nicole dusted off her packsack. No use bringing a suitcase. Dawn's End must be the name of an abandoned village or mine site no longer listed on the map.

The packsack had never been used. Her old one had fallen apart. She'd purchased a state-of-the-art backpack, assuming hiking and travel would be lifelong interests she would share with Randy. The backpack now smelled of storage. Inside, she stuffed a first-aid kit, a raincoat, a thick Canadian Wildlife Federation hoodie, snap-together warm-up pants, underwear, dried food, a bottle of water, bug repellent, matches, a flashlight, vitamins, a whistle, and an assortment of personal toiletries. She wished she had some water purification tablets, but it was too late to buy them now.

She wondered what she should write to her stepmother. What could she say? She remembered Carmen was going camping with friends this weekend and scribbled an evasive note about joining her. Carmen would be out of cell phone range so Gloria couldn't check out her story, and Nicole doubted she would bother even if she could. Her stepmother had been pushing her to get out more. That was about the extent of her involvement in Nicole's world.

Nicole did decide to burn one bridge behind her. She dug out paper and an envelope and wrote a letter of resignation to the manager of the book store where she worked. It would save him the trouble of firing her when she didn't show up for work tomorrow. No great loss. A part-time job she hated was probably worse than being unemployed.

She'd never wanted the job in the first place. She'd wanted to be a flutist, but her father said she lacked the required talent. Business, not music, was where the money was. Randy had told her to keep up with her music studies anyway; maybe she could give lessons. Randy. She wondered if he was happy with Andrea. Or was he already telling the same lies to Andrea that he had told to her?

Nicole felt her confidence fading as she slipped on her warm hoodie. Her enthusiasm dwindled further as she drove to the park. She wasn't used to making these kinds of decisions.

As she parked, she noted the presence of two vehicles. A young couple approached, entered their truck, and drove away. Nicole slipped on her packsack and locked her Sunfire.

Dusk sprinkled over the park like pepper as she walked down the path. She passed the last visitors heading toward the parking lot, a couple in their forties with an adolescent daughter. They looked curiously at her, probably wondering why she would be heading into the park so late.

A young goose glided over the pond, sporadically dipping for roots. It bobbed to the surface, its little splash the only sound. Nicole climbed onto the quartz rock and waited. Slowly, her mind cleared, as though she woke from a long dream.

Was last night a hallucination? Perhaps she was having a breakdown. Perhaps they would find her in the morning, smearing mud on her face and talking to imaginary people. Was the dark man real? If so, who was he? A crazy person, too? Perhaps a dangerous person. A criminal who hid in the woods watching for lonely women. This whole Dawn's End idea could be a trick, an attempt to lure her away from the safety of her home. Perhaps he planned to make her his personal slave. Chain her in his basement. The only thing that would make this more classic was her being barefoot and wearing a skimpy night shirt.

What am I doing? Nicole thought. *No one will even miss me. I've put myself in the perfect position to disappear. I've got to get out of here!*

She leaped to her feet. A passing blue jay startled her, interrupting her flight. "Ready to go?" The man's deep voice came from the woods.

"No!" shrieked Nicole. Then, realizing it would not be advantageous to appear hysterical, she continued speaking in a more normal tone. "I've changed my mind."

"Why?"

"No reason. I just don't want to go." She edged down the path, her steps slow and careful, and her eyes scanning the bushes.

"I told you she was useless." It was Larina's voice.

Who is Larina, Nicole thought, *and why does her voice sound half-child, half-woman?* Nicole didn't care what Larina said. She was concentrating on each step, on reaching her car as quickly as possible without drawing an attack.

"Are you sure that is what you wish?" asked the dark man.

"Yes," said Nicole, her steps quickening. She hurried toward the parking lot, shoulders tense, expecting a man's hand to grab her any second. Nothing happened.

Street lights shone on the lot, which was now empty of all cars but hers. A cool breeze blew. Night had settled in.

As she hurried across the pavement, Nicole heard a shuffle behind her Sunfire. A muscle tensed in her chest in a spasm of pain; her heart thumped. Eyes sweeping the lot, she paused. She remembered the key was hidden under the front bumper. She cursed her lack of foresight.

A low growl reverberated from the other side of the car. It wasn't the dark man; it was a wild animal. A massive shaggy shadow rose above the hood. A large predator! Nicole recalled stories of people mauled by huge black bears, dragged into the woods to a brutal death. Eaten alive! Ever since the spring bear hunt had been cancelled, the bruins had become bolder and more aggressive. She had jumped from the frying pan into the fire.

She knew better than to run. She froze, trying to remember all the rules about encountering a bear—make a lot of noise, look big, move slowly while keeping an eye on the animal. When the animal growled loudly again, she backed away. With a primeval roar, an enormous, black body lunged toward her.

Nicole screamed, spun around, and raced back down the path. There was no way to stop a charging bear without a weapon. Her only slim hope was to find refuge. The animal pursued, its claws churning up the gravel. A few meters before the pond, Nicole left the path in search of a tree to climb. White and black birch and rough maples loomed within reach. She scanned their trunks for a foothold. Useless! She tore into the blackness of forest.

Branches whipped against her body. She would never be able to outrun a bear. A stiff limb poked her face just beneath her eye. Her breath came in harsh, dry gasps. She stumbled over stones, mounds, roots, and fallen wood until her foot caught on something. She went down. Hard. A sharp pain shot through her knee. She locked her hands defensively over the back of her neck and curled into a ball, expecting the bear's leap any second. She kneeled, panting, her body shaking and sweaty. The woods were silent. How could she have lost it? Bears could outrun a horse.

She listened, trying to quiet her breathing. Finally, she rolled over to a sitting position. She waited until the trembling stopped, then dug out her flashlight and flicked it on. The white beam arched back and forth, silhouetting an entanglement of growth in the ghostly quiet forest. The strangely gnarled tree trunks were discomforting. Which way was the path? Her leg throbbed and burned. She tasted vomit in the back of her throat.

She was lost. The only sensible thing was to sit it out until morning. It seemed a good time to start being sensible. What had she been thinking? What had she done?

Chapter Three—Jiminy Cricket

Tucked into a windbreak between two coniferous trees, Nicole tried to wait patiently until the sun rose. She shivered, hugging her knees tightly to her chest, and then remembered the extra clothing in her pack. She slipped on the hooded sweatshirt and the raincoat over that, and then snapped on her warm-up pants. Still, her feet were cold. She considered starting a fire, but she was afraid of injuring herself in the dark again looking for firewood. Besides, she might attract the bear or cougar or whatever beast had chased her. Luckily, the night temperature was not as cold as it would have been a month earlier. At least it was not hypothermia weather.

She waited for the onslaught of mosquitoes. She knew moose dashed heedlessly into oncoming traffic trying to flee the relentless bloodsuckers. She tightened her hood and tucked her hands into her sleeves. Nothing. Not a single buzz.

Once, she thought she heard a snap of brush to the right. Quickly switching on the flashlight, she pointed the beam in the direction of the sound but saw nothing. A little later, the beam shone on a pair of small eyes. A stoic blue jay blinked in response. She dozed fitfully, for only a few minutes at a time. By dawn, her nerves were as brittle as three-year-old kindling.

When the sun rose, she realized nothing looked familiar. The sky was gray and dismal. The forest was dry, with only a light morning dew. But, if it rained, she would be miserable. She removed her extra clothes and stuffed them back into the packsack. She would generate heat hiking. Sweat could dampen her clothes, causing problems if the weather cooled.

Eventually, someone would notice her abandoned car, and Carmen would return from camping without her, but it would be a long time before they searched the woods. She had no idea how far she had run. After climbing a ridge for a better look of the landscape, she searched for the usual landmarks, Mount McKay, Mount Baldy, and Candy Mountain, but the countryside was completely unfamiliar. How was this possible? Survival advice said to stay put, but she felt as though she was jumping out of her skin just sitting there.

She looked at her wrist. Her watch was gone, probably torn off in her frantic flight. She hiked back and checked the ground around where she had removed her clothes, but she saw nothing.

I can't stand another night in these woods, she thought. *The mosquitoes are bound to show up, if not the bear, and my supplies won't last long.*

A small drink of water and some dried apricots served as breakfast. She would save as much food as possible. Stretch it out just in case. Her rumbling stomach complained as she staggered stiffly to her feet. Her torn knee protested. She should make a fire. That would attract attention. She would build it so high no predator would dare approach her.

What if she was close to the trail? It would be stupid to spend an unnecessary night in the bush. She decided to walk for a while in the direction she thought she had come from. She needed to stretch anyway. If she couldn't find her way out in a couple of hours, then she would bunker down and build some kind of shelter.

Threading her way carefully through the brush and trees, Nicole noticed a curious absence of the usual insects. The mosquitoes had stayed away all night. That surprised her since the days had been warm enough to hatch the eggs. People in the bush ran themselves to exhaustion in the north woods, trying to escape the persistent vampires. Where were the dragonflies, the butterflies, and the clouds of black flies?

She walked for hours, pausing only for a drink of water and a granola bar. Still, nothing looked familiar.

The trees seemed different, too. Their branches and leaves were more droopy than usual, and the forest floor was covered with a vine she had not previously encountered. Coniferous trees were unusually scarce in this section of the woods; the surroundings lacked the rugged appearance generally associated with the northern Canadian Shield. Although Nicole had felt cold last night, the temperature should have been much colder.

Her musings were interrupted by a familiar smell—a campfire!

Controlling the urge to run, Nicole stumbled toward the smoke. She staggered into the clearing, fully expecting to see a cluster of men drinking coffee. What she saw instead brought her to a surprised halt.

No one was in the clearing when she entered it. A circle of stones enclosed a tidy campfire on which sat a brass pot, and a neat pile of wood sat nearby. Someone had cleared the plants away from around the fire and prepared a seating area with a blanket. On the blanket rested a wooden scoop and a small bowl. A tidy respite in the middle of nowhere.

Nicole called out. "Hello. Is anybody here?" Her shout was swallowed in the stillness. She called again. Nothing.

The clearing looked like a camp for one person. She assumed that person would be back soon. She approached the fire. The warm crackle beckoned like a lover's arms. Now that she had stopped moving, she realized it was dusk. *What is going on?* she thought. She had been grateful for the lengthening days in spring, but now the sun seemed to have reverted to winter behavior. *I've probably just lost track of time,* she thought.

With an exhausted sigh, she shrugged off her pack and collapsed onto the blanket. She took out her mirror and first-aid kit. Examining her face, she carefully rubbed her scratches clean with a cotton ball and water and then coated them with ointment. One scratch was dangerously close to her left eye. She rolled up her pant leg and cleaned and bandaged her knee.

Peeking into the pot, Nicole discovered a savory vegetable stew. It smelled delicious. She thought the owner would not begrudge her a little, considering the circumstances. Northerners followed a code in the woods, caring for each other in distress, knowing that, with a change of weather, accident of circumstance, or trick of the human body, they could be in need themselves the next time.

When she picked up the bowl, Nicole found a gold bracelet inside. Its wide band was embellished with tiny fanciful engravings of animals and mythical creatures. The dominant figure was a side view of a leaping leopard, its eye a black crystal. Nicole traced the shapes with her fingers, the closely bitten nails contrasting with the band's elegance. She was astonished that anyone would leave such expensive-looking jewelry lying around. It was so attractive she could not resist trying it on. Hinged in the middle, the bracelet snapped into a perfect fit on her wrist. She admired it for a few seconds, but then, regretfully, attempted to remove it.

It would not unlatch! Nicole struggled frantically, but the band would neither unclasp nor slide over her hand. Embarrassed, she abandoned her efforts. The owner would have to show her how to release the catch. She pulled her sleeve over it. She did not want the returning camper's first impression of her to be that of a thief. She would explain first and reveal the obstinate bracelet afterward.

After a restorative meal of the thick stew, Nicole lay back to await the return of the mysterious traveler. Although she felt trepidation about encountering another stranger, it seemed the best alternative. The treetops swayed hypnotically, playing hide-and-seek with the sun, sending dappled light dancing across her face. The fire crackled as she threw on another log, sparks streaking upward. Her satisfied stomach and a sense of security drew over her like a charm, lulling her to sleep. She curled up on the blanket as exhaustion gave way to slumber.

A bright blue jay flew down and landed beside the blanket. The bird ambled around her sleeping figure, thrusting its head forward and back with each step. It halted by Nicole's face, head cocked. Its bright little eyes stared at the wisp of reddish hair lying across the young woman's cheek and the worry wrinkle on the bridge of her nose.

Nicole began dreaming of the bird man again. In the dream, his feathers tickled over her skin like angel's kisses. His voice was the voice of the man in the park, no longer pleading, but softly sensual and deep with arousal. His breath seared against her cheek as he nuzzled her. She arched against him moaning, feeling his manhood hard and hot against her thigh.

"I'm ready, for you, for all of it," she whispered.

Nicole shifted in her sleep. Immediately, the jay took flight, heading toward the woods south of the clearing. Waking with a start, Nicole checked the position of the sun. She had been asleep for hours. But she still felt tired, muddle-headed.

The fire still burned! The last log should have been reduced to smoldering coals by now.

She checked the wood pile. Sure enough, it looked smaller. Someone had fed the fire. A small hard loaf of bread, studded with an unfamiliar nut, was in her bowl. Someone had come into the clearing and gone again, leaving her asleep.

Nicole considered the meaning of this behavior. The camper couldn't be gone for good. He would have to return for his belongings. After all, she was still wearing the valuable bracelet. The mysterious camper's kindness in providing food, warmth, and rest overcame her apprehension. He must have realized how exhausted she was and let her sleep. Perhaps his vehicle was only a short walk away.

"Hello," she called. "Is anyone there?"

"Yes." A deep voice answered from the woods.

"Thank you for all your help." Nicole strode in the direction of the voice. "I'm afraid I'm lost, and I've had a horrible night." She reached the edge of the forest, but no one was in sight. "Where are you?"

"Please sit and eat while we talk." This time, the voice came from the opposite side of the clearing. "Have some bread. I have to gather more firewood."

Nicole frowned, but returned to the fire. She sat again in the clear spot and bit into the bread. It seemed to be her week to meet weirdos. Why was he alone in the woods anyway? It wasn't hunting season. A poacher! She was probably still within the park boundaries. Open fires were not even allowed here. He was probably keeping his face hidden so she wouldn't be able to identify him to the authorities. Still, he hadn't shown any malice.

No. That didn't make sense. A poacher wouldn't leave a gold bracelet lying around, except by accident. A thief! Hiding out from the cops? She took a deep breath. She was getting paranoid. She hadn't slept enough. She'd had a terrible scare last night when she had suddenly realized she was about to head into the woods with some hidden man, as though she had awakened from a dream to find herself in a nightmare. Being hunted by a bear had just been the icing on the cake. She rubbed her eyes, trying to clear her tangled thoughts. Too much adrenaline and not enough sleep had left her befuddled.

Cooperating with the camper, or whoever he was, was probably her best strategy. She'd figure out what was going on soon enough. If she cooperated, she was sure he would at least point her in the direction of home.

"This is delicious," she said aloud. "An unusual bread."

"I am glad you like it, Nicole."

Nicole froze, the bread now a dry lump in her mouth. He knew her name! That voice! The man in the park! The man who had almost convinced her to go with him into the woods. She had fallen right back into his grasp. Had he been following her this whole time? Herding her like prey! She jumped to her feet and reached for her packsack.

"Please do not run again," he pleaded. "You will only hurt yourself more. I swear I am not going to harm you."

Nicole hesitated. Her knee throbbed. She could not face bolting through the woods again. He was right; she probably would only injure herself. She obviously couldn't outrun him.

She looked at her wrist. "Is this your bracelet? I couldn't get it off. When you get it back, will you let me go?"

"Go where?"

She sank to the blanket. Her eyes stung with suppressed tears. "What is going on? Where am I? What do you want?"

"Oh, sob, sob," said a female voice. "Poor little bunny."

"Be quiet, Larina," admonished the man. "She has good reason to be upset. Nicole, please do not go charging off into the woods. Next time, your injuries could be worse than a torn knee. Don't cry. It's all right, really, I would never harm you. You are invaluable."

"I'm *not* crying." Nicole took a shuddery breath. "How did you know about my knee? Did you see me bandage it?" Nicole felt the hair on her neck stand up at the thought. How long had he watched her?

"I saw when you fell. I was right behind you."

"You saw the animal chasing me? What was it? A bear?"

"No."

"A cougar? It seemed sleeker than a bear, like a cougar."

He chuckled. "Something like that. Actually, it was me."

"You! Why?" Her voice rose. "You said you wouldn't harm me."

"I never will. It was unintentional. I am not proud of the ruse, but I was desperate. When I saw you leaving in such a panic, I thought you might stop coming to the pond. I would never have the opportunity to see you again. You need to understand. There is not much time. I need your help now."

"My help! You terrorize me beyond endurance, get me lost in this God-forsaken bush, cause me to almost blind myself and break a leg in the dark, and then you want my *help*! Why the hell should I help you?"

"I did not know you could get so angry." He sounded intrigued.

"I can if I have a good reason, and you've given me plenty," Nicole shouted. "Who the hell are you? And no bullshit! No more lies."

"I did not lie." He sounded insulted. "I am exactly who I say I am. Let yourself see. Stop shouting, and listen to your inner self. You slept just now. You dreamt of me."

Nicole blushed. "Lucky guess, considering what happened last night."

"I always know what you dream. Awake, you confuse me. But when you sleep, you truly live. I follow you better in your dreams than in your waking state."

Nicole scoffed. "Tell me something from my dream."

"I'm ready, for you, for all of it."

Nicole was thunderstruck. "It's not possible."

"You are wearying. I have told the truth. I need your help to fulfill a quest."

"I might have talked in my sleep. How do I know you didn't hypnotize me and plant that dream in my mind? Maybe you're some kind of mentalist. I think that's what you did last night. That's how you got me back to the park. Maybe I've just popped my cork, and you're not even here. Maybe *I'm* not. Maybe I've fallen down the rabbit hole."

"I think you are too large for a rabbit hole," he replied.

"Enough!" Larina's little voice screeched. "It's time *we* had a talk."

A flutter of wings heralded the arrival of a cocky blue jay. It landed in front of Nicole and strutted back and forth. "You are an exasperating woman."

The voice came from the bird's beak.

"Stop it!" shouted Nicole. "It's just another trick."

"For such a dreamer, you show little imagination." The bird ruffled its feathers indignantly. "I am no trick. I am Larina, girl of the forest and calia to the Alaric. Things you are too stupid to appreciate."

"Larina," chided the dark man.

"What is her problem anyway?" continued the blue jay. "All she's been doing is moping around and wanting something to change her life. Now that she has the chance, she gets hysterical. I knew she would be useless. She *is* damaged."

"Who asked you?" snapped Nicole. "God, I feel like I'm talking to Jiminy Cricket."

"Quit wasting our time," said Larina. "We cannot go back and forth to Dawn's End like it's a holiday trip. It is a world difficult and costly to enter."

"World? What are you, some kind of alien?" snickered Nicole.

"No, stupid girl, we are of the same earth as you, just not in it," said the jay.

"So, how'd you get into my world?" asked Nicole.

The dark man spoke. "The bracelet opens a hidden door."

"You mean this?" Nicole extended her arm.

"One like it," he said. "That one is for you, for the time being. I used mine to hold the door so you could enter Dawn's End."

"Enter? Your world?" Nicole's panic rose again. "Was that why the woods looked . . . off, somehow?"

30

"My bracelet will allow you to leave through the door as well. You agreed to help. I am holding you to it."

"I said I changed my mind." Nicole passed her hand across her forehead. She felt lightheaded. "Besides, I think you hypnotized me."

"Do not deny yourself this chance," said the man. "You need something to make you feel alive again. To feel strong. This will do you as much good as it will us."

"She's gutless," taunted Larina. "Gutless and empty."

Nicole ground her teeth. She wanted to believe she had somehow left the stifling monotony of her futureless life. That this man was truly providing her with an opportunity, a distraction. Yet, why had he frightened her so much? His deception infuriated her. She had had more than enough of deceptive men.

Still, she was sick of being rational and holding a brave face to the world. She felt like a starving seagull turning a bare fish bone over and over in hopes of finding something that wasn't there. What if this man was telling the truth? Would she regret throwing away this once-in-a-lifetime chance?

She had always felt, deep in her core, that there had to be more to the world than she saw with her modern eye. It wasn't that she had much choice in the matter anyway. She had no idea where she was. The best tactic would be to play along until she at least got her bearings.

"We can find someone better," said Larina. "Easily."

Nicole hated that snotty blue jay. She would show her. She'd go along with this for a while, just to see what it was about, and she'd keep her eyes open for a way home at the same time. Larina would be shocked at her resourcefulness and gumption.

"All right, I'll do it," said Nicole, half meaning it. "So, when are you going to show yourself?"

"Finish your meal," said the dark man. "We will start in the morning. I think you've had enough excitement for one day."

The shadows were long. A strangely short day for spring, but perhaps the days were different in Dawn's End, wherever the hell that was.

"I will keep the fire going," he said. "Larina and I will take turns keeping watch, just in case a real bear shows up."

Even though she was disoriented and frightened, Nicole did sleep. Her mind and body were drained from stress.

She awoke at first light. The fire was burning cheerily. Nicole wondered if he had slept in the woods all night and only warmed himself when building the fire. Probably afraid to frighten her off if he came too close. Served him right, being cold. Tricking her and chasing her. She would put on a cooperative face until she reached safety. She'd convince him she had accepted all this. If she was lucky, she might have a chance to wring that stupid bird's neck. She wondered how blue jay tasted with orange sauce. Blue jay under glass. How appetizing.

"Good morning!" she shouted.

There was a rustle at the edge of the clearing. Larina flew out of the woods, calling, "New day! New day!"

"Good morning," called the dark man. "Keep the fire going while I gather some food, please. I have no more supplies."

"I do," said Nicole.

"Save them for our journey," he said. "You'll need them then."

"Okay," said Nicole. "The nights are sure long here." She was hoping he would give some clue as to where they were.

"They will grow longer if we are not successful," he replied.

"They will? Why?"

There was no response. Evidently, he had gone in search of food. Nicole hoped he had more skill than she did. She was seriously hungry. She knew wintergreen and the leaf of a blue-beaded lily were safe. Sarsaparilla roots and Labrador tea leaves could be boiled for a drink. But she saw none of those plants around the clearing. Once she ran out of food, she'd be helpless. She wondered if she had passed out the first night and been transported to another country. Maybe chloroformed in her sleep. Perhaps more time had passed than she thought. She was not going to spend every minute helpless, ignorant, and panicked. She needed to get herself together.

Nicole sighed and adjusted her socks. She went into the bush for a private moment, then brushed her teeth and combed her hair. Whatever happened today, she was finished with panic. No more hysterics. That just drained her energy and focus. She needed to hold it together if she was going to get home in one piece.

Larina will be deeply disappointed, she thought. *What an irritating creature. How does the dark man stand her?*

"Well, what do we have here?" asked a gruff voice from the woods.

Alarmed at such a strange question coming from a new voice, Nicole remained silent. Into the clearing stepped three men. Each wore a jumpsuit made of dark green fabric with deep pile. Around their waists, they wore thick belts stuffed with sheathed daggers of various sizes and shapes. They carried bags slung over one shoulder. All had thin lips, light brown skin, and thickly matted shoulder-length hair. Nicole knew instinctively that none of the three was the dark man.

"Who are you?" she asked.

"Who am I?" mocked the largest man as they approached. His face was pockmarked and filthy. An old scar ran across part of his forehead, over his temple to his left ear, where the top piece of the lobe was missing. "Why, my brothers and me are to be your traveling companions, pretty lady. I am Gaul."

The shortest man grabbed her arm roughly and searched for weapons. His hands were grimy, his nails black and broken. Nicole squirmed as he ran his hands over her breasts.

"What'sa matter, missy? Don't like Camm?" Gaul asked. "Prefer me?" He laughed.

Nicole raised her hand to strike. He seized her wrist but then felt the bracelet.

"What's this?" He examined the wide gold band. A flood of unfamiliar oaths followed. "It's got the sign of the panther. Where'd you get this, woman?"

Nicole cringed at his foul breath. She felt spittle on her face and shuddered, turning away just as Larina flew past.

"I found it," said Nicole.

"Found it? That's mighty strange. These things ain't just lyin' around." He struggled futilely with the clasp then snarled when it refused to budge. He glanced around the clearing. "I don't like the look of this campsite either."

"Let's go," said Camm. "There could be one of them things lurking in the woods."

"Move, girl," ordered Gaul as he pulled Nicole toward the bush. Camm picked up her packsack and tossed it into her face. "We'll check out your bag later. Carry it." She slipped it on.

"Help!" she shouted as they dragged her forward. "Help me!"

They stepped onto the path, Gaul holding her close, followed by Camm and the third brother.

"Who do you think is going to help you?" snorted Gaul. "We checked. There's nobody here but you. You're all alone, girl."

Chapter Four—The Dark One

The path was overgrown, obviously seldom used. No birds sang; no chipmunks or squirrels gamboled in the trees. As Nicole stumbled down the path, her knee still throbbing, her captors discussed strategy.

"That there bracelet is worth a fortune. We oughta just cut it off," urged the third brother. "She'll slow us up anyhow."

"No, Rolf. We ain't gonna spoil it, or her," said Gaul. "She's too fine to let bleed to death. I owe some men a favor. I think they'll accept her in payment, iffen we keep her undamaged."

"Little bit 'o damage won't lower the price," snorted Camm. "She only needs one hand to do a man's biddin'. Maybe we oughta test her out first. It's been a long time since I've been with a pretty girl."

"When have you *ever* been with a pretty girl?" challenged Rolf.

"Shut up!" ordered Camm.

"We'll settle this when we break camp," said Gaul. "We'll look through that packsack then too. She might have a few things worth selling. First, let's put some distance 'tween us and that clearing. I got suspicions 'bout that bracelet. I don't feel right her wearing it. I never saw one b'fore on the likes of her."

"Think it's real gold?" asked Camm.

"For sure," said Gaul. "But it may be worth more than gold with that panther on it and the black stone. A lot of people would like one of these. They's supposed to have power. I'd like me some of that. B'fore we go selling it, I'm gonna find out about the power. Iffen we can harness it, we might be able to settle a few scores. Hell, who knows what we could do? But, for now, we're leaving it right where it is, got that Rolf?"

When he heard no response, Gaul looked back over his shoulder and then stopped, his mouth hanging open. Rolf was gone. He swore and drew his enormous dagger from his belt. Camm did as well.

"Where he be?" said Camm. "You think the dark one got him? I never heard a damn thing."

"Shut up!" Gaul hissed and then shouted into the woods. "Stay away, or I'll kill the woman." He stepped closer to Nicole, pulled her toward him and moved his knife to her throat. She whimpered as his bruising grip tightened.

"Can't travel like this," said Camm. "It's one 'o *them*. Hunting us. We shouldn't of touched her. She must belong to him. Damn. It'll pick us off, one by one. They got the strength of three men. Let her go. I'm not dying for some bitch."

"Let her go, my ass," said Gaul. "She and that bracelet are worth more money than we've seen in many a season. I bet it gave her the bracelet. Must care about her a lot. That's the weak spot. Even them things got a weak spot."

He shouted, "No more sneakin' around. You surrender, or I'll slit her throat. Don't think I won't. Come out, now, and bring back my brother."

There was silence for a few moments, the only sound a slight rustle of leaves in the wind. Nicole shivered, both from the knife at her throat and the tension in the air. She heard a crackle in the canopy of the forest, then a crash of breaking branches and a thump on the path behind as a body fell to the ground. It was Rolf. His throat was encircled with blood, and his eyes were closed.

"Fornicatin' animal!" screamed Gaul as he dug the knife point into her throat. "Step out 'fore I count three, or else I carve up this little fishy."

Soundlessly, the dark man dropped to the path. Nicole gasped. Gaul hissed, and Camm made a choking noise. This was the mysterious man of Nicole's dreams. She felt certain of it deep within her bones. He was over six feet tall and powerfully built. He wore a loose shirt and breeches. His feet were bare. His arms, chest, throat, and much of his face were covered in short, gleaming black hair. His eyes were almond-shaped, piercing black with white diamond-shaped pupils. His nose was flat and broad, his cheekbones high, and his teeth sharp. He was human, but yet not. Now Nicole understood the symbol of the panther on the bracelet.

"Tie him up, Camm," ordered Gaul. "And give me his knife."

The smaller man dug through his bag for a rope. Hesitantly, Camm approached the dark man, removed his knife from a leather sheath tied to his belt, and then passed it quickly to Gaul. Gaul wrapped the knife in a dirty rag he pulled from his pocket, and then tucked it under his own belt. Fumbling, Camm bound the dark man's wrists behind his back. Camm then hobbled his legs with enough space for walking, but not enough for running or climbing.

Camm approached Rolf's body. He kicked it softly, and then harder. He glanced over his brother, noting that the body had been disarmed. With a shrug, he took a few coins from Rolf's pocket.

Camm flinched when the dark man spoke. "Do not be frightened, Nicole. No harm will come to you. I will protect you."

Gaul snorted. "Big promises. Let's go."

Taking the lead, Camm shoved the bound dark man while holding a knife to his back. Gaul removed the knife from Nicole's throat, but continued to hold it as he prodded her along behind Camm. No one looked back at Rolf.

Although Gaul gradually relaxed and fell further behind her, Nicole's terror increased. Her sore knee burned, lightning jolts of pain spreading up and down her leg. After being jostled along for hours, she collapsed with relief when the men paused for a rest. Camm drank and passed the flask to his brother. He wiped his mouth and laughed, displaying badly rotting teeth, as she watched. Even with a parched throat, she would not have drunk from the same container had they offered it to her.

The route slowly headed downhill, periodically joining with other paths. The trees no longer crowded in, snatching at them with multi-fingered branches. Nicole found walking easier as the trail widened. She wondered if they had entered a more frequently traveled area. Would they meet up with the men Gaul had spoken of?

Gaul and Camm became talkative now, their confidence increasing as they neared their destination. Gaul delighted in pushing Nicole, even though her pace had not slackened. He yanked her hair and laughed. Once, in an act of bravado, Camm pushed the dark man, but Nicole could tell it made him uneasy.

"How come you always get the pretty girls?" complained Camm. "I'm always stuck with the ugly brutes."

"Like with like," said Gaul.

"Aw, come on. I'm tired of guarding this creep. Your turn."

"All right, switch if it'll stop your whinin'."

Gaul grabbed Nicole's hair, holding her while he changed places with his brother. He shoved the dark man, who was looking back at Nicole. As they continued, Gaul strutted, laughing and telling crude jokes to his brother.

Both Nicole's legs were now racked with hot slivers of pain. It took immense willpower to keep moving. She had been fairly inactive for the last year and could not keep up this pace for much longer.

The path came out along a stream. To the west was thick forest. To the east was a steep, eight-meter-high embankment sloping into the waterway below. The deep, muddy water flowed slowly. Nicole trudged along, tripping and staggering. Her breath was dry, and her chest ached. Her knee felt pierced by hot glass. Her legs and feet were swollen and heavy. Anxious to reach their destination before nightfall, the men picked up the pace.

Nicole's head spun. She suddenly sank to the ground. It was all the distraction the dark man needed. He shouldered Gaul into the water and jumped in after him.

"Butt-licking animal," yelled Camm.

He and Nicole stared into the churning water below. The dark man's hands and feet had been bound; surely he would drown. Seconds passed without either one surfacing. Camm jerked Nicole to her feet and raised the knife to her throat.

"Where they be? Where they be?" he mumbled. "Damn Gaul and his big plans. Never shoulda messed with a dark one. Where they be?"

The water exploded. The bandit emerged, held aloft by the dark man as he stepped onto the embankment and roared with triumph, the cry echoing and vibrating deep in Nicole's guts. Gaul's clothes were shredded, and he lay flaccid as a rag doll over the panther man's head. The dark man tossed the body into the air and into the mud embankment. He drew his recovered knife.

Larina suddenly screeched from the trees. "You've had it now, tough guy. Today you die an ugly death."

Camm made a strangled sound, stepped away from Nicole, and bolted for the forest. Nicole watched him crash through the trees until he disappeared from sight, the sound of cracking branches continuing for a while longer.

A chuckle by her side made Nicole turn. The dark man, dripping wet, was standing next to her. He shook his head like a dog, spraying water.

"Do not worry," he said. "He will not return. Camm was the weak one. I waited until he was your guard before acting. He was more smoke than fire."

Too worn-out to respond, Nicole nodded.

"I expected you to stumble much earlier. You were very resilient and brave. You never screamed."

"I almost did when the other brother, Rolf, fell out of the trees. I never saw a man killed before," she whispered.

"You still have not." The dark man laughed. "He was unconscious. The cut on his throat was just a scratch. For effect."

"What about him?" Nicole gestured toward Gaul.

"Unconscious." The dark man leaned over the body. "He's still breathing, unfortunately. Of course, he has a chance of drowning if he rolls back into the water, but I doubt Dawn's End would be so lucky."

"But how is that possible?" croaked Nicole. "Your hands were tied. They took your knife."

The dark man held out his hand. His nails shot out to three times their length. They were thick, curved, and sharp as daggers. Retractable claws. Useful as a panther's and just as dangerous. The hair on Nicole's arms rose.

Larina fluttered down and landed on the dark man's shoulder. "They'll have quite a story to tell their fellow bandits," she said. "About their fierce battle with the dark man. I'm sure it will grow with the telling."

Nicole swayed. The dark man steadied her and took her packsack.

"You are faint. You need water. This river is unclean, and I would not risk using the rogue's canteen."

Nicole nodded in agreement.

"I can carry you the short distance to safety, if you do not mind. We will reach fresh water and be able to rest more quickly."

Nicole shook her head, but her knees buckled with her third step. The dark man scooped her up in a single, swift, smooth motion. Limp in his arms, Nicole noticed that, although he was soaking wet, somehow warmth spread from him in waves. As long as she did not have to walk another step. She closed her eyes and sank against his body.

The rest of the journey was a tired blur. Finally, she heard a knock on a door and words exchanged between the dark man and another. She was carried inside a small house and up the stairs, and placed gently into an armchair.

"I would put you straight to bed, but now you are wet as well as dirty," said the dark man. "You should undress. I will fetch you a drink while you do. Can you manage on your own?"

"Yes." Nicole avoided looking at him. It was all too much to deal with right now. He paused in the doorway.

"My name is Morrel, Alaric Morrel. You may call me Morrel because we are quest-mates."

"I'm Nicole Newman. Pleased to meet you." She giggled at her own automatic but incongruous statement.

Morrel laughed. It was an oddly comforting sound. It made her think he must be human. Animals couldn't laugh, could they? After he left, she struggled out of her clothes and pulled on panties and a sweatshirt from her pack sack. She stumbled to the bed and crawled in. Then she heard a soft tap on the door.

"Come in," she said.

Morrel entered carrying a chunky mug. "Drink this broth," he said, setting it on the low table beside the bed.

Nicole gulped it down as he gathered up her muddy clothes. She was asleep seconds after the door shut.

The clank of a buckle woke Nicole. She rubbed her eyes and looked around. The room was small with log furniture—a small night table and an armchair with a brown, stuffed cushion, feathers poking through the fraying seams. The two outside walls were chinked logs, one of which held a small window with closely spaced metal bars and inside shutters. Planed logs and white plaster formed the inside walls. The floor was wooden, and the bed was made of hewn logs.

Morrel opened the packsack, which was propped against the wall, and then folded and placed her washed and fireside-dried clothes inside. Lying quietly under the covers, Nicole studied his appearance.

He *was* the being who had appeared as a shadowy figure in her dreams all these months. Tall and unearthly, he moved with fluid grace. The muscles in his neck and arms rippled as he buckled the straps on her pack. He walked soundlessly on bare feet, which had thickly padded soles.

Morrel's hair was gleaming ebony and straight, and it hung to his jaw line, full and sleek. He wore a small coal goatee, and his skin was shining black. He had the powerful build of Wesley Snipes in *Blade,* the smile of Will Smith, and the height and speed of an NBA star. He wore loose, tan trousers, tied at mid-calf, and a roughly cut white vest, both made from linen-like material. A white headband completed the arresting contrast of black and white. He stood more than a head taller than Nicole.

Task completed, Morrel turned and smiled. "Feeling better?"

Nicole was captivated by his most startling feature—his eyes. Astonishingly bright, they held a gleaming black iris with a diamond-shaped white pupil. She had been staring into their beauty for several seconds when she realized she hadn't answered.

"Yes. Amazingly so," she said as she swung her feet over the edge of the bed. "Even my knee no longer hurts."

Morrel sat down in the armchair. "It was the herbs I added to your broth. They ease muscle aches and the pain of cuts. We will travel slowly until you are fully recovered."

"I feel fine now." She stood and picked up the packsack. "Whatever those herbs were, you could make a fortune marketing them."

"Does making a fortune appeal to you?"

"Sure. Everyone would like to be rich."

"Rich in what?" He titled his head in puzzlement.

"Money, silly," replied Nicole.

"Why?"

"Why! So you wouldn't have to worry," she said. "So you could be secure and independent."

"Money brings this? Security. A worry-free life."

"Well, not entirely I suppose," said Nicole. She finished brushing her hair. "Still, it beats being poor." She buckled the packsack closed.

"Do you have any other injuries besides your knee?" asked Morrel.

"No, I think I'm okay. Stiff and sore, but no cuts or broken bones. Nothing that will scar me anyway."

"How did you get that scar on your lip?"

Nicole's hand flew to her mouth. She touched the scar. "An accident when I was little. Tobogganing."

"Tobogganing?"

"Sliding. On hills of snow." She smiled at his puzzled expression. "No snow in Dawn's End, eh?"

"High in the mountains, but I've never been there. I have not seen snow up close."

"I've seen plenty," she said.

"What does it feel like?" he asked.

"Newly fallen snow is like cold, wet, tiny feathers. It changes when it reaches the ground. It can be wet and heavy, sticky. Or it can be grainy, almost like sand. It changes with the weather and other variables." Nicole paused. "I can't believe we're sitting here talking about the weather. Seriously. About this quest. It doesn't seem like you know what you're doing."

"We will talk more over breakfast. You might like to wash up at the well."

Nicole agreed, although a hot shower sounded even better. She followed Morrel downstairs. He handed her a bar of green soap which smelled like mint and a linen cloth Nicole assumed was a towel.

"The well is out back," he explained. "Pull up whatever water you need but don't dump the dirty water back in the well. Toss it further away."

Nicole nodded.

Larina was perched on an odd red-barked tree by the well. "Good morning, lie-a-bed," she chirped.

"Good morning," answered Nicole. She was determined to avoid arguing with the testy blue jay.

"I must say, Nicole, you handled that experience with the three ruffians admirably yesterday," said Larina. "When I flew off to find the Alaric, I had no idea what you would do."

"I *thought* it was you I saw flying off," said Nicole.

"I wanted to make sure he hadn't gone too far to hear your calls for help, even though he has excellent hearing. He is as fast as an arrow when he travels alone. He covers much terrain when hunting for food."

"You saved my neck," said Nicole. "Thank you."

"The Alaric did *that*. I was but a messenger."

Larina clasped each tail feather in her beak, one by one, and scraped it along the shaft, preening. Nicole thought of the cormorant, the bird she had loved so much. Maybe Larina wasn't such a bad old bird, just scrappy.

"Why do you call Morrel 'the Alaric'?" asked Nicole.

"Because I understand the sacrifice. You may call him Morrel because you are the chosen one. Morrel is his personal name. It is an honor to use it." Larina nodded solemnly, ruffled her feathers, and then flew off.

Chosen one? thought Nicole. *I'd like to know who the heck chose me and why they didn't bother to ask if I wanted to be chosen. I'm not too crazy about* the sacrifice *either. The whole thing gives me the creeps. The sooner I get out of here, the better.*

At breakfast, Nicole met their host, Chas of the Glen. They ate downstairs at a log table with two log benches. Nicole sat as close to one end as she could. Morrel sat at the other, and Chas sat across from them. He was a burly man of Nicole's height, with a shock of sandy hair falling continually into his eyes. He seldom spoke and subtly watched Nicole as she ate.

Chas treated Morrel with friendship tempered with respect. He quietly served the simple, but filling, breakfast of a hot grain cereal and offered food for their journey.

"Are there many bandits around?" Nicole asked Morrel after her hunger slowed.

"I honestly do not know," he admitted. "This is all so new to me. Strange things are happening in Dawn's End now. Since darkness is once again consuming our world, we must expect anything."

"Again?"

"I was not yet born the last Nightfall, but my grandfather told me how it changed Dawn's End forever."

"Forever! Then what's the point of this quest? And what is 'Nightfall' anyway?"

Morrel scraped his spoon back and forth along the bottom of the wooden bowl. "When the dark things grow, Dawn's End changes. The land and the people submerge into their darker selves. If The Meeting is a success, the night retreats, and our world returns to balance."

"The Meeting?"

"I can't explain that yet."

"Why not?" Nicole's voice snapped with impatience.

"Partly because I don't know that much about it myself yet, and partly because only those who attend can learn the details."

"Okay, so somehow this meeting solves the problem of Nightfall?"

"Yes, but Dawn's End is scarred. There are echoes of Nightfall left. The longer the dark things roam and the stronger the power they gather, the deeper and more plentiful the scars."

"What do you mean?"

Morrel sighed.

Chas responded. "Before the last quest, there were no bandits. It never occurred to people to take what was not given willingly. The bandits are new to the last two generations."

"The bandits are something that grew out of the darkness?" asked Nicole.

Chas looked at Morrel. The dark man spoke. "They are humans but affected by the change. Before the waves of darkness, Dawn's End had never seen greed and violence."

"So," said Nicole. "I'm guessing this is not normal darkness."

Morrel and Chas nodded.

"Where does it come from?"

Chas shrugged.

"We don't really know," admitted Morrel.

"I'm going to feed the animals," said Chas. "You two take your time."

He left his bowl and spoon on the table, took a straw hat from a peg by the door, and left. Nicole looked back at Morrel.

"So, this darkness leaves residue?"

"Yes. After the last darkness was dispelled, shadows were left. When light was restored, not everyone returned to their former state. This handful of deviants have bred and formed new threats to our society. The longer darkness grows, the more new evils will form. Even if we succeed, they leave their shadows behind."

Nicole shook her head. "I didn't understand half of that. But, I'm even more amazed that bandits did not previously exist. You must be a young society."

"Legend says our land was pristine before the first threat. Some say it was then called Dawn's Cradle."

"How lovely. It sounds like paradise."

"There is still much that is innocent and beautiful. My village, for example."

"Hmph." Nicole frowned and absently rubbed the spoon on her bottom lip.

"Grandfather believes our people lived longer lives with old age scarcely different from youth. Crops were easier to grow. There were no devastating parasites. People were peaceful, happy. It was, indeed, a paradise."

Nicole put down her drink and raised an eyebrow. "What snake got in your garden?"

"Snake?" Morrel frowned in puzzlement.

"In our legends, humanity was expelled from paradise for eating the fruit of knowledge. A snake convinced them to eat the forbidden fruit."

Morrel nodded. "To think we may be following your world. No! I won't allow that to happen. We must succeed!" He clenched his spoon. "I cannot complete The Meeting alone. You have been chosen as well. It is vital that we both attend, else nothing will stop Nightfall."

Nicole looked away, took a deep breath, and said, "Not *we*. I want you to take me home."

"I can't. You must see how desperately I need your help," he pleaded.

Nicole shook her head. "Not a bit."

"You will. Today, we visit—"

Nicole interrupted, "Today, I go home!" This was no dream, and she didn't need any more scars.

"The piece—"

"You are not listening. I will not stay here and have my throat slit by a bunch of creepy outlaws. I didn't sign on for all this."

"You are safe with me, Nicole. I swear it."

"Yeah, sure," Nicole declared sarcastically. "Look, I can see you're strong and kind of ninja-stealthy, but nobody's invincible. Maybe next time you go off looking for mushrooms, you won't get back in time. What would happen to me then? I'm alone here. I don't have a black belt in bandit-busting. I don't know how to get home. And, to be honest, I don't know why I should even be here."

"Trust me."

Nicole snorted. "Trust you? Why should I?"

"Why not? I could have left you to the bandits." Morrel touched her arm, his fingertips hot through the fabric of her shirt.

Nicole jerked away. "Only an idiot or a child would trust a strange man."

"Or *any* man?"

"I'm outta here," said Nicole bristling. "With or without your help." She pushed back her chair and stood.

Morrel crossed his arms. "Go then. How long will you survive in my forest with no idea which direction to travel and no way to open the door should you miraculously find your way back?"

Nicole clenched her jaw. She'd be lost once she ventured three steps from this building, and he knew it.

Chapter Five—Threats

Nicole packed her back pack, refilling her water bottles from the well and adding bread and cheese provided by Chas who had returned. Chas kept giving her hopeful looks, but she studiously avoided eye contact.

As she and Morrel stood at the door, Morrel asked Chas how they could repay his generosity.

"No need, Alaric," said Chas. "I am honored by your company."

"I am honored by your service," said Morrel. "Still, it is difficult to travel the roads with the lengthening darkness. Is there anything you lack that we might provide?"

"Well." Chas hesitated, glancing at Nicole. He smiled. "I was wondering if the lady might have medicines and the like in her bag. I have no emergency supplies left, and it is a long way to the healer's cottage."

Before she could open her first-aid kit, Morrel took the entire thing and pressed it into the cottager's hands. "I hope this will do."

Nicole floundered, mouth open, then thought better of protesting and fastened her packsack. She had plenty at home, and she planned on being there soon. Very soon.

A short distance down the path, Morrel halted. He pointed to the left. "This fork takes us to my village. Grandfather waits there. He can explain much to you better than I can."

"Not interested."

"Nicole, give us a chance. Grandfather will know if you are suitable and ready. If he says you aren't, then I will take you home."

"It isn't up to him to decide."

"If you just listen to him, and promise to think deeply on his words, I will agree to your decision."

"I've already decided. That way must be home," said Nicole pointing right. "That's where I'm headed."

She marched off in the opposite direction from the one Morrel indicated, refusing to look back. Morrel watched her go. Breakfast and determination fuelled her long strides. Her body felt no effects from the exertions of yesterday, but her mind was churning. *Who does this guy think he is anyway? Some physical throwback tricking and manipulating me to his own ends? Putting me in danger from a gang of mental throwbacks? Paradise lost. Yeah, right. Delusional. That's what he must be, expecting me hike off into the woods, like Little Red Riding Hood and the big bad panther. What was that?*

She stopped abruptly. There it was again. A strange noise.

She listened, her throat constricting. Not another chain gang. A shuffle. A low snort. It sounded like . . . no. Couldn't be. Just like the nasty rooting boar in the Old Yeller movie.

She stepped backwards with small, quick steps, looking left and right, anticipating the charge. *Where was it?* She screamed when the movement came from behind. As a dark figure rushed past her, she turned and ran back in the direction of the cottage. A high-pitched squeal rose behind her, followed by thrashing.

"Oh, shit," she gasped. "I'm going to be chomped like truffles by some overgrown pig. Damn you, Morrel."

She fell, started to scramble to her feet, and then shrieked a dry, strangled cry as someone grabbed her elbow.

"Why do you damn me?" asked Morrel.

"You!" She punched his arm. "You! You!" She hit his chest, over and over. "What kind of sick game are you playing now?"

"Did you not hear the dark creature?" he asked, grasping her wrists.

"I thought it was something *terrible*."

"It was," he said, his face sorrowful. "I had to kill the poor thing."

"The poor thing! Enough. I want to go home," wailed Nicole. Even to her own ears, she sounded like a lost child in a shopping mall.

"Home to what?" he asked.

"Sanity." She twisted out of his grasp and flung her arms expressively. "Peace and quiet. Safety."

"So, you're safe. Is that all you want from life?" His forehead furrowed.

"Shut up!" She clenched her fists, and her voice rose. "I don't want to die in some pointless quest I don't even understand or care about!"

"Everyone dies, even you," he said, in a matter-of-fact tone.

"Not today." She poked a finger into his chest. "Not for a freak like you." She froze, stunned by her remark.

Morrel studied her face, his diamond pupils like shards of glass. "I've protected you every time you needed it," he said softly.

Nicole lowered her hand and looked away. "I wouldn't have needed it if you'd left me alone."

"Yes, alone. Alone, bored, going nowhere and doing nothing. The worst you've gotten is a scraped knee, and it is more living than you can stand."

Nicole blinked back the tears. "Stop it! Don't say those things."

"Please, Nicole, I'm begging you. Listen. Find out the whole story before you decide. I will not force you to stay. But, if not for me, or my grandfather, or all the ordinary people like Chas, then stay for the difference it can make to you."

"I'm . . . I'm afraid."

"I know. But will you be any less afraid at home?"

Nicole buckled. Her tears dripped into the dry earth in ink-like splotches. She sobbed, silently. Finally, she wiped her nose on her sleeve and whispered, "If I talk to your grandfather, will you take me home if I still want to go?"

Morrel sighed. "I will obey my grandfather's wishes. He is much kinder and wiser than I."

"If I convince him to let me go, will you see me through the door? Back to the park?"

Morrel nodded. "Yes, I swear it."

"All right, let's go see your grandfather then."

To pass the time as they hiked, Nicole questioned Morrel. It wasn't that she really cared about his crazy quest, or even believed there was a quest for that matter, but the silence was unnerving.

The days in Dawn's End were becoming shorter as the dark hours were lengthening, an unnatural occurrence for spring. Once The Meeting was held, he explained, the progression of Nightfall would stop, and time would revert to its normal pattern.

Nicole wondered if there was a board of directors that looked like Morrel. She had a sudden vision of the painting of dogs playing poker, only this would be cats passing around file folders. She stifled a nervous giggle. Fear was making her giddy.

Nicole and Morrel made camp in a clearing at the base of a rock face. The gravel around the rock was littered with broken stone and punctuated by a few tired brown weeds. Morrel watched while Nicole cleared a few plants from the space and made a stack of twigs and branches. As Nicole arranged her pack sack to serve as a seat, Morrel squatted on his heels. He nodded, satisfied with her tepee of kindling, but, unimpressed with her matches, he used flint and steel to strike the spark.

"Cold?" he asked.

"Aren't you?" asked Nicole. She dug out her hooded jacket and put it on.

Morrel shrugged as if bare arms and feet were of no consequence. When Nicole still trembled, he moved closer to her side. She felt the draw of his body heat. Huddling against him would be better than putting on the raincoat. In so many layers she felt like a pig in a blanket waited to be stabbed with a giant toothpick. She moved closer to him. He wrapped his powerful arm around her back, watching her expression carefully.

Strange, how cozy it felt. Nicole even felt content, cuddled up to this dark creature who was not quite man and not quite animal. She rubbed her hands. Morrel took one in his own hot, black hand. A tingle traveled up her arm. She met his eyes, which were so unique, yet somehow so familiar. Looking into them was like peering down a long, dark tunnel toward a lantern. Or walking toward a lighted entrance. She was pulled down, inside their otherworldly depths. The diamonds' brightness blazed into her. Soothing. Welcoming. Peaceful. Sensual.

Morrel looked away. The spell broke.

"If you lie between me and the fire, you should feel warmer." He stretched out, his face toward the darkness.

Nicole was conscious of the hard muscles in his buttocks against her. She had a fleeting vision of them flexing beneath her hands, slippery with sweat. She shivered. Morrel, interpreting this as cold, pressed closer against her. Nicole gave a small gasp, and then shut down her thoughts.

Sandwiched between the sources of heat, Nicole drifted to sleep. She dreamed of the large bandit with the knife and awoke feeling weak and vulnerable. It was still night. Morrel turned over and reached for her in the darkness. He wrapped his arms around her, positioning himself so that his thigh was against her buttocks. Grateful for this discretion, yet feeling a little cheated, she settled against him.

"No one will harm you while I am here," he whispered. "Sleep well."

Am I delusional? she thought. *I never expected to feel this way again about a man. But then, he isn't a man. Is he? Part of me doubts any of this is real. Any moment I'll wake up in my own bed, or in a hospital room. Either way, what is the point of resisting? Why not live a little adventure? Maybe there's a unicorn right around the corner. Not that it would come to me. Randy took care of that. Besides, I forgot how comfortable it is to spend time in the company of a man. I didn't realize how much I missed that. Why are relationships always so complicated?*

Later that day, they followed a beaten path through a thinning forest. The trees seemed heavy, as though weighed down by invisible ash. The sky was leaden overhead, and the air felt thickened with industrial smog. The trees diminished, giving way to brush and stubble. As they traveled, Nicole asked, "Why does Larina call you 'Alaric' instead of 'Morrel?' She tried to explain, but I didn't really understand."

"'Alaric' is a title."

"The dark things, are they real living things or just imaginings of frightened people?"

"They are as real as nightmares."

Nicole laughed. "On Elm Street?"

Morrel continued. "As real as I am."

"Hmm." Nicole shrugged. What he was saying was too deep for her. "So why hasn't everything changed? How come you and Chas are still okay?"

"Some were twisted by the abnormal nights early on. They are enlarged, crueler, deformed. When the balance of day and night is restored, so will they be. Unfortunately, some trace of evil will remain. I suspect the longer they are changed, the deeper the changes run. I do not know if the change comes at different times to different beings because of where they are or who they are. I know certain groups, such as my people, seem to suffer less from the effects, but, eventually, we too will fall."

Nicole did not understand how her presence could have any impact on the situation Morrel described. "So why me?"

"The bracelet steered my choice, but it was, still, my choice. You came to me in my dreams. It led me to the pond. I watched you there and became part of your dreams. I am drawn to *you*, Nicole." They stopped walking. "I fill a void in your life and that gives me satisfaction. There is something inside me that I do not understand that responds to you as well. We are drawn to each other, even though you rebel against it."

Nicole stared at his bare feet. "I'm not interested in a relationship."

"Every action is a result of a relationship. Without relationships, you are dead."

Nicole brushed past him and continued walking.

"Human women are strange," said Morrel. "The bracelet makes us understand each other's language, but sometimes the meaning is still unclear to me. I do not understand women."

Nicole laughed. "You haven't said anything every human male hasn't said as well."

"I never meant to terrorize you," said Morrel. "I did not know how to approach you. You are like a magnet, sometimes attracting, suddenly repelling. Strong-willed, yet easily frightened. I did not want to make the same mistake as my grandfather."

"What mistake was that?" Nicole asked as she carefully threaded through a loose pile of stone.

"He selected a woman from your world, thinking she was ready, but he had not prepared her well enough before they met. She was to be his helpmate in the quest, his partner for the meeting. But, he could not connect strongly enough to her in her dreams. When they met, she fled in terror. Grandfather had no idea how horrible his features would seem to a person from your world. That he would be considered a freak."

Nicole stumbled to a stop. She turned and faced him. His eyes were large and sad. "I apologize for that remark, Morrel. I'm so not like that. I'm not racist or anything. I have a sneaky temper, I guess. I'm sorry."

A slow smile brightened Morrel's face. "Good. If I am rejected, I am glad the cause will not be something I can't change, such as my appearance."

Nicole pressed her lips together tightly. She picked up a cloth strip from his vest and rolled it back and forth in her fingers. "I know about rejection."

"There can be no deeper scar than being rejected by someone you love."

She dropped the strip, and they resumed their hike. This Alaric Morrel had an uncomfortable way of bringing buried things out into the light.

"What happened to your grandfather's quest when he couldn't get the woman's help?" continued Nicole.

"I think he ran out of confidence as well as time," sighed Morrel. "He selected the most exceptional woman he could find in Dawn's End, a panther woman of great intelligence and strength. But, bringing her to The Meeting held back the

61

night for only a short time." Morrel paused. "It becomes more and more difficult to find a woman from your world as the years pass. With the changes in your world—cynicism, loss of magic, corruption, spiritual impoverishment, mistrust . . . . "

"Why does she have to be from my world?" asked Nicole.

Morrel frowned. "You ask so many questions. I am neither a historian nor a wizard. I do not know everything. I just know what is required of me. I do not endlessly quiz my elders. I just do what is needed, grateful I can serve."

He stopped when he saw Nicole glancing at him with a frown.

"With your help," said Morrel, "I will be able to protect my people for hundreds of years. Eventually, other peoples may have to take up the responsibility. I may be the last of the panther people. That makes our meeting special. I guess I am hoping fame will appeal to your sense of pride."

Nicole snorted. "Pride! Not much of that these days. But why me? There are many far more special women in my world. Women of great talent, beauty, strength, courage, intelligence."

"All women are special," remarked Morrel. "You seem to think I need a princess. It is much simpler, yet much harder to see, than that."

Nicole shook her head. "You're not descended from a Cheshire cat by any chance?"

"Pardon?"

Nicole giggled. "Nothing. How do you get into my dreams anyway?"

"Through the bracelet. Through destiny. Through the links in our worlds and our own desires. I do not understand it all myself."

"Is all you know about my world what you learned in my dreams?" she asked. "That would be a pretty distorted view, I'm afraid."

"No," said Morrel. "I watched people by the pond. I found scraps of writing, with pictures, that showed me about other parts of your world. Also, my grandfather has told me what he learned. The bracelet allows me to enter your world, but staying there too long weakens the bracelet's power. If I spend too much time there, it will not have enough power left to open the door for my return."

"Then you'd be trapped!"

"I do not think I would enjoy the reactions of humans who happened to see me if I became trapped in your world."

"Not likely," admitted Nicole. She touched the beautiful bracelet that now seemed a part of her. "How do the bracelets come off?"

"Only I can unclasp yours. I ensured it could not be removed while you were here. You would be too vulnerable without it," said Morrel. "If you brought it into your own world, it would lose its power over time, of course. Then you could remove it yourself. It would eventually become ordinary jewelry."

"Not like any ordinary jewelry I've ever seen," commented Nicole. "How did Larina get into my world? She doesn't have a bracelet."

"On my shoulder. She is my calia."

"Calia? A pet?"

"More like a supportive companion."

"Why isn't she traveling with us?" Nicole glanced overhead.

"She is following," said Morrel, nodding. "You will see her when *she* wishes."

"She's kind of a snappy little thing, isn't she?"

Morrel gave a gentle laugh. "Larina is caught in an impossible, but once feasible, dream. She understands me as no one else can. She is a reminder of what is to come."

Nicole glanced at him, her forehead furrowed. Morrel frowned, sighed deeply, and then shrugged. She realized he was losing patience. She had enough to think about for the moment anyway. Besides, her body had been flooded with adrenaline so many times in the last two days, she wasn't sure she could absorb or deal with much else.

 They continued on in silence. Nicole's hiking boots made soft thuds on the hardened path. Morrel's feet were as soundless as a cougar's. The quiet settled on her like a drug. On and on they walked, the sun slowly sliding across the drab sky. There was no breeze, no birds crying overhead, just the relentless padding of Nicole's boots, scuffing up the gray earth. Twice, she spotted Larina in the distance.

The brush thickened and increased in height as the pair entered a deep forest. Like jungle foliage, the branches drooped toward the ground in gestures of defeat. Black mold grew in every crease and bend of their trunks. Bark glistened with a gray slime. Light was scarce, and the path was thickly carpeted with fallen, wet leaves that absorbed all sound. Sight and sound were muffled, almost choked. Nicole considered taking out her flashlight, but Morrel confidently took the lead.

He picked his way through the trees in near darkness. Nicole stumbled twice. The second time, he reached behind and took her hand. She mimicked the sways and turns of his body as she continued forward. She was so in step with his movements that she collided with his back when he abruptly stopped.

"What is it?" she asked.

"Listen."

All she heard was their breathing, overly loud in the heavy silence.

"I thought I heard something. My error."

They began again but froze in mid-step when Larina screeched her warning.

Chapter Six—Alaric Morrel

They had reached a point in the path where tired light filtered through the tree tops. Nicole wished for a second that she could not see what was coming. Out of the gloom rumbled a monstrous, snorting animal. It bellowed as it charged. A ton of fury on four hooves. Triple horns spiraled out from its forehead. Drooping spaniel ears flapped. Its back was encased in black plated armor. Its glaring orange eyes riveted Nicole in place. It was so close now she could see the pus oozing down its cheeks from its red, irritated eyes. Morrel threw his arm around Nicole and hurled them both off the path, taking the impact of the beast's charge on his right shoulder.

Momentum propelled the beast past its targets. The pair scrambled to their feet, wet leaves and twigs clinging to their bodies. Adrenaline pumped through Nicole, numbing her to the sting of her fall. Morrel quickly steered Nicole to a large tree with thick, widely spaced branches.

"Climb. Remain hidden until I call for you," he ordered. "Larina!" The bird lighted in the tree above their heads. "Stay with her."

As he disappeared, Nicole's hands began to burn from the impact of hitting the ground, and her wrists ached. After three attempts, she finally managed to pull herself up onto the first heavy branch of the tree. She scaled the slippery bark, struggling for toeholds and grips. As she climbed, she remembered a time when she found a forgotten margarine tub of wild strawberries under her bed. The fruit had been covered in furry fungus and smelled of decay. This tree smelled just like the strawberries, yet she wrapped herself around it and did not look down. She heard the animal turn and renew its charge.

Morrel drew the beast away from her refuge. She stiffened and held her breath as the creature tore past, intent on its mark. The very tree she hugged trembled with the next crash.

The battle plunged into the thick woods. Nicole heard a savage scream, part human and part feline, wild and fearless. She imagined Norse warriors, the Berserkers, from English history. She clung to the tree, trembling, her face pressed against the damp trunk. She knew Larina was perched on an adjacent branch, but Nicole could not meet her eyes. Her tensed hands throbbed and perspired.

What if Morrel never called for her to come down? How long should she stay hidden like a quivering mouse? Would she climb down to find his ravaged remains? Would the beast devour him?

She resented his trickery, yes, but she would never wish for Morrel to die, especially not in such a gruesome way as being shredded by a triple-horned beast. Even though she had known him for only a short time and their relationship so far had been overshadowed by deception, the intimacy of their shared dreams colored her emotions.

The sound of fighting rose and fell, like an impish child with a snare drum. Morrel shouted, once, unintelligibly. The beast bellowed triumphantly. Without a word to Nicole, Larina flew off.

"Alaric!" Larina cried out in the distance, her voice fearful.

Nicole whimpered, straining her ears. The sounds of battle ceased, and the forest quieted. The heavy thud of the beast's hooves drew closer. Nicole lifted her head from the tree and looked down toward the trail. She saw the black armor covering the animal's back as it passed her hiding place in the tree. It stopped a few steps further down the path, and then returned. The beast raised its head, sniffing, its long horns bobbing. It looked deeper into the forest, and then back toward her tree. Nicole tried to breathe soundlessly, frozen in place. The beast slowly raised its head until its orange eyes met hers. Nicole swallowed. Sweat was running into her eyes. She blinked, but dared not move her hand to wipe the moisture away. She struggled to stay still. Nevertheless, even such a small gesture as her blink enraged the beast. It waddled backward, making space to charge, lowered its head, and thundered forward like a rabid rhinoceros.

Nicole screamed in terror, clutching the tree with all her strength. Just as the beast's head bent to meet the tree trunk, Larina appeared, screeching and flapping her wings. Although this did not slow the beast, the distraction diverted its aim. It hit the trunk with a glancing blow, crushing its own ear, and howled in pain.

Larina assaulted the creature's face with insistent jabs and swoops. The beast lunged and twisted, chasing the blue jay back to the path and out of sight. It emitted a roar of pain. Again, the beast tore past Nicole's place of refuge. Snorting and huffing, the creature rumbled down the path. Finally, the animal's sounds faded into the distance. Nicole whimpered. Then silence.

"I told you to stay with her."

It was Morrel's voice! Nicole let out a deep breath, realizing she had been holding it.

"I do as I please," snapped Larina. "You can't deny I helped. That disgusting creature did not like having his beady eye pecked, I can tell you. I will not cower in a tree while you are stomped and gored to death."

Nicole felt a flush of embarrassment. She would have cowered in the tree until doomsday.

Morrel came in sight and glanced up at her to reassure himself that she was safe. Then, he continued scolding the bird. "You are too stubborn for your own good. If it had caught you once on a horn, you would be but a pile of crushed feathers."

Morrel and Larina reached Nicole's tree. Larina lighted on a nearby branch. Morrel looked up again at Nicole, gave her a small smile, and beckoned with his hand.

Nicole suppressed a shriek, which transformed instead into a nervous giggle. "Good Lord, what's going on?" she asked as she descended. "Monsters on parade?" She jumped from the lowest branch, Morrel steadying her. "I feel like I've died and been sent to Muppet Hell. You sure it's gone?" She knew she was babbling, but she couldn't control her nervous habit of making bad jokes in uncomfortable situations.

"It's gone," said Morrel. His vest was torn, and a sleeve hung from one arm. Nicole placed her hand on his chest to steady her landing. When she pulled it back, blood covered her palm.

"You're injured!" she cried in dismay.

The sleek, black hair on his chest was streaked wet with blood.

"It is not serious," he said. "A bit of missing skin. It knocked the breath from me for a few moments."

Nicole looked into his face, its expression so matter-of-fact.

"How can you still be alive?" she said. "That animal was like a rhinoceros on steroids."

He shrugged.

"Let me see the cut," she ordered.

Nicole wished she still had her first aid kit. Larina nervously fluttered from tree to tree. Nicole realized the bird could do nothing at this point to aid Morrel and was distressed by her helplessness. If he was ever seriously injured, the best Larina could do was go for help. Nicole removed her jacket and tried to rip a strip off the bottom of her shirt to use as a bandage.

"Stop tearing at your clothing," said Morrel. "I am all right. The bleeding is slowing. Anyway, there is not enough fabric in that entire shirt to make a decent bandage."

Nicole looked at the broad, muscular expanse of his chest and silently agreed that her shirt was inadequate. "I wish I had my first-aid kit."

"Chas of Glen may have need of it should he encounter the dark things," said Morrel.

"That beast was a dark thing? It looked and acted like that because of Nightfall?"

"Yes, and the dark things are increasing."

"My God. Nobody's safe. How can people move about? How can we stop it?"

"So." Morrel smiled. "You show concern for others."

Nicole bit her lip and turned away. *Damn. I said we.* Silently, she wiped her bloodied hand on some large, low-hanging leaves.

That was no renegade pig, she thought. *Morrel's crazy story seems true. It's highly unlikely that Dawn's End is somewhere outside the city limits. More 'third star to the right and straight on until morning.'* Was she the Wendy, come to save the lost boys?

For years, she had been frustrated by her inability to make any true difference in the world. Signing petitions to stop the stoning of women in the Middle East, writing letters to free prisoners of conscience, donating to environmental causes, walking for cancer, supporting schools in Africa, bringing clothes to the women's shelter . . . . It all seemed like a drop in the bucket. Watching the news—crude oil spewing into the Gulf of Mexico, never-ending wars in the Middle East, dictators crushing human rights around the world, the increasing rate of climate change—made her feel completely helpless. But here was an opportunity to make a profound difference in the lives of a multitude of living beings. Even the trees were suffering. What caused all that mold? And the drooping branches, the off-kilter smell. If she turned her back on Dawn's End now, would she ever be able to look at herself in a mirror and not feel shame at her own hypocrisy and cowardice?

Morrel was crawling on his hands and knees, collecting bead-like green spores from the underside of ferns. She watched as he crushed the beads and mixed them with a few grains of white powder from a small pouch he had withdrawn from his pocket.

"What's that?" she asked.

"The powder is from the root of the Lilyvern. The spores will make it sticky. It will speed the healing of my wound and prevent infection. I only have this one dose. It is very rare, almost impossible to acquire, but I can't take any chances of becoming ill now." He rubbed the paste into his chest wound.

71

As they serpentined through the forest, Morrel held Nicole's hand in the overgrown, dark parts, occasionally warning her of holes and other obstacles underfoot. After a while, the canopy of treetops thinned. They rested and ate in a small clearing.

Determined to be of some use, Nicole gathered a pile of the strong, flexible straw growing around them.

"Give me your vest," she said.

Morrel complied, watching closely. Nicole used her nail clipper to create little holes along the torn shoulder seam. She braided the straw into a lace and threaded it through the holes, weaving the vest back together. She tied off the end, leaving a tassel of straw dangling over the shoulder.

"Impressive," said Morrel as he eased back into his vest.

Nicole smiled. "And somewhat stylish. The stitches won't last. I could have done a better job with the needle and thread in my first-aid kit."

"But it would not have demonstrated your ingenuity, nor would it have looked so unique."

Nicole laughed. "I also know how to finger crochet. You never know when *that* might come in handy."

At the next crossroads, they veered east. The depressing woodland abruptly opened into a sweet-smelling meadow. The air cleared. A weight lifted from them, and they breathed deeply. Nicole felt the way she used to on the first warm day of spring, like a survivor, a northerner who made it through another winter without crashing her car, getting frostbite, or going crazy.

When the greater part of the day had passed, Morrel said, "We are entering the area of my village. It is over the next hill."

On the next rise, she spotted it. Gleaming, rectangular buildings were surrounded by fruit and shade trees. A well worn path led straight into its center. Pale rock buildings were bricked with white mortar. Each home was rectangular or square, one level only, with a large wooden door and no windows. Small ventilation holes ran below the overhanging roof. A covered well stood on one side of the square. Here and there were empty benches. All the inhabitants seemed to be indoors.

Morrel led Nicole to a small building. "This is my home. I live alone."

Light seeped through the rock ceiling. Thinly sliced, translucent slabs of marble in various shades of white, cream, and apricot formed a skylight.

"Rest, Nicole," he said, "while I greet my family and community. Explore. Sleep. Do whatever you like. I will not be long."

Nicole discovered an orderly room with a table and bench, dried food, and cooking utensils. Another room contained a wash tub and cleaning supplies. Nicole looked longingly at the basket of soaps. A small, stark room contained a straw mat and a black and white sketch of a leopard leaping in front of a rising sun. Or perhaps it was the moon?

In the sleeping room, clothing hung on pegs. A thick, oval rug, braided from rag strips was rolled against the wall. Beside it sat two neatly folded quilts. On a lidded wooden box sat a trinket-sized cube. In each room, there was a lantern with some type of oil. Returning to the entryway, Nicole tried to relax on a chaise-lounge. Struggling to find a comfortable

73

position, she finally stretched out on her back. She felt as though she was waiting for the dentist.

Morrel returned, followed by a dignified, older female carrying a tray of food. The panther woman set the tray on the small table and approached the rising Nicole, her arms extended.

"Welcome," she said. "I am Alaric Sabella, mother of Morrel. I bring you refreshment, greetings, and gratitude from the villagers."

Nicole looked into her proud face and striking eyes and knew this was a woman of merit. Alaric Sabella had an alien beauty. Her facial features resembled Morrel's. Her deep black skin had a navy undertone. Her fur was glossy, though sparse, and she had little facial hair. Her body hair was shiny blue-black. The hair on her head, a bluish-gray, was neatly brushed back. She was tall and small-busted, but feminine. Her warm smile softened her imposing figure.

A finely woven gold headband encircled Sabella's hair. She wore a sleeveless, gray suede gown, with a simple V-neckline. Though small facial lines and her silvery hair betrayed her age, her powerful body, poised on bare feet, did not. Her gold wrist band was identical to Nicole's and Morrel's.

Morrel and Nicole sat on low wooden stools by the table. While they ate the plants and breads, Sabella expounded upon their plans. "The villagers will not visit tonight since it will soon be dark. Before then, hot water will be brought for you to wash. You will speak with Morrel's grandfather tomorrow. He has gone to meditate in seclusion. The bracelet told him of your arrival."

Nicole frowned at her bracelet.

"Thoughts appear in the mind," explained Sabella. "Occasionally, the bracelet foretells something of importance to an Alaric, even one as worldly as I. I knew I would become pregnant and bear an extraordinary son two years before Morrel's birth, for example."

Nicole nodded, somehow able to accept these odd remarks as truth.

Sabella continued. "Tonight, you must rest and recuperate. Tomorrow, everyone will want to meet Morrel's companion for The Meeting."

Nicole grimaced, but she was too tired to question further. She was more concerned that this woman seemed to expect her to spend the night alone with Morrel in this bedroom than she was about The Meeting. She had mixed feelings about staying with Morrel. Alone by the campfire, her body had been aroused by his masculine one, but the physical discomfort and dangerous situation had dampened any response. Here, in this private, clean and comfortable home, she wondered what might happen.

Nicole heard a soft scratch at the door, and a lovely young panther woman entered. She was in her early teens, dressed similarly to Sabella, an apple-green gown over her black fur. She and Morrel touched noses.

Morrel smiled. "This is my younger sister, Linnel. She is my only sibling."

The girl carried soft breeches and tunics. "These are fresh clothes for you both. You may put them on right after you wash and sleep in them as well. Please place your dusty clothes outside the door. They will be clean and dry by morning."

Nicole smiled at the word 'dusty'. She felt like she had wrestled with a greased pig.

After their baths, Morrel carried a second mat and a pile of quilts into the sleeping room.

"These are for you. It is best to snuggle in before darkness. That way, your body builds up warmth in the quilts. You seem vulnerable to changing temperatures without enough fur. I mean, with your naked skin. I mean . . . . " Morrel cleared his throat.

Nicole giggled. His nervousness reassured her.

"Now that the nights are lengthening, they are also becoming colder," said the dark man. "Soon, my people may have to provide a source of indoor heat."

"How do you manage in the winter?"

"Our winter is not like yours," he admitted. "I hope we will have completed The Meeting before it becomes a serious problem."

Morrel smoothed the last quilt in place and stood. It looked so inviting that Nicole didn't hesitate. She climbed into one of the pallets. Morrel wiped his feet with a cloth by the bed and climbed into the other.

She yawned, folded the edge of the bottom quilt into a makeshift pillow, and yawned again. In his blankets, Morrel lay on his back, his hands clasped behind his head. He was as stiff as the chaise lounge. Perhaps, he was no more experienced with physical intimacy than she. He lived alone. Perhaps less. She had at least had a fiancé. Morrel stared fixedly at the ceiling. Nicole suppressed an urge to shout, "Boo!"

"Morrel?" she whispered. He twitched in reaction. She waited, stifling a giggle. "I felt uncomfortable before about us sleeping in the same room."

Morrel waited, not moving, not speaking.

"But I don't now," she said.

His shoulders relaxed. "Why not?"

"One, because I think you're more nervous than I am. Two, because I don't think it has to be any different than on the trail. Does it?"

"No." He sounded relieved.

"I'm kind of glad you're here," she admitted.

"Does this mean you trust me to keep you safe?" he asked.

"I suppose so," she agreed.

Morrel looked at her and smiled. His dark eyes were pinpricks of light in the twilight. "Good. Without trust, only darkness can grow. We must trust each other if the quest is to succeed."

Nicole listened to his breathing deepen. Why had she let that remark about the quest go? She was not sure she was going to be part of any quest. As much as she wanted to help, she was not the stuff of legends. She was no Amazon with bullet-repelling bracelets and a lasso of truth. Tomorrow, she would convince Morrel's grandfather this was all a mistake, and she would be escorted home. She rubbed the scar on her lip, and then she closed her eyes with a tired sigh.

Chapter Seven—Shadows

Nicole dreamed again of the dark man, but this time his features cleared and she could see it was Morrel. He smiled and called her, reaching out with his brawny arms.

She hesitated, but the light in his eyes beckoned. A shiver ran down her spine. Something lurked nearby. Something dark. She stepped into Morrel's arms, a circle of protection. His embrace was warm, his fur like a blanket against her cheek.

The darkness reached them. It poured over Morrel, turning his skin cold. It seeped from his body. She was bathed in his burning coldness, like dry ice. She dissolved, melting into the ebony gleam of his skin and fur. She no longer recognized herself.

Who was she? Could she remember who she was before Dawn's End, before Randy, before the change in her father after her mother's death? Where was that confident, energized little girl she had been with her mother? She felt lost.

In her dream, Morrel ran his arm down her back. A sudden flare of warmth spread through her body. His lips brushed her cheek.

"Trust me," he whispered. His voice was husky, sensuous.

She wanted to be what he needed, but she knew she would disappoint him. Once he knew the real Nicole, he would be gone.

I would never survive, Nicole thought. *Look at him. Masculine, strong, pure animal passion. Look at me. Wilting.*

"Enough," growled Morrel. "I will show you."

Nicole struggled in his arms. He could no longer hold his feline desire in check. He would explode over her in a fury of muscle and teeth. He would release himself like a mating animal, base and swift. Resistance was hopeless.

Morrel looked at her, eyes sad. "So little trust."

Nicole awoke bathed in sweat. She sat up. Morrel was no longer lying on the pallet beside her. He stood in the doorway, silhouetted by the lantern he held in his hand. His eyes were twin candles.

"Are you all right?" he asked.

"Yes," she whispered. "Just a bad dream."

"I'll bring you some water."

Nicole wiped her face with the quilt. Images of the dream fled from her thoughts like shadows in the noon sun. Morrel handed her a cup without speaking and waited for her to finish. Then he took the cup, crawled into his pallet, turned his back to her, and turned down the lantern. She had the uncomfortable feeling of having done something wrong. She sighed, trying to sleep but wide awake, listening to Morrel breathe. Finally, he moved. She heard him turning on his side to face her.

"Why do enjoy going to the pond so much?" he asked.

"It's quiet, beautiful. I love watching the wildlife."

"Like the cormorant."

"Yes," said Nicole. "He was injured. I took him to the vet and tried to nurse him back to health, but he died anyway. I named him Caller because I felt like he was trying to call me, to make contact. It started to get pretty strange."

Morrel rubbed his forehead. His expression seemed uncomfortable.

"I feel responsible for some of your confusion," said Morrel. "My linking to your dreams and your stress may have caused you to think the bird was trying to communicate. I think that was me."

"Oh," said Nicole. "Is that why you seem familiar sometimes?"

Morrel nodded.

"I did dream about you, too, though. Often," said Nicole. "You and Randy and the bird, all muddled up together."

"You've had a hard time," said Morrel. "I'm sorry for that. But you can't shut down, turn away from people. You're too special. The world needs you."

"Dawn's End?"

"Yes, but your world, too," insisted Morrel. "You are beautiful, Nicole. Inside and out."

"Oh," Nicole warmed at the compliment. "You're beautiful too, Morrel. Exotic."

They both stared at each other, comfortable, but unsure what else to say. Finally, Morrel broke the silence.

"I'm also very tired, as you must be."

"Of course," said Nicole as she settled back into the quilts. "I think I can sleep now. Thank you for keeping me company. I guess I just used too much adrenalin today."

"Too much of a lot of things, I suspect." Morrel turned down the lantern again and also prepared to sleep. "Sweet dreams, Nicole."

She gave a quiet laugh. "They'd better be."

And they were. Dreams of the dark man covering her in kisses, licking all her private places with his rough tongue, nibbling her skin, but this time she could see his face, smell his musk. It was Morrel, and they moved together like lusty, blissful cats.

Chapter Eight—Dance of Passion

When Nicole awoke the next morning, Morrel had already folded his quilt and rolled up the pallet. She felt oddly disappointed; the dream had seemed so real. She wandered into the eating room where he was slicing fruit into two bowls. He looked well-rested and alert. The sleeveless tan tunic emphasized his powerful deltoids and triceps. A shudder threaded through her body as she imagined how it would feel to touch them.

"Good morning," she said.

"Dawn's brightness," he replied, before sliding a bowl down the table in her direction.

"Thanks," she said. "It smells good. Everything here smells good. You, too." She inhaled deeply.

"I already washed," he replied.

A fleeting image of his soapy chest flashed through her mind. *Oh, my,* she thought as she stepped beside him and took a deep breath. "Like blueberries." It's nice to see you looking so clean. You were pretty ragged when we arrived last night."

"You also look much better," said Morrel as he pushed her loose, tangled hair back over one shoulder. He twirled a strand of her hair around his finger and then traced her cheekbone. Their eyes met. He dropped his hand and stepped back.

"I am going to have my shoulder treated," he explained. "We will arrange supplies and spend the day resting."

"In here?"

"No. The villagers need to meet you," he said. "After all, you will be spoken about for generations to come."

Nicole frowned. "I will. Why?"

"As the one who saved our world . . . . "

Nicole tensed.

"Or," he continued, "the one who let it die."

Nicole paused, a fruit halfway to her mouth. She dropped it back into the bowl.

"What if I say yes, and then we fail?" she asked. "Will I be known as the one who tried and fell on her face?"

"No more than I," he said. "Please, Nicole. Do not speak of this to my people. Let them have this one day of hope."

Nicole nodded. "Okay. So what now?"

"Today, my simple people are going to be unusually elaborate in your honor. Everyone will dress in their best clothes and prepare their most delicious dishes," said Morrel with a devastating smile. "And, I have a surprise for you, a present. But first, you had best clean and groom. As lovely as your auburn hair is, it could still use a comb."

Alaric Sabella was first to arrive. She brought Nicole to her home where black and brown females were fussing about with preparations for Nicole.

"This is Linnel, Zareen, and Patia," said Alaric Sabella. Nicole was shocked when she saw the first tawny face and blurted out, "You come in different colors!"

The girls giggled. "Don't humans?" said Zareen.

Nicole blushed at her own stupidity. "Of course. I just thought everyone looked like Morrel."

"Now, wouldn't *that* be wonderful!" said Linnel, giving Nicole a conspiratorial wink.

Linnel ordered the women about with light-hearted gaiety. Nicole chose a warm cloak, coated in waterproof oil. It would keep her dry in wet weather and become a warm wrap at night. She picked a pair of suede overpants and an extra sweater knitted from a fuzzy yarn.

"I have everything else I need," she said. "I just didn't anticipate snow."

The girls were clearly anxious to be helpful but unsure what to do.

"I do wish I had my first-aid kit, though," said Nicole.

The girls jumped at the chance to provide. They offered bandages, powders, a curved needle and thread (which gave Nicole goose bumps knowing it was for stitching flesh), ointment, pads, and a painkilling draught.

Morrel arrived bringing a bundle of food and a sheathed knife. The girls stepped back in awe, exchanging large-eyed glances, when he announced, "I've brought Nicole a gift."

The girls rubbernecked as Nicole unwrapped the rectangular cloth. Inside was a soft, white ankle length gown elaborately patterned with hand-stitched black panther silhouettes. She felt a rush of pleasure and wondered if Morrel had chosen it. There was a rustle of admiration as she held it up.

"It is for you to wear during the celebration," he said, smiling. "There is a belt to help it fit better. I tried to convince them you had a tiny waist but I think it is still a bit too loose. The neckline, however, should be very flattering." His smile widened, showing the tips of his pointed fangs. Nicole shivered, thinking of those teeth against her breast.

Suddenly, Linnel snapped into movement, ushering the other two women out of the room, exiting herself, and shutting the door behind her.

Nicole ran her fingers along the deep pile of the fabric and detailed workmanship. She smiled at the long sleeves, the first she'd seen, probably a concession to her lack of body hair. She lifted the dress to her chest. It was the perfect size.

She stepped up to Morrel and kissed his cheek.

"Thank you," she said. "It is spectacular."

"You are most welcome." He stroked her hair once. They smiled at each other.

"I must go," he said. "I too must change clothes and look my best, though no one will be looking at me once you arrive."

As soon as he left, Nicole said, "I will."

The excited chatter of the returning young women filled the room. Zareen packed Nicole's travelling gear and scurried off to deliver it to Morrel's home. Then, Linnel and Patia filled the tub in the next room with floral-scented water.

I feel like a queen, thought Nicole. *I just hope they don't intend to wash me, too.*

Fortunately, the girls wanted to prepare themselves as well. Only Linnel and Patia stayed, but they allowed Nicole her privacy. After the bath, the women returned with hand fans and dried her hair, raving over its thick natural curl. Nicole realized every panther person she had met had straight hair. Then Patia started to braid her hair in sections.

"No," said Linnel. "We must not hide all the lovely waves."

The two girls argued loudly and finally compromised. Part would be braided and part would hang loose. Nicole didn't dare voice an opinion. It was as though they were two little girls deciding how best to dress their doll. Zareen returned with tiny, stiff white flowers. Linnel threaded them into Nicole's hair as the other two cleaned up. She helped Nicole slip into the beautiful gown.

"I have no dress shoes," said Nicole.

"Shoes?" said Linnel. "Oh, of course, your feet are bare and tender. We do have footwear for the cold season."

Nicole glanced at their furry, thickly padded, clawed feet. *How sad,* she thought. *No shoe shopping.*

Zareen dropped to the floor, measured Nicole's foot against her hand and hurried off. "Such little feet for such a tall woman," she said.

Nicole shrugged. She watched Patia wipe the tub dry and rub it with pale leaves, refusing any help. After Patia departed, Nicole heard the hum of voices in the square.

"The villagers are already arriving," said Linnel.

"I could go barefoot," offered Nicole. "It's no problem, really."

"No, no. That will not do. Do not worry," said Linnel, tapping her own foot nervously.

Zareen burst through the door, two pairs of slippers in her hands. The second, made of black felt, fit beautifully. The two young panther women sighed with elaborate relief.

Linnel touched Nicole's shoulder. "Morrel will come for you. We will see you later." She left with Zareen.

After all the hustle and bustle, time seemed to stop. Nicole wandered about the waiting room examining tapestries and sculptures until Morrel finally returned.

"The way you look, you will be subject of legend and song for centuries to come," said Morrel, as he looked her up and down approvingly.

Nicole smiled and looked down at the dress. It was certainly nothing like what she usually wore, but she did feel pretty.

Morrel wore black pants and a short white tunic with a leopard embroidered on the chest. A gold headband encircled his full, black hair. His midriff was bare. Even below the hair, Nicole noticed the tight muscles. She wondered how those abdominal muscles would feel beneath her hand or pressed against her belly.

She swallowed and said, "You look wonderful yourself, Morrel."

She spun round in her dress feeling the urge to dance. "I don't know why I feel so giddy," she said.

"You have been too despondent for too long. And since your arrival, you have been mostly frightened. Your spirit yearns for a lighter heart." Morrel moved beside her and inhaled deeply. "Now, you smell good, too. Even the Virgin's Bloom."

"What?"

"The flowers." Morrel pointed to her hair. "They're called Virgin's Bloom."

Nicole laughed into her hand. "I hope that's not intentional. That bloom has passed."

Morrel laughed loudly, open-mouthed. Nicole realized the roof of his mouth was also black and stared in fascination. He clicked his mouth shut, conscious of her reaction.

Damn, she thought. *I'm such an ass.*

Then, Morrel winked, and they both laughed.

"I love the needlework your people do," she said, stepping toward him and touching the stitched panther on his tunic. "Such skill."

Morrel examined his powerful hands, turning them over and back, flexing his claws in and out. "You would not think hands like ours were capable of such delicate, gentle work, would you?"

Nicole took his hands in hers. "I think you are capable of doing anything you set your mind to."

"Even look suitable enough to escort a beautiful human woman to the festivities?" he asked.

"Very suitable," she said. A tautness filled her abdomen. "You're striking in these austerely elegant clothes, Alaric Morrel, and you must know it." Her voice took on a teasing note. "They show off your strong, perfect body." She dropped his hands and ran them over his shoulders.

"I will dress like this every day if it pleases you," he whispered.

Nicole ran one finger down the hair of his arm. He took her hand and brought it to his face, barely touching it with his soft lips. She shivered.

"Time to go," he said. His voice was husky, strained.

Nicole concentrated on moving her legs in a controlled manner, watching the way the muscles in his neck flexed as he led her outside.

Then, she was lost in a swirl of faces in a variety of shades of gray, black, brown, tan, and even orange. Everyone wanted to meet her. The villagers smiled and hugged her gently in greeting, until Morrel intervened. He sat her on the grass between himself and Sabella. The panther people settled into a rough circle, and music began to play. Wild rhythm pounded from drums and three stringed instruments. Pleasantly surprised, Nicole was soon caught in its grip.

First, a throng of young females danced. Linnel moved with innocent grace. When the dance ended, Nicole waved to the girls she recognized. They giggled, waving back excitedly. People applauded the dancers by humming, grunting, and growling.

Each dance began and ended with a bow toward first Morrel, then Nicole, and finally Sabella. An elder male danced ceremoniously. Nicole recognized much of his movements as a mixture pantomime and dance. He was telling a story with his body. The mood of the audience turned serious, and Nicole felt several inquiring and piercing looks aimed in her direction.

Four dance selections followed; the dancers were a mixture of ages and sexes. Nicole was particularity impressed with a provocative performance by a brown and black female. A knot of jealousy formed in her stomach when the dancer cast 'come hither' glances at Morrel. He gave a polite nod, but he remained impervious to her charms.

During the next number, Larina soared past and perched on the edge of a roof. Nicole waved. The feathered lady hesitated and then bobbed her little head in return. Children performed a simply patterned dance, weaving strips of white cloth around each other. As the youngsters cleared the square and scuffled with one another for seats, Nicole felt the crowd adjust. They were expectant, chattering with anticipation. She recognized the buzz as the excitement that builds just before a star performer takes the stage.

Pound! Pound! Pound! The slow insistent beat of the drums threaded through Nicole's body. The crowd hushed. She waited for the dancer to appear where the dancers had entered the clearing , but, instead, a bright figure leapt over the seated villagers into the square. He flung his arms wide, head back, and drank up the crowd's response. His skin and hair were pure white.

A black jumpsuit, cut low in front, deep in the arm holes, and high up the calves, flattered his muscular body. He wore his thick, wild, ivory hair long and loose down his back.

He danced in jerky, muscular movements around the square, throwing himself face down in front of Nicole. He arched upward, then forward, and met her eyes. Nicole gasped. The irises were deep red with white-diamond pupils.

Nicole was mesmerized by this albino dancer. Everything about him was exotic and vibrant. Launching into back flips, he increased his pace. Bare feet flashing in the dust, he urged the drummers to harder, faster rhythms. Leaping, spinning, bending, stamping, he drew the crowd like asteroids to a black hole. Sweat ran down his face and spun off his hair.

Again, he paused in front of Nicole. His chest heaved, the soaked hairs plastered to his muscular body. The drums beat softly, urgently. Strings tiptoed along the surface of the music. Deliberately, provocatively, he stretched, swayed, and churned for Nicole. *First a gymnast, then like a Chippendale, and now almost ballet!* she thought.

Leaning forward, Nicole swallowed; her lips and throat were parched from shallow mouth breathing. Her eyes were riveted on the dancer. He smiled, teasingly, extended his hand, and then leapt away, ending in frantic lunges and kicks, before vanishing over the crowd.

Nicole sat, hammered in place, while the crowd roared. Cheeks flushed, she gave a long exhale, and turned to Morrel. He stared straight ahead, lips tightly pressed together, eyes narrowed.

A young couple performed a gentle duet. An elderly male danced ritually, telling a story of spring planting. Gradually, other seniors joined him, building on the story. When their performance ended, the crowd moved toward the tables. There was laughter and much chatter.

Where the edge of the forest met the border of the village, an unobserved dark creature stood. The pounding rhythms had tortured its mind, filling it with the urge to charge, but a small instinctive recognition of danger made it wait. Saliva dripped from its slack jaw as the scent of food reached it from the banquet table, but, still, it hesitated. It hated the happy sounds, the laughter. It hated the light. But more and more the ooze of darkness spread, and the creature felt its own power increasing each nightfall. All memory of the creature's former self had disappeared, leaving only instinct, anger, and hunger in its place.

When the music resumed, the creature clawed into the earth, trying to protect its ears from the sound. Fortunately, it had come alone. Frenzied by the music, it would have torn to bits any fellow creature, drowning out the piercing sounds with its victim's squeals of pain and the taste of its blood. The other creatures were banding together in the forest, forming an invincible assemblage, preparing to attack the beings who threatened their existence, the panther people who refused to be subdued. They did not speak to each other. Communication was subliminal, simple. Yet, they knew the power of groups and when to join together. Soon, they would be on the move. Waiting was so difficult. The creature shook its head, spittle flying. It needed the taste of blood now.

Morrel handed Nicole a plate and watched her choose from the vast array of dishes. Breads, puddings, fish, shellfish, fresh and dried and steamed fruits and vegetables. Some foods looked slightly familiar, but most were strange. To her surprise, she loved everything she tasted.

Sabella joined them on the bench. When Morrel carried away their plates, stopping to chat to others along the way, Nicole questioned Sabella.

"Morrel has tried to explain the threat facing your land, but little else. May I ask you some questions?"

Nicole nodded. "Does the magic work for you too?"

"Magic?" Sabella wrinkled her nose.

"Of the bracelet," said Nicole. "Morrel said it opens the door to my land. Some bandits we encountered wanted to use its power."

"Fools." Sabella shook her head in disgust. "Power comes with a price they may not wish to pay."

"What price is that?"

Sabella looked away. Her expression softened. "Each generation, the children are altered. We were not always thus." She gestured at her own face and body. "Once, my people looked like you. Each generation is born more panther-like when we use the bracelets. As our bodies devolve, so do our minds, and our attitudes. We do not use the bracelets lightly. They are not trifles." Her voice lowered, flattened.

"It changes your genetics!" gasped Nicole.

"Eventually, my people will cease to exist. We will become one with the leopard."

Nicole's eyes widened. "Larina? How does she fit in?"

"Larina comes from a family more ancient than ours. Her family wore the bracelets before we did. Then, they held the image of a blue bird," explained Sabella. "Her family saved Dawn's Land repeatedly from the eternal darkness. Slowly, they shrank, grew feathers, beaks, wings, until they became like you see her now. I believe her influence is strong on my son. She inspires him."

"Is that why he connected with me through the cormorant?"

"Cormorant? I do not know what this is."

"A black water bird."

"Ah, possibly. But, perhaps its qualities were the closest he could find to himself. Perhaps he thought you already had a fondness for the creature and would be more open to it than a wild feline. Do you encounter many panthers in your world?"

Nicole laughed and shook her head. "So, Larina's ancestors were human?"

"Yes. Larina is a throw-back. She is capable of thoughts and emotions largely unknown to her people. She is brave and wise and would do anything for Morrel."

"I think she loves him," said Nicole.

Sabella nodded.

Nicole continued. "Morrel and the white dancer are the only ones I have seen with the white diamond shape in the pupils of their eyes."

"Morrel's eyes changed when he entered manhood. That is how we knew he was suitable for The Meeting."

Chapter Nine—Scars

Morrel looked in Nicole's direction. She smiled in return. He nodded, understanding she was comfortable talking with his mother, and joined another group.

"If Larina's people were once human, and now they are birds, does that mean there was an in-between stage as there seems to be for you, the panther people? If that isn't too personal to ask."

Sabella smiled. "No need to be self-conscious. Yes. Legend says the bird people were quite beautiful. I imagine they were less frightening to those of your world than we are. Sharp claws and fangs signal predator to humans, whereas beaks and four-toed bird claws are bizarre but not threatening. When the last of her line became like Larina, none of her people could wield the power of the bracelets any longer. Then the wizards reforged the bands, and our family was entrusted with their responsibility."

"When was that?"

"Eight hundred years ago, the Alaric clan began the descent into oblivion," said Sabella softly. "Like Larina, we will eventually be trapped inside the bodies of animals. The bracelets will again be reforged into a new species."

Nicole's eyes filled with tears. "This is horrible. Can't you get rid of the bracelets?"

"Then who would stop the night?" said Sabella. "Instead of the destruction of some, it would be the destruction of all. To desert our cause would bring us great shame. Morrel does what he has to do, with honor. We know no other way."

"I guess I understand." Nicole chewed her lip and then added. "But it's horrible."

"It is not all sacrifice," said Sabella as she patted Nicole's hand. "Legend states that The Meeting allows the Alaric to experience human emotions to a depth never before achieved, a fascinating thought."

"What is this meeting, anyway?" asked Nicole.

Sabella shrugged. "You will have to find out for yourself. It is part of your quest."

Nicole opened her mouth to protest but then stopped.

"Besides, all I really know is rumor. The keepers are so secretive." Sabella gave a little grin.

Alaric Sabella rose as a male approached them. With a flutter, Nicole realized it was the passionate dancer, now wearing a scarlet jumpsuit and a gold headband and bracelet. He nodded, with cocky confidence, to young admirers in passing.

"Stop strutting and sit," said Sabella as he reached them.

Aubin smiled and kissed their hands in turn, lingering over Nicole's.

Zareen called from across the village square, "Alaric Sabella. We need your advice."

"Coming, dear," Sabella turned to the dancer and said, "Try to behave, Aubin."

"Aunt, you wrong me," he said as she departed. He sat beside Nicole on the bench. "Well, she of the sunrise hair, did you enjoy the entertainment?"

"Excellent," said Nicole. "I can see you're the star of the show. I enjoyed it very much."

"I thought you did," he responded, lowering his voice and moving closer.

Nicole stiffened, realizing he was coming on to her. Her eyes searched the crowd for Morrel.

"Relax," purred Aubin. "I am Alaric too." He held up his panther bracelet.

"You're Morrel's cousin, aren't you?" she said.

"We are of the same lineage," answered Aubin. "But I am not innocent, dull, and serious like Morrel. A woman with fire in her hair would enjoy my company. I would make sure she found it . . . satisfying." He slid closer to her until their thighs were touching on the bench. His musky scent flooded her nostrils. "I could Meet with you instead," he whispered, his breath on her cheek. "It would be such a Meeting that you would wonder what you ever saw in Morrel. We would experience great enjoyment."

"But you would not enjoy the challenges along the way," said Morrel, suddenly over their shoulders.

"I could face any challenges you could," snapped Aubin as he stood to face him, the bench in between.

"Perhaps," say Morrel. "But would you learn from them?"

Aubin snorted and said to Nicole. "Always a scholar. Even in this."

"Especially in this," said Morrel. "And *you* are always rash."

Aubin jumped over the bench and faced Morrel. Aubin's face was flushed and contorted; Morrel's was calm and steady.

97

"What's wrong?" asked Nicole, getting to her feet.

"Nothing. Right, cousin?" said Morrel.

Aubin hissed like an angry cat and strode away.

"Whew," said Nicole as she sat down. "What was that all about?"

"Aubin becomes worse with each passing year," said Morrel. "We used to be the best of friends."

"He has a bracelet too. And the same diamonds in his eyes."

Morrel nodded and sat beside her. "Once, I thought it was good for Aubin to also have a panther bracelet, to share the responsibility. But now . . . . He is changing. He uses it as a toy, not caring about the consequences. If I could remove his . . . . " He shrugged. "Forget him. One cannot live the life of another. We have time for a bit of Telling before nightfall. Come and sit again in the circle."

"Telling what?" asked Nicole.

"Stories, poems, news, whatever anyone wishes to tell. Do not be surprised if you are asked to speak."

Nicole sputtered as she stood. "Oh, no."

"You must not worry." Morrel patted her shoulder reassuringly as they headed toward the gathering. "Just tell them about your world."

As everyone settled, Nicole sat between Morrel and a light brown pregnant female. She wondered if the female had ancestors who had worn a bracelet. Would the child be more feline than its mother? Morrel introduced her as Dorinda.

"Hasn't this been a marvelous day?" Dorinda said. "Not a cloud in the sky and a smile on everyone's face."

Nicole agreed. Dorinda spoke of the upcoming birth with happy anticipation just like any other mother.

The children joined in the circle. The pre-adolescents were almost smooth-skinned, their body hair light and sparse. From afar, those with typical skin colorations could pass for children of Nicole's world.

Dorinda's husband was a quiet, smiling, gray being. The two of them sat close together, holding hands. *How wonderful to have a relationship like that. Someone who loves and cares for you, that you trust in return*, Nicole thought.

"I ache from sitting so much today," complained Dorinda, arching her back.

Her husband moved behind her and pressed his knuckles into the small of her back. She moaned gently. Then he massaged her shoulders. He winked at Nicole.

"Isn't she beautiful?" he said. "My lovely mother-to-be, ripe as an autumn fruit."

Nicole felt a stab of envy.

The elder, who had danced with such dignity, organized the Telling. He started with a poem, his eyes roving from one listener to the next. He chanted in a raspy voice,

"Black on white, white in black,

Shades of night grow in attack,

Silhouetted by the sun,

Comes the darkest chosen one.

The wizard's stone is his device.

What does he have to sacrifice?

Eternity within the band.

For her, a chance to understand.

Their final selves infuse in light,

United, they push back the night."

Again, Nicole felt the curious villagers assessing her. She fidgeted. Morrel put his arm around her shoulder, casual yet comforting.

Others told stories and poems. Some were humorous, teasing tales, veiled references to people in their midst. These caused raised eyebrows, giggles, and a few pokes. There were also poems of beauty, death, and mystery. Finally, Dorinda asked Nicole to tell about the other world.

What could she say? She was at a complete loss.

"Tell them about the cormorant," suggested Morrel.

She smiled at him gratefully. She described the winter turning into spring, the growth of grass, trees, and flowers, the return of the animals, and the special cormorant. She meant to stop there, but the people encouraged her to go on. She spoke of the beauty of the Sleeping Giant in its many moods, back lit by an azure sky, drenched in the gray of a thunderous day, or floating on a cloud of mist. They applauded and chattered about how fortunate she was to live in such a beautiful place.

"Yes," agreed Nicole. "I am very fortunate. I would not want to live anywhere else." She gave Morrel a pointed look.

"Should we give it to her now, Alaric Morrel?" interrupted Zareen.

"Yes." He took the bag from her hands. "This is for Nicole. When I first saw her, she was playing one of these. She left it behind at the pond, and another person took it. I know she will say she is out of practice, but I would be pleased to hear it." He handed the bag to Nicole.

She opened the drawstring, took out a bundle and unwrapped it with a sense of awe. "Morrel! Wherever did you get a flute?"

"I need not tell all my secrets. It is the only one I know of in Dawn's End, so do not leave this one carelessly lying around," he teased.

"Thank you!" She flung her arms around him and kissed him on the lips. The villagers hummed. Nicole laughed, and covered her mouth at her own audacity.

"Please play it," requested Morrel.

She tried the scale. The pitch was perfect. She started with a simple tune, then a few favorites, and then copied a section of a dance the villagers had performed. The audience responded enthusiastically. Morrel rubbed her shoulder proudly.

The Telling ended, and people prepared for the night. As the villagers cleared away the last of their things, Nicole heard screams from a small group of children heading toward the buildings. Morrel, Aubin, Dorinda's husband, Zareen, Linnel and others, dashed to the call, unsheathing their knives. The sounds of shouting and crashing followed as Nicole sought the comfort of Dorinda's company.

"What is it?" Nicole asked.

Dorinda shook her head. "I dread to think."

When the villagers returned, one woman had a small cut on her cheek, and a man clenched his bleeding arm. Their families rushed to administer treatment. No one was seriously hurt.

"It was a thing of the night," said Morrel. "They have never ventured into the village before. It is not even dark yet. This worries me greatly. Fortunately, it was no match for all of us."

Sabella approached. "From now on, the villagers will travel in groups," she said. "Two adults for every child as well, until The Meeting is completed."

Aubin snorted. "If The Meeting *is* completed. I have my doubts. The scholar and this confused, frightened creature he has chosen."

"Be quiet!" ordered Morrel.

"You are wasting time while our children are endangered and our people wounded," insisted Aubin. "I should have been the one chosen. The woman I picked would have been willing and committed, not hesitant and afraid like this one."

"That is enough!" snapped Sabella.

Aubin whirled on his heel and strode away.

Morrel turned to Nicole. "Are you still frightened, Nicole?"

"I'd be lying if I said no," she answered. "I'd probably still hide in a tree if one of those things came at me. I'm not a fighter, and I don't have claws and fangs to defend myself."

"No matter. You are not here to slay beasts. That is my job. Do you not think I can protect you?"

Nicole smiled. "I think you can, but I'll probably still be scared all the time while I'm here, and I still want to know what I'm getting into." *If I'm getting into anything at all*, she thought. *Why do I say things that sound as if I am staying?*

Morrel looked downcast.

"It's not your fault," she continued. "It's me. I just . . . . It's hard to explain. I don't really understand what I feel or what I want. And I'm not too good with trust."

"I'm not invincible. But nothing will harm you as long as I can still breathe. I cannot guarantee what would happen if I fall."

"There's always Larina," laughed Nicole.

He smiled and stroked her cheek with his knuckles. The soft hair tickled, like a butterfly kiss.

Later, as they crawled into their pallets, Nicole spoke. "Why is the other room so bare, just a mat and a wall hanging of a leaping leopard?"

"It is my meditation room."

"That's where you converse with the bracelet?" she asked.

"Not exactly. Meditation is a large part of our culture, especially for the bearers of the bands."

"So, what does the bracelet do?"

Morrel replied, "At times, it sends me thoughts, warnings, clues really. The more one meditates, the more one is in tune with all aspects of Dawn's End, and, of course, one's self."

"Does everyone have a room like that?"

"Some have just a corner. Grandfather meditates out of doors. It does not distract him when children run by or animals call. He is completely grounded, focused. He teaches me, and I, in turn, teach those with less experience."

"Is that your job then?" she asked.

"Job?" asked Morrel.

"Role in this society. How you make your living."

"I do not understand," he said.

"How do your people survive? Who makes the clothes you wear? Provides the food? Do you have a monetary system? A barter system? What?"

"I see. We all do what we do best or enjoy best. We trade, share. At harvest time, though, everyone must help. We are gathers of wild food as well. We trade with other villages, those not of the panther," explained Morrel.

"What do you give to the other villages in exchange?"

"Although the bracelet takes away, it also gives," said Morrel. "Our panther qualities provide us with skills other races lack. We trade our skills."

"I know you are amazingly strong. Is that a skill you offer?"

"Yes," said Morrel. "Also, our people run quickly and are often used as messengers. We work well with animals. We gather herbs and precious stones and sell these. We can climb anywhere, sniff out anything, and cover large territories quickly."

"Wow, that's impressive."

"My tribe has other crafts as well, original talents of our family. Our working of marble and our embroidery of cloth are widely respected."

"Interesting," Nicole nodded. "Other than Aubin's outburst, your people seem very harmonious."

"Why should we not be? We have all we need and more. Food, shelter, strength, companionship, art, freedom, and— until the growth of darkness—peace."

"Many people in my world would still not be satisfied. There are some who think power is the most important. They would destroy those wonderful things in order to have power or wealth."

Morrel wrinkled his forehead in puzzlement. "I wonder if power is what Aubin craves. I do not understand its allure."

"Yeah, I don't get it either," agreed Nicole. "I hope it all works out for you, Morrel. Dawn's End is worth preserving."

"I will protect it with everything I have, no matter what the cost," he said.

"Don't say that. You should protect yourself too."

"Can we not all protect each other? The weak help the strong, the adult the child?"

Nicole absently rubbed the scar on her lip and rolled away. Morrel reached over and rolled her back.

"What is it?" he said.

"Nothing."

"I promised no more deceits. You must abide by that as well," chided Morrel.

"Not all adults are capable, or even there," said Nicole.

"Tell me."

Nicole twirled her finger in the quilt, thinking. "My mother died a month before my eighth birthday. She was struck by a car. I felt like a turtle that had been flipped on its back and left to dry out in the sun."

"I know turtles. You are very much like one."

"Slow?"

"No. Drawn into a hard shell," he said. "Keeping your softness hidden."

"Hang your softness out and it's liable to be stepped on," said Nicole.

"Or cared for. Did your mother not care for you?" asked Morrel.

"Yes. My mother was wonderful. She had the sweetest voice. She used to read me bedtime stories. When I was six, I got a book called *Twelve Faerietales.* I loved it so much; she read it over and over. After a while, I knew parts by heart. We'd recite it together, changing our voices for the different characters, and laughing."

"You miss her."

"Not now," said Nicole. "I'm a grown woman. I did when I was little, sure."

Morrel put his hand under her chin and looked into her eyes. "You miss her," he said. Nicole nodded.

"I don't have any brothers or sisters," she said.

"Your father?"

"We were never really close. It was my mother who kept things smooth between us. Kept nudging us toward each other. She could make him laugh. She had the best sense of humor. He loved her like I never saw him love anyone else, even my stepmother."

"He married again?"

"Yes, when I was fifteen. She's okay. Her name's Gloria. She's a very busy woman, hard-working. Well meaning."

"But you don't have much of a relationship with her."

Nicole tipped her head in an "I don't know" gesture.

"How did you get the scar?"

She touched her lip quickly. "I told you before. Tobogganing."

"How?" he asked.

"I got it the winter after Mom died. It was a beautiful day. Dad and I had a distant relationship, but I think he felt it was his duty to do things with me. He wasn't much for winter activities, but, once we got outside, we always had a good time, at least when Mom was around. I had asked Dad to take me tobogganing. I don't know why. It just seemed important that we do the things we used to do with Mom. So we could remember her, you know? But Dad didn't want to go."

"Did he?"

"I made a slide in the snow banks of our driveway, but I was too big for such a little hill. A neighbor came by to borrow something from my Dad and said he'd take me sliding if Dad didn't have time. Dad got all indignant and said he could take me himself. We went to Thunder Park."

"Good," said Morrel.

"There were wide rolling hills filled with kids and three iced sled chutes. My father wanted me to use them. Mom always let me go on the hill. Parks and Rec had built the chutes out of wood and iced them so the toboggans shot down like bullets. The sides kept you straight, but they scared me. My father got angry because I wouldn't go. I started to sniffle. He said he never should have brought me. It was a waste of time, and he had so much to do."

"Did you go down the chute?"

"No. I went to the top of the chute and sat down. I started thinking about what Mom would do, and then I started really crying. My father finally came to the top. He told me to stop carrying on. That I could go on the hill if I wanted. Then he picked up the toboggan and dragged it to the top of the hill. He told me to get on, and he gave it a running shove."

"What happened?"

"I hung on with all my might. The wind stung my eyes. I blinked and blinked, trying to see. Suddenly, there was another toboggan beside me. We collided. Their front end flew over mine and hit me in the face. I remember my head snapping back and children screaming. Afterwards, I realized no one had been hurt but me. They were having fun."

"They did not realize you were injured."

"I know. One of my teeth was knocked out, a baby tooth luckily, and I needed stitches in my lip. My father kept saying that, if I'd gone on the chute like he wanted, it never would have happened."

"Is that true?"

"Maybe. Kids get hurt on the chutes too. I just wonder why he had to push me so hard. Didn't he see the other toboggan?" Her voice was small.

"Do you think he did it on purpose?"

"No, I suspected for a long time, but probably not."

"Perhaps he was hurting as well."

Nicole sniffed. "Yeah, but he never said he was sorry."

Morrel drew her into his arms. He didn't seem to mind the tears on his chest. Finally, she fell asleep.

Chapter Ten—Death of an Age

The gray, overcast morning smothered Dawn's End in dreariness. The trees encircling the village began to droop, and wildflowers clutched their petals tightly closed. Yet, it did not feel like rain. It reminded Nicole of the heavy smog of large, car-choked cities. No birds broke the dull stillness with song. Even the wind was sluggish.

Nicole and Morrel packed and left the village in silence. Alaric Sabella and Linnel saw them quietly off. The gloom had kept most people indoors.

The land was lightly forested, hilly, and interspersed with stone formations. A few moments outside the village, they saw a mound of pale limestone topped with a small figure sitting cross-legged and staring into space. Nicole hesitated, reluctant to disrupt his meditation, but Morrel strode forward eagerly.

"Grandfather," he called.

As the elder man stood, Nicole realized he was as large as Morrel, but thin and slack. His body was covered with white hair, tinged with yellow from age. Calm, gray eyes with white diamond centers in a wrinkled, smiling face lit up at the approach of his grandson.

"Welcome, Morrel." His voice was deep and still strong. He clasped Morrel on the shoulder and then turned to Nicole. "You must be the woman from the outworld. Brave *and* beautiful, a rare combination."

Nicole flinched at this undeserved praise.

"This is Nicole Newman," said Morrel. "She has *not* decided yet to participate in the quest."

The old man's face fell. "But she is here. You have done well, my grandson, and now so must I. I will explain to Nicole why we need her. I will help her to understand. If she has the potential you feel she has, then all will be well." He smiled at Nicole. "Come and sit with me young lady."

Nicole sat opposite the grandfather, setting her pack beside her on the ground.

"My name is Alaric Bethane." He gave a formal nod. "I am Morrel's Great-Grandfather. I have outlived both my son and my grandson, who died together in an accident."

"I'm sorry," said Nicole. She looked at Morrel, realizing that would be his father. He had never said anything about losing a parent of his own.

"I was very young when it happened," said Morrel. "They were erecting a marble ceiling when the entire building collapsed. Father, Grandfather, and Uncle were all killed."

"I am sorry for you, Morrel. That is tragic," said Nicole. She took a moment to absorb this. "You said Uncle? Aubin's father?"

"Yes," answered Alaric Bethane. "Aubin has not handled it well. He is all charm and flash on the surface, but beneath that is hurt and anger. His impulsiveness has made him unsuitable for the quest."

"But I'm not suitable either," said Nicole. "I think Morrel has made a mistake. There must be hundreds of woman far more capable and suited to a challenge. I'm physically out of shape. I've been emotionally scattered this year as well, unfocussed, even depressed. My adventures in life have only been in books. I'm the last person equipped to take on a risky quest."

111

Alaric Bethane smiled. "Both Morrel and the bracelet were wise in their choice. I think you are exactly the right person."

"But—" Nicole protested.

Morrel interrupted. "I am very satisfied with the choice."

Grandfather nodded and took Nicole's hand. "You could not have come even this far if you were truly incapable. You can succeed if you wish. All you need is confidence and determination."

"But why should I?" blurted Nicole. "I mean, why should I risk my life, and it seems that's what I'll be doing if I say yes."

She expected anger in return, but the elder chuckled. "Why indeed?" He settled back, his voice taking on the tone of the storyteller. "You need a personal motivation. Perhaps duty to your own kind might appeal to you. Dawn's End is not your land, yet it is of value to you and your people. Although you are not aware of it consciously, our lives filter through to your world. That is how Morrel was able to contact you, through your dreams."

"Yes, I understand that," she admitted. "I've seen him in action. Do other people in my world dream about Dawn's End?"

"In a way," said Bethane. "Our vibrations reach the minds of those in light sleep, the stage when you are fully relaxed and your mind is open and vibrant. With the increase in numbers of the dark things, I believe many people in your world are experiencing an upsurge in nightmares. Even in dark thoughts during their waking hours. They will be more curt than usual, squabble more. Crime will rise, especially domestic violence."

"Really? Dawn's End is like our dream world? I can't see people's behavior changing because of a few nightmares. They don't affect us that much." Nicole shrugged.

"Don't they?" continued Bethane. "But it is not as simple as that. We are real, but your people are so afraid of our reality that the only time they allow themselves to see us is in the twilight of dreams or the subconscious expressions of art. How will they feel when they are forced to see the dark things every time they fall asleep or let their minds wander during their waking hours?"

"I see. So, if I don't help your people, my people will become afraid to fall asleep because of the growth of dark things? If they do sleep, they won't sleep well? As a result, they will be more prone to behave in negative ways. Is that it?" asked Nicole.

"It may be much worse than that," said Bethane. "I am not positive the doors to your world will hold against the dark things once Nightfall gains full control."

Nicole's eyes widened. She leaned toward Bethane. "What? Morrel said the bracelets control the door."

"Doors can be shattered as well as opened," continued Bethane. "I may be completely wrong, but the power of Nightfall worries me. I am unsure of the limits of the dark things. If we can't stop them from destroying Dawn's End, what is there to stop them from spreading any way they can?"

"Are you saying they might invade my world?" asked Nicole.

"Perhaps, or slip through a little at a time, until your night lengthens out of season," said Alaric Bethane. "My son believed it would affect your world differently since you already have so many varieties of evil. He thought that, instead of night lengthening, there might be weather and

113

climatic changes. Flooding, tornadoes, drought, wildfires, uncharacteristic temperatures."

Nicole's eyes widened. "Like climate change?"

"He called it the growth of heat. I did not think it could be as bad as the darkness, but . . . . " He shrugged.

"It could," said Nicole. She rubbed her forehead anxiously. "It has already begun, but because of things we have done, not because of the dark things. I think. But any more impact on our environment could cause massive problems."

The men exchanged worried glances. Grandfather continued, "I am not saying that, in saving Dawn's End, you *will* save your own world. I have no wish to deceive you. It seems your people have their own battles to fight. But, if our world falls, it may cause negative vibrations in yours which will only intensify your problems. All I know for certain is that no good will come of it, and I'm not sure how far and how deep the negative changes will make themselves felt."

Nicole sighed. "My world has been on the brink of destruction for most of my life. I doubt if it could take any extra weight. Why didn't you tell me these things, Morrel?"

"I did not know them." Morrel shook his head.

"There is much Morrel is too inexperienced to grasp," said Bethane. "His knowledge of your world is even more limited than mine. He thinks he knows more than he does."

Morrel squirmed, uncomfortably, as Nicole tried, but failed, to suppress a grin.

"Besides, it seemed better to have you see our world and the growing Nightfall for yourself," Bethane said. "There was already so much you had to accept on faith."

"Nicole is not prone to accepting things on faith," said Morrel.

It was Nicole's turn to squirm in embarrassment. "I have encountered some of the dark things here," she said. "I believe they are real."

"I know," said Alaric Bethane. "The bracelet allows me to see when others with the band are in danger. A curse, in a way, since there is nothing I can do to help from a distance. It stretches my vision in many ways."

"Grandfather is far beyond my skills," said Morrel. "He can tell us what is happening in distant corners of our world, and sometimes he can tell us what the future holds before it happens."

"Can you tell what is going to happen to us?" asked Nicole.

Alaric Bethane smiled sadly at each in turn. "Alas, I can only see part of today. My vision ceases. I will not be able to help you in the future."

Morrel's brow furrowed in puzzlement. He seemed to be struggling with a question, but Nicole spoke first.

"Tell me what we need to do," she said. "I'm not agreeing to anything, mind you, but I'll hear you out."

"That is fair," said the elder. "In order for the power of Nightfall to be defeated, the prophecy says Morrel and an outworld woman must complete the quest together and arrive at The Meeting on time."

"On time?"

"Before the sun sets at midday, when the darkness rules three-quarters of the time. By then, we will have lost. It will be too late to turn back the damage." He frowned. "The chosen woman must be committed to the quest, so, if you decide to leave, Morrel will need to return you to your world quickly and try to find someone else."

Nicole clenched her teeth as a tingle of jealousy passed through her. She bristled at the thought of another woman cuddling up to Morrel by a campfire. *Why does that bother me? I didn't want to be here in the first place,* she thought.

"If I agreed," said Nicole, "couldn't we get the villagers to help? It's a lot safer traveling in groups."

"You may bring anyone you like," said Bethane. "But it is important to the success of the quest for the two of you to spend time understanding one another. The internal growth is crucial. How easy would it be to accomplish that in a crowd?"

Nicole nodded in understanding.

Bethane continued, "Also, if a villager was in danger, neither of you could put yourselves at risk to help."

"What?" said Morrel. "Of course, I would help."

"Of course, you would *not*," said the grandfather. "*You* are irreplaceable. To protect Nicole is one thing, but to die for a villager is to sentence all the villagers to darkness. Once Nicole is committed to the quest, she too becomes indispensable. She must not be killed."

"Be killed!" said Morrel. "Why do you say these things? You know I would never let that happen."

"As strong and quick as you are, my grandson, you are not infallible. None of us is." He paused, lost in thought. His expression was sad. Morrel and Nicole glanced at each other. "The two of you must survive. If ever the odds are in favor of the dark things, you must leave any companions behind and take Nicole to safety."

Morrel's brows were folded into fierce ridges. "I have never run from danger to leave others behind."

"I know, and I am sorry, but you must give me your oath that you will this time. No matter who it is. The quest comes first before personal desires and duties."

Morrel stared at the ground, his eyes narrowed in frustration. Grandfather glanced uneasily toward the woods. Nicole felt as though someone had walked over her grave.

"Give me your oath now," ordered Bethane. "As an Alaric and as my precious grandson. Commit yourself completely. Partial obedience is useless." He waited in silence for a few seconds. Then, in a pleading voice, he added, "We have so little time."

Morrel opened and then shut his mouth.

"Do you no longer obey and respect your grandfather?" asked Bethane.

Morrel looked up. "I . . . I give my oath."

The elder released a long breath. "Good. I trust you to keep your word, no matter what." His voice quickened. "Now, there are three objects you must gather to complete the quest. It was my duty to scatter them for safekeeping after the last quest. They fit together to form a talisman against the darkness. It is a symbol from Nicole's world, so she will explain its significance."

Nicole nodded. She hoped it was something obvious.

The elder continued. "One of the shapes is in the care of Queen Melita. You must convince her to surrender it. This may not be easy since she has had it for a long time and does not trust the big people completely. She may even feel she can protect her own people more effectively from Nightfall than we can. You must convince her otherwise."

Grandfather paused and glanced again toward the woods. Morrel stiffened and sniffed the air. He fingered the hilt of his dagger. Nicole shivered.

"If you anger Queen Melita," Bethane warned, "she will disappear without a trace. Appeal to her personality, Morrel."

"Yes, Grandfather. I know her moods."

"Good. The three objects, two gold shapes and a silver arrow—" An unearthly howl interrupted him. "Forgive me, grandson, I overestimated our time. There is still much I have to tell you, but I may not be allowed."

"What is it?" asked Nicole. But, all too soon, she knew. From the forest charged three large beasts like the one that had attacked them on the forest path. Nicole jumped to her feet in terror and then saw that Bethane was looking in the opposite direction. She screamed as a flock of condor-like birds flew toward them, claws extended.

"Take Nicole and flee," ordered Grandfather as he stood. "I can use the bracelet to keep them here until you are safe."

"No," shouted Morrel, unsheathing his dagger.

"At first opportunity, you disobey," said Bethane. "Is this the man I have put my faith in?"

Morrel hesitated.

"Go," said the elder. "Do not fail your first test. I would not be a helpless old man, even if I did not have a bracelet." He pushed Nicole into Morrel's arms. "Do your duty, Morrel. Do not shame me." He turned to face the birds. They were flying fast and would reach the mound before the beasts.

Morrel groaned. "Goodbye, Grandfather. By panther's strength. I will not fail."

"I know, grandson of my son. Travel with my blessing and my love."

Nicole screamed as the first bird came close enough for her to see its black eyes. Morrel threw her over his shoulder, whirled and ran. Her breath was sucked away.

Oh, God, thought Nicole. *They've already won.*

The world went black.

She woke in darkness. Complete, cold darkness. She screamed.

"Shh!"

"Morrel?" She tried not to shriek.

"We are safe," he whispered.

Nicole took a few deep breaths, steadying herself. The smell of rich earth filled her nostrils. "Where are we? Have they won? Is this how Dawn's End will be forever?" Silence. Nicole reached out, searching over the earth floor until she found him. He was trembling. She traced her fingers up his hairy arms to his face. It was wet with tears.

"Oh, Morrel. Your grandfather? Is he . . . . "

"Dead."

"How do you know for sure?" she asked.

"I know. I know." He curled into a shivering ball.

She pulled him close, stroking his hair, and rocking him gently like a child until the trembling stopped. She suspected it was as painful as when he lost his father, perhaps more so. Morrel had been close to his great-grandfather for so long. Bethane had been a surrogate father to him. He was also a tower of strength, a symbol of agelessness. It must have shaken Morrel to the core to know the dark things could kill a panther man of that stature. To know that now everything now rested on his shoulders. But, mostly, she knew he felt grief at losing someone he loved deeply.

Eventually, he gathered himself together. "I am all right now," he whispered. He sat up. "They have killed my grandfather, but they have not won."

"I'm so sorry, Morrel."

"Sorry enough to help?" he asked, his voice bitter. "Please, do not let his death be for nothing."

Nicole paused. "Where are we?"

"In a tunnel," he answered. "I played here a child. I blocked the entrance. I needed rest, and you had fainted."

Nicole shivered at the remembrance. "I never fainted before. I thought the world was ending, and when I woke in this darkness, I thought Nightfall had come."

"It is coming. Just not this minute," said Morrel. "The group that attacked Grandfather will not find this spot until after we have left. We are too far away. But there may be other dark things about. We need to be quiet and cautious."

"If I hadn't fainted, you might have been able to help your grandfather. I'm sorry. I guess I'm a pretty big coward."

"No. That is not what happened," said Morrel. "Grandfather was right. Even with the two of us and our bracelets, you might have been harmed. It was too many. I had to get you away as quickly as possible. You did not faint from fear. You fainted because I carried you."

"I don't understand."

"I moved too fast for your body to cope. Bent over and in my wind stream, you did not get enough air. You fainted from lack of oxygen. I will be more careful in the future. You might have suffocated."

"No one can run that fast. Not even a panther."

Morrel explained. "We have used the bracelet for generations. It does not give us the characteristics of an ordinary panther. Some are distorted, exaggerated. One is speed."

"Then you could always outrun the dark things. You are safer than I thought."

"I could if I was alone," he admitted.

Nicole felt a cold chill at the thought of being left behind to the mercy of the beings of the night. "I could never outrun one. Is that why your Grandfather didn't run away?"

"He wanted to be sure they would stay to fight him and we would have the chance to slip away. He used the power of his bracelet to attract them. Even if he hadn't, I would have died myself before I let them have you. For Grandfather, my world, and myself, I must succeed, and I need you alive and well to do that."

"Indispensable but useless," muttered Nicole.

"I am a fool." Morrel fumbled in the darkness for her hand and then gave it a gentle squeeze. "I am explaining this all wrong. You are not a burden. I brought you to this hostile world through trickery and have done little to help you understand your worth. You are valuable for yourself as well, Nicole. I want to succeed for you, too. I care about you. I am glad I did not have to choose between you and Grandfather. I have feelings for you that I cannot express or explain, but they are there nonetheless. Grandfather was wise to make my duty to the quest unconditional. It would have torn me in half having to choose between you."

"I have never been so terrified in my life," she said. "Even in the tree. Your grandfather was extremely brave. I liked him. He showed such calm courage, it shames me."

Morrel patted her hand. "I could say many things to build on that shame, all trickery, and I might thus succeed in convincing you to help me. But I cannot. Doing so would be dishonorable. Either you come, or you do not. Tell me now. When we leave this cave, it is either back to your world or on to The Meeting. I do not have time for delay. It is probably already too late to find another. Choose now."

Nicole thought of the old man, standing on the mound, his arm lifted. The way he smiled at Morrel with pride. Morrel, no father, grandfather, great-grandfather. All the responsibilities for Dawn's End on his shoulders. No one but a little bird to share them. And maybe a frightened human girl. She whispered, "I can't promise that I would ever do anything but scream and cry. I'm still terrified."

"Of course. It would be foolish not to be. If that is your choice . . . . "

"No, wait. I'm still afraid, but I don't want to go home—"

"Nicole! Do you mean it?"

She put her finger tips on his lips. "Hear me out. I might spend this whole quest hiding up a tree. I can't guarantee I'll behave any better next time. I haven't exactly been trained for this. Will that be of any use to you?"

"Yes. Hide up all the trees you want. Just come *with* me, and I know we can succeed." He squeezed her hand twice.

Nicole tried to sound determined. "Okay. I'm in."

Morrel hugged her in a crushing grip.

"Tomorrow," he whispered. "Tomorrow, we face Melita, Queen of the Valley People. She may well be the most daunting little thing in all of Dawn's End."

"Why do you say that?"

Morrel sighed. "Because she is a beautiful, vain female in a position of power, and she is intelligent enough to know it."

Chapter Eleven—Little People

"Where's Larina?" Nicole asked when they emerged into the dim light.

"After the Telling in my village, she went off by herself," said Morrel. "We are not always together. She is a free creature with her own life." His voice was flat. Nicole could tell he did not feel like talking.

They hiked in silence. It seemed as though cotton had been stuffed in her ears. The world was muffled in dank dimness. When they stopped for lunch, Nicole struggled for a way to break the gloom. Morrel sat with his knees tucked under him. When he finished eating, he kneeled with his hands resting on his thighs, staring off into the sickening trees.

"You remind me of a sphinx kneeling there," said Nicole.

"What is a sphinx?"

"An enormous, wise creature with the body of a lion and the head of a man."

Morrel cocked his head, interested. "Have you ever met a sphinx?"

Nicole smiled. "No. A very long time ago, people called the Egyptians made all sorts of statues and drawings that were part animal and part human. They thought that cats were sacred, too. Egyptians were often buried with small carved cats. I don't really know much about their myths."

"Egyptians." Morrel rolled the word around. "I have heard that name in some of our legends. There was a door into Egypt a long time ago."

Nicole looked askance at Morrel. She studied his furry features and then laughed. "I'd better take myths more seriously from now on."

Morrel gave a small smile. They ate in silence for some time before he spoke again. "I should not grieve. I was fortunate to know my own great-grandfather so well. Not many have such a wonderful relationship in their lives. He took the place of my father in many ways."

Nicole nodded. "Losing a parent is the hardest thing any child has to face."

"Yes," said Morrel. "Our relationship with our parents is the closest we experience."

"What about a man and wife?" asked Nicole softly. She looked away when he tried to meet her eyes.

"We do not have that the same way you do," said Morrel. "As generations change, so do our traditions and attitudes. I know we feel affection, love, possessiveness, and sexual desire, yet, there is something missing from relationships between my people. Larina seems to carry a hint of it, yet I cannot describe it."

"Larina," muttered Nicole.

"She is unusual," said Morrel. "A throwback. More human emotionally than the panther people. We are more like animals than you realize. We protect our young, obey our parents, value our blood-line, but . . . . Well, we do not understand much of lifetime commitment. Our people do not view a joining as permanent."

"But, how . . . I mean, you have children."

"We value our blood-line, and we care for the community. We care for each other."

"I don't believe that for a minute," protested Nicole. "I saw Dorinda and her husband."

"Perhaps," said Morrel. "Perhaps it is just my own outlook. I am in a direct line of many who wore and used the bracelets. Perhaps I am more changed than others. I do not know. But I suspect I have a little too much tom cat in me for most human females." He grinned. "Aubin has elevated it to a fine art."

"I suspected as much," said Nicole. "Your grandfather said you were inexperienced. I think that also means in matters of the heart. Maybe you just need time. Or to find the right person. Dorinda and her husband were as humanly bonded as I've ever seen."

Morrel shrugged. "She is with child. Maybe it is hormonal."

"Possibly, but her husband isn't pregnant."

Morrel nodded thoughtfully.

Nicole continued. "I've seen a fair bit of flirting, the young girls, and Aubin. Would none of them want to keep him as their mate for life?"

"That is physical. Like the peacocks in your world flashing their feathers. I would not depend on Aubin to stay around one peahen very long no matter what she might want."

"Like a lot of men in my world," Nicole muttered.

"Really? But they stay together to protect the offspring like we do, do they not?"

"Not all," admitted Nicole.

"Perhaps we have not lost as much as I thought. Or maybe I do not know what I am talking about. You had a long term intimate relationship with a man, did you not?"

"I thought I did. He turned out to be . . . false."

Nicole finished her dried fruit in silence, thinking, *The panther people mourn their loss of humanity, their decreasing ability to feel emotional bonding. I, on the other hand, have the ability and reject it, refuse to risk feeling either again. Isn't life funny?*

As they were packing up, she asked, "After Queen Melita, what then?"

"I am not sure. There is one piece that could be anywhere in Dawn's End. I have no clues where to search."

"This is like looking for a needle in a haystack," said Nicole.

"You store your needles in animal feed?" Morrel's forehead furrowed.

Nicole laughed. "It means trying to find a small item in a huge search area that resembles the item. It is like looking for a tree in a forest, or a piece of trash in a dump."

"A dump! I saw one in your world. That might just be it."

"What?" asked Nicole.

"You have given me an idea. Would it not be a good idea to check a place containing hundreds of unusual items?" he asked.

"I guess," said Nicole.

Morrel nodded, thoughtfully. "The Hoarder might have a piece."

"A hoarder? Does that mean the same as in my world?"

"The Hoarder, not a hoarder. That is his name. At least he has been called that for so long no one remembers any other," said Morrel.

Nicole gave her hair a quick comb. "Okay, so who's *The Hoarder?*"

Morrel followed the comb with his eyes. "He is a being who lives for things. He collects."

"Baseball cards? Stamps? Spoons? What?"

"I do not know what baseball cards and stamps are, but, if he ever found one, he would hoard it." Morrel smiled. "He saves everything he finds. Anything that can be picked up and carried. Even rocks, if they have a quality that catches his bugged-out eyes."

"That's impossible," said Nicole. "He can't collect *everything*. Where would he put it all? How would he pay for it?"

Morrel shrugged. "He collects anyway he can. As for storage, that is a challenge. He keeps blasting tunnels into the mountain and filling the spaces with junk. The problem is, he often finds interesting ores and crystals during the excavation and winds up putting rock back."

Nicole laughed. "He sounds like a true eccentric."

"If he has seen one of the pieces of our symbol," said Morrel, "you can be sure he has it stashed away in a cave."

"Should we go there first or to Queen Melita?"

"They are equal distance. We will see the queen first."

Crisp, yellowed brush lined the fawn-colored paths. The cloudless sky hung overhead, a lifeless blue-gray. Plants were scarce in the barren, rocky soil. Larina could be seen flying point. Other animals remained hidden. Morrel said that the area had not been this barren before the coming of the darkness. To Nicole, it appeared as though it had suffered years of drought.

Dust settled into the crevices of Nicole's shoes and seams of her pants. The countryside was stunted and dull. Nicole was relieved when small blossoms on tiny green plants appeared.

"We are getting closer," confirmed Morrel, also noticing the small signs of life.

Soon a few small shrubs dotted the landscape. In between them grew moss, threaded with silver.

"Before the darkness, the fragile glow-moss grew everywhere. It is endangered now," said Morrel.

At the next crossroads, they veered east toward a hill. For several miles, they walked through woods with no signs of animal life. When they reached the crest, the depressing woodland abruptly opened into a meadow. A weight lifted. Nicole reached for Morrel's hand.

They gazed over the gently, undulating meadows, a sea of lime-green foliage, dotted with a multitude of lemon and bronze flowers. Here and there a blossoming bush or deciduous tree accentuated a small hill or ravine. The air was honey sweet. They soaked in the rich beauty, letting their eyes adjust to the bright sunshine echoed in the brilliant blossoms.

"Wow!" said Nicole. "It is beautiful."

"There were many such places before the growing Nightfall," said Morrel.

"I wish I could have seen them," said Nicole.

Morrel took a deep breath and called, "Larina!"

The blue jay alighted on a small, white-barked tree. "Yes, my Alaric."

"You are to stay here," he commanded. "Large, aggressive birds will cause havoc in this glade. Do not follow me and ruin our chance to get the first piece of the key."

"But, Alaric!" She sounded petulant. "I am *not* aggressive."

"Do not argue." Morrel's voice was firm. "I will be upset with you if you follow. The valley people may be frightened."

Larina ruffled her feathers irritably. She turned backwards on the branch and preened, ignoring them.

"Mind me now," said Morrel as he and Nicole started across the field.

"Aggressive, indeed!" muttered Larina.

Twenty paces into the field, Morrel halted. "Stay here, Nicole. I wish to speak to Larina alone. I am going to try to convince her to return to the safety of the village." He walked back to Larina's perch.

Nicole nodded. "Good luck with that."

Morrel's low voice carried across the field. "I am sorry to leave you behind, brave calia, but you can no longer travel with us."

"I can meet you on the other side of the valley," argued Larina. "I can fly around."

"I want you to return to my village," said Morrel.

"Why? You have a long way to go yet. I have stayed out of the way. *She* won't even know I am around."

"I know, but I would. I care about you, Larina. Nightfall strengthens. I do not know what lies ahead for us. I cannot protect both you and Nicole."

"I can take care of myself," snapped the blue jay.

"No doubt, but you did not see the flying dark creatures. I do not need the extra worry. I cannot choose between you and Nicole should danger threaten." His voice softened. "I made an oath to Grandfather, and then I had to leave him. I do not want to face that again. Please do not put me in that position."

She bobbed her head. "Very well, my Alaric. I understand. But I care for you as well, so don't treat your life cheaply."

"I will be careful." He held out his arm. Larina flew to it and hopped up to his shoulder. "It is not the threat of death that fills me with doubt, but what I must do. I may not find the pieces in time. Or at all. And The Meeting. Agh! I am so ignorant."

"Shh! You will succeed, Alaric. Have you not always found the rarest herbs and most valuable gems to trade with the out-villages? As for The Meeting." She bobbed her head. "There is more human in you than you realize."

"Thank you, my calia. I shall miss you," said Morrel. "Fly straight to the village. You will be safest there. Tell my mother we are well."

"Succeed in safety, Alaric Morrel," the blue jay called as she soared into the air. In a brief moment of defiance, she curved out into the meadow and over Nicole, calling, "Find strength, outsider, and you find it all." She headed toward the village, Nicole and Morrel watching until she was a dot in the skyline.

If she were in my place, thought Nicole, *they would succeed for certain. To have half her pluck! Morrel is less assured than I thought. Has he lost heart because of his grandfather? Or because of me? His little calia brings him confidence. If he loses hope? I guess it's up to me to make sure that doesn't happen.*

"I'm surprised you convinced her," said Nicole when Morrel joined her. "I didn't think anyone could order Larina about."

"I would not even attempt that," he admitted. "It was an appeal."

"Still, she wouldn't have left if she didn't think we could make it on our own. Right?"

Morrel nodded and then smiled. "She is a good judge of people." He looked over the valley. "This is the land of the little people."

Nicole scanned the plants of shrubs for any sign of inhabitants. She wondered if their homes were underground.

"It will be the last place to give way before total Nightfall," said Morrel. "Queen Melita and the faeries create a protective aura."

"Faeries!" exclaimed Nicole. "That's what you meant by little people? The size of my thumb? With wings?"

"Actually, they are a little larger than that, but only a little, so you can see why Larina would intimidate them. Only the females have wings. But look for yourself."

He pointed to a spot of thick flowers clustered around a boulder. On top of the rock, stretched out in the sunshine, lay the most lovely, delicate creature. Nicole gasped, grabbing Morrel's arm in surprise.

The faerie was about four centimeters tall. Her skin was golden, with a luminescent glow. Fluffy, white hair crowned her round face, setting off her bright, green eyes and her miniature, pink lips. Silver-pearl feathers fanned out from her back. They glistened and tinkled as the faerie moved into a sitting position. She tossed her autumn-dandelion hair and spoke. "Alaric, why come thou here?"

Her melodious voice was small but clear.

"I am just Morrel to a queen such as you," he responded with a small bow. The tiny creature laughed with delight.

"Come now, Morrel. Why dost thou journey so far to see us? Or art thou on thy way elsewhere?"

"Both, Queen Melita. We seek your aid."

"I have no interest in the tedious problems of big people," Melita sighed. "Hast thou nothing wonderful to share with us on this blissful day? Nothing amusing or interesting or novel?"

"Alas, Queen Melita," said Morrel, "if we do not stop Nightfall, there will be no more blissful days."

Melita made a small noise of irritation. "Who are thou, lady of the firenut hair?"

"This is Nicole Newman from the outworld," said Morrel. "She travels with me."

"To The Meeting," giggled Melita.

"Yes," Morrel replied. "And whatever gossip you have heard about the quest is best left unsaid."

"Do not be cross with us, Morrel, or we shall fly away, and we don't think thou would like that." Melita bent her leg and tilted her head coyly. "We can tell when someone wants something badly, and thou hast that look."

Morrel nodded. "Most perceptive, little one. We need something that was entrusted to you a long time ago."

Melita shrugged. "We do not know of what thou speak. We have nothing to give thee. Thou mayst well go on thy way."

Nicole was bewildered by the faerie's change of mood. "Why are you upset, Queen Melita? We need your help to complete the quest. It will protect the faerieland from the dark things."

"Dark things!" snapped Melita. "They will never enter our valley. Our meadow would dazzle them into fleeing to the dismal forest."

"During the day," said Morrel. "But, with the lengthening Nightfall, daytime will cease to exist. Then, even this magical land will be overrun. How can the flowers thrive without sunshine? How can the faeries live in eternal darkness?"

Melita twitched.

Morrel continued. "Alaric Bethane said you were entrusted with an important piece of the key we seek. The faeries were selected because their magic was strong and good."

Melita sighed, heaving her body dramatically. "Very well. Your grandfather spoke correctly. We were once given something for safekeeping. It pains us to part with it. It has been made part of my throne. I do so love it. But if thou really need it . . . . "

"I am sorry, sweet queen, but we do."

The faerie stretched her wings and flew into the air, soft tinkling notes sounding from her wings. Her lithe, little body glistened and weaved in the sunlight like a summer dragonfly.

"How lovely," breathed Nicole. "Even her flight is spellbinding."

"The wings of each faerie play a different melody. They are all very distinctive and personalized. One can learn much about a faerie by analyzing her tune."

"Are they born like that?"

"No. At the beginning they make a cacophony of tones, like a baby babbling, but eventually it is sorted out into a pattern. It is a sign of development into mature faeriehood. Their kind of maturity anyway. The tune is unique, yet it must blend with the whole of all the faerie melodies."

"I feel bad taking away part of her throne," confessed Nicole.

"I, too," said Morrel. "But since she gave it up easily, she must understand the danger. I am relieved. She can be a mischievous tease."

The faerie returned, followed by two others carrying a golden shape and four following. Seven pairs of wings beat out a musical arrangement of twelve to fifteen notes, repeated with each stroke. The notes blended together symphonically, a harmonious mixture of spirits. The females laid the gold shape on the small boulder and flew off, while Melita landed.

Nicole picked up the gilt form. "Thank you," she said. It was a small, spiral shape, thin as a dollar coin. Now that she could see it clearly, Nicole examined the artifact. The centre held an engraving of a tiny sun. A row of jagged holes ran across its reverse.

"Take care of it," said Melita. "From what we know of the quest, it may be returned to faerieland one day. We would like the next queen to enjoy its beauty."

"We will," said Morrel.

"We'll do our best," said Nicole. "After The Meeting, Dawn's End will be safe again. Things will be happier then."

"Especially thee," giggled Melita. "Meeting with Morrel." She winked at the dark man.

"Me-li-ta," he growled.

"We didn't say anything," said the faerie queen as she raised her hands in protest. "Thou are such a dull, old grouch. Take our treasure, and go on thy silly quest." She waved them away.

Melita flew into the air, soared energetically once around the couple, and zipped off.

"Goodbye, Queen Melita," called Nicole. "It was a thrill meeting you."

"Farewell," called the faerie. "And better thrills at better meetings."

Morrel laughed and shook his head.

"What was all that?" asked Nicole. She knew a sexual innuendo when she heard it.

"Melita is an incurable tease with an exotic imagination. Take no notice."

Nicole put the spiral in her zippered jacket pocket. "The Hoarder now?"

"Yes," said Morrel. "It is as good a place as any to search."

As they walked, Nicole fingered the spiral through her pocket. Something poked at the back of her mind. She took out the shape and examined it. She stroked the gleaming surface, scratched it with her fingernail, and then stopped walking.

"What is it?" asked Morrel.

"What was it your grandfather said about the three pieces?" she asked. "Exactly."

"He said, 'There are three objects, two gold shapes and a silver arrow."

"Two gold shapes and a silver arrow," said Nicole. "Two gold shapes—That's it! He said gold, not golden. We've been had."

Chapter Twelve—Hoarders

Morrel snatched the spiral shape from Nicole and examined it. "You are right. This is not real gold."

"Did we ask the wrong faeries?"

"There are no other faeries," snarled Morrel. "The little vixen tricked us."

"But, why?"

"When it comes to dealing with big people, the faeries have no scruples."

"Then why was she entrusted with the shape?" Nicole asked.

"Probably because no one would ever get it without her consent. Grandfather did not realize she would care more for the shape than about the threat of dark things. We have to go back and get the real piece."

"What if she won't give it to us?"

"I will see that she does," said Morrel, striding back determinedly.

The faerie queen was not sunning on the rock.

"Melita!" shouted Morrel. "Your ruse has failed. Give me the gold shape."

Nicole glanced around. Morrel's demand was met with silence.

"I mean it, Melita. This is no time for games. Dawn's End will not survive without that shape. I will not leave without it."

There was no response.

"Please, Queen Melita," called Nicole. "It is the noble thing to do."

The silence burned like poison.

"Now!" shouted Morrel. He whirled about, watching for movement. "This shameful act will never be forgotten. You will be isolated from everyone in our world. The faerie people will be despised for eternity if you do not return the shape immediately."

Nicole touched his arm, but he pulled away.

"Damn you, Melita," he shouted. Nicole's eyes widened as he picked up the boulder she had used and flung it across the field. He ripped up the plants and bushes with the fury of a thunderstorm. "Answer me, you little witch!"

Nicole stepped away, shocked at the violence. Morrel saw her expression and froze. He released the shrub he was holding and sank to the ground. "It is I who am shameful," he said and buried his face in his hands.

Nicole approached. She touched his shoulder and sat beside him.

"It is no use," said Morrel. "We cannot even get the first piece. I do not know where the other two are. My world is doomed."

"I didn't think you were such a quitter," said Nicole.

He looked up at her, his brow furrowed and eyes narrowed.

"I also didn't know you had such a temper," Nicole continued in a scolding voice.

"I knew I had a temper," said Morrel. "It is one of the worst side effects of the bracelet. Passions are amplified. If I harmed a faerie, I will live in shame forever. How could I have done that? They are so little and helpless."

A twinkle of light caught Nicole's eye. She gave Morrel a hug, and, without seeming to, she slowly looked toward it. Melita was standing in the grass, most of her body hidden. The tips of her wings caught the light. Morrel might be able to catch her if he knew.

"It's not your fault, Morrel," Nicole said. "Alaric Bethane overestimated the faeries. He thought they were people of worth. Perhaps *they* are, but they may be led by a bandit queen."

Melita shifted her position.

"I knew she was a trickster," said Morrel. "But I thought she had honor."

"It seems not," said Nicole. "She reminds me of a black bird we have in our world called a crow. Crows are very clever animals, but nasty little thieves. Perhaps we should call her Queen Crow."

"No," said Morrel. "She is a good queen. There must be a reason why she did not give us the shape. Perhaps she thinks we will fail, and this piece of the key will be lost."

"No matter," said Nicole. "If we fail, everything will be lost. The valley, the faeries, even her lovely throne. We are her only hope."

Morrel nodded and pushed back his black hair. "I could never convince her to trust us after what I've done."

"You could put everything back," suggested Nicole.

"Of course," said Morrel. "I would have done that anyway."
He leapt to his feet, picked up the bush he dropped and
replanted it.

Nicole opened her packsack and took out the flute. She sat
for a moment, recalling the arrival of the faeries. She blew
the first notes, nodded, and then played Queen Melita's
signature. She followed it with the other melodies she had
picked out and ended with a medley of the faerie tunes.
Suddenly, Melita was standing in front of her.

"We are not a crow," she announced.

"I know," said Nicole. "You are a guardian. But a guardian
must know when to expel and when to admit entry."

Melita wrinkled her tiny nose. Morrel stepped up behind her.
She zipped off.

"Wait!" he called. "I will not harm you. I am deeply sorry."
He shrugged at Nicole. "Everything is repaired. Thank the
light, I did not find any crushed little bodies. I could never
live with that. I have behaved badly. Even Aubin could not
have been more hot headed."

"Neither would he have cared so much," said Melita as she
popped up beside him. "My people are bringing the spiral.
The *gold* one." She smiled at Nicole. "We think it is the right
thing to do. We may have underestimated you. Together, you
just may return the balance."

"Thank you, gracious queen," said Morrel. "I am in your
debt."

"We will not hesitate to remind you of that," said Melita.
"Thank you, lovely Nicole, for the music. That was most
precious. A faerie cannot hear her melody the way others do.
It is changed by the wind and our closeness to the wings. It

sounds hollow and distorted. We are overjoyed to hear it clearly."

"You are welcome, your majesty. It was wonderful beyond words to meet so beautiful and rare a queen."

The faerie smiled.

Nicole and Morrel returned to the last crossroads and headed toward The Hoarder's Mountain. Nicole felt oddly comfortable as they traveled. She should have been scared out of her wits. They could meet a pack of dark things on the next bend. But, somehow, she felt safe with Morrel. She knew he would not let anything happen to her. He had learned from the battle with the black-armored creature. He was less cocky about defeating the creatures because of his grandfather's death. He would be more cautious.

The path narrowed. She pushed back the forest growth in spots, picking her way along. Morrel seemed to melt through the forest, disturbing little. Soft, deep moss sank underfoot. Occasionally, she heard the sound of a small animal and a quick movement.

They ascended into a cluster of small mountains, Nicole attempting leaps and scrambles that would usually have made her muscles lock and face clench in alarm. If she stumbled, Morrel's swift support eased her through. She learned to find stable foothold whenever the passage became difficult. Her hands sought firm grips. Morrel sent her ahead, not wanting to knock a shower of loose rocks down upon her head. He scaled close behind, ready to help should she fall.

As the day progressed, Nicole's movements became more confident, and, as a result, more adept. She and Morrel reached midway up the slopes and then followed a well trodden path encircling the cliff face. Only scruffy, stunted plants grew in the open space. The slate-like stones underfoot allowed to them to stroll at a steady pace.

Nicole took out the flute and played a few of the more difficult tunes from her past. It was becoming easier each time she lifted the instrument to her lips, like an unused muscle regaining its former strength. She ended with the faerie tunes.

When the ground steepened, she reluctantly packed the instrument safely away, vowing never to let a day go by again without enjoying the music. In fact, when she returned to her world, she was going to start exploring options.

She hummed songs from the top forty and then her favorite campfire songs.

"Pretty sounds," commented Morrel. "Are there words to go with it?"

"Campfire tunes are about the only songs I know all the words for," laughed Nicole.

"Sing them."

Morrel was bewildered by the brutal "What Do You Do with a Drunken Sailor?," moved by "Farewell to Nova Scotia," and laughed at "There's a Hole in My Bucket." Soon, he was singing the male parts in a perfect bass, enthusiastically continuing the rounds over and over. Nicole begged for mercy when he started "There's a Hole" for the fifth time. They were still laughing when they reached the entrance to the caves.

143

The Hoarder had attempted to hide the entrances to his storage tunnels with rocks and uprooted branches. Nicole was thrilled to discover one by accidentally plunging her hand into a space in the cliff face. Morrel powerfully tossed aside the rubble blocking the entry. Nicole switched on her flashlight and closely followed him inside.

The dank smell was almost overpowering. Mildew and dust covered everything. Repressing her revulsion, Nicole searched through the junk, like a homeless street person in a dumpster, for anything gold or silver that looked like it might form part of the key. Morrel rummaged on the other side of the cavern.

A decaying suitcase lay on top of the pile, one side rotted open with its lining hanging in tattered strips. The inside was coated with green fungus. A large wooden wheel poked through the pile, four spokes broken. Candle holders, rocks, clothing, cheap jewelry, furniture, and tools were tangled together. She spotted an undamaged smaller case on the stockpile, the familiar shape enticing her over the debris.

"Look!" she called. "A flute case." She flipped open the metal latches. "It couldn't have been here long. It's beautiful. The velvet is clean and dry. I wonder if he would trade it. It would protect the flute."

"Do not show him the flute, or he will want that in exchange," said Morrel.

"That would be crazy," said Nicole. "Then I'd have to trade the case for the flute."

"Like a hole in my bucket," said Morrel. They both laughed.

Nicole tucked the case under one arm and scanned the room with her flashlight. "There's so much stuff, even if it's here, how could we ever find it? It's impossible."

"Find what?" bleated The Hoarder from the entrance. As he shuffled into the cavern, Nicole stepped back. He walked with small steps, bent over as if clutching invisible treasures. An enormous nose with a long flap of hanging skin twitched between two bulbous eyes. His ears were twice normal size. Nicole's flashlight revealed green skin on his disfigured face.

"What do you have? What do you have?" he demanded, poking and tweaking at her.

"Stop that!" Nicole pushed his hands away.

He touched the end of the flashlight with his fingertip. "Light that does not burn." A long sliver of saliva dripped from his cracked lips. "Give it to me."

He snatched at the flashlight. Nicole jerked away.

"Won't give it to you," he said. "Come to take my things, eh? *Take my things.* Sneaking around like dirty thieves." He pushed her.

"Touch her not," growled Morrel from the other side of the cavern.

The Hoarder jumped then peered into the darkness. "A panther man," he stammered. "What do you want with me? I haven't taken anything of yours."

"Maybe. Maybe not."

The misshapen man regained his confidence in response to Morrel's nonchalance. "You want something. I want something. An even trade."

"You are unworthy of the light without heat," said Morrel. "It comes from another world."

"Agreed!" shrieked The Hoarder as he snatched away the flashlight.

He thumbed the button on and off, laughing wildly, as Nicole stood, stunned, with the flute case under her arm. "No," she protested. "I didn't want the case. We wanted something else."

"Too late! No reneging." He hunched and glared at Morrel. "No bullying, panther man, no stealing."

Morrel hissed. "Keep the flashlight, but you must listen to us."

The Hoarder tipped his head back and forth and rolled his eyes.

"We are searching for a silver arrow," said Morrel.

"There's plenty of arrows," said The Hoarder. "All kinds. Silver. Gold. Wood. Metal. Some are useless, cannot be shot. Some are fine, fine weapons."

"Not a shooting arrow," said Nicole. "It is like a decoration, or an ornament. It's little. It should fit in my hand."

"Maybe," said The Hoarder. "Maybe not. You must have something good to trade. Silver is expensive. Something better than the light."

"She has many wonders," said Morrel.

The Hoarder poked at her pack. Smacked his lips and then ordered them to wait and then shuffled out of the cavern.

"Where is he going?" asked Nicole.

"He has dozens of caverns like this one. I hope he is going to find the arrow. Quickly, put the flute in the case. He will not look inside it."

Nicole complied. The Hoarder shuffled back in.

"No silver arrow," he said.

Morrel sighed. Nicole frowned, studying The Hoarder's expression. He didn't meet her eyes. She opened her pack, took out the cloak, and spread it on the floor. She had heard her father wheel and deal on the telephone and sometimes in person. She knew when someone was holding out for a bargain.

"Common," said The Hoarder as he waved his hand with disdain.

Morrel crossed his arms, puzzled. Nicole dumped the contents of her pack and laid them out neatly. The Hoarder squeezed the raincoat between his fingers and snorted. He sniffed at the can of bug repellent.

"It goes on your skin, but not your eyes, and stops the bugs from biting," explained Nicole.

The Hoarder dropped it and picked up the box of matches.

"Instant fire," said Nicole.

She took the box and lit a match. The Hoarder pulled back, his eyes bulging further. Nicole blew out the flame and put the box on the cloak. The Hoard pushed it to the edge. He set aside the dried food, flicked the bottle of water disdainfully, and shook the bottle of vitamins.

"One a day keeps you healthy," said Nicole. "Helps you live longer. But only ever take one or the powerful medicine will make you ill instead."

The Hoarder set the bottle beside the matches. Nicole blew the whistle. He set it beside the vitamins. He rummaged through the box of toiletries. Nicole resisted the urge to slap his hand. He set aside nail clippers, two safety pins, and a tube of lip gloss. Nicole wondered what he could possibly use it for. She tried not to giggle at the thought.

"Not enough," he sniffed.

"For what?" asked Morrel. "I thought he did not have the arrow."

"He didn't say that," said Nicole. "He's waiting for the right trade."

"I have food, clothing, and a knife," offered Morrel as he slid his pack from his shoulder.

The Hoarder sniffed disdainfully and waved away the dark man. He flicked the flashlight on and off, waving it over Nicole. He stopped at her hair. He reached out, took a section and let it fall slowly through his fingers in the beam of light.

"Beautiful," he said. "Soft, long, an unusual color."

"Let me see the arrow," said Nicole.

Morrel's face puckered in bewilderment. The Hoarder reached into his shirt and pulled out a small, bright object. Morrel stepped forward. The Hoarder squeezed his hand shut.

"We have to see it first," said Nicole.

The Hoarder hesitated and then held it out, shining the flashlight into his palm. It was about three centimeters long, slightly tarnished. Nicole and Morrel exchanged glances.

"Deal," said Nicole.

The Hoarder gathered up the lip gloss, nail clippers, food and safety pins. He pulled a knife from inside his shirt and took Nicole by the hair. Morrel snarled and grabbed his arm.

"It's all right," said Nicole. "I agreed."

Morrel released The Hoarder, confused. Nicole stood beside The Hoarder as he raised the knife to her hair. Morrel's mouth dropped open as The Hoarder sawed off Nicole's hair about five centimeters from her scalp. She scrunched her eyes up tightly and gritted her teeth against the pain as he continued clutching and sawing. He gathered the hair into a bundle and shuffled out. Nicole bit her trembling lip and packed her belongings away.

"Oh, Nicole," said Morrel as he hugged her.

"It'll grow back," she said. "It's just hair. It doesn't matter."

"In the meantime," said Morrel, "you are still beautiful."

Nicole smiled and whispered into his ear. "Besides, the flashlight batteries won't last long."

Chapter Thirteen—Messages

It was a relief to breathe the fresh air. They dusted themselves off and wiped their hands. Nicole put the hood up on her jacket. Morrel picked leaves for them to rub on their skin and clothes. The minty scent removed the stench.

The silver arrow was about three centimeters long, engraved with cryptic symbols on one side and lined with tiny castle-top shapes on the reverse.

"It doesn't look like much of a key," said Nicole.

"I have never seen it before," said Morrel. "I only know what Grandfather told me. My people do not record things on paper like yours do. Everything we care to pass on to our children is memorized or woven into the tapestries. That way it cannot be put on a shelf and ignored."

"Perhaps the third key will explain it all."

"Assuredly," agreed Morrel. "It is supposed to be an obvious symbol to the people of your world from antiquity. First impressions are seldom valid anyway. In order to understand the truth of something, we must make an effort to understand it at its deepest level. It is the same with people."

Nicole nodded. "But now it will get harder since we have no where to look."

"Do not worry," said Morrel. "We have been blessed finding two pieces so quickly. I believe we have a good chance of success."

"I'm glad you're feeling better," said Nicole with a smile.

"I appreciate the sacrifices you have made Nicole. Don't think I didn't know Melita was nearby and that you were leading the conversation in a direction to draw her attention and gain her support. You were amazing with the Hoarder as well. Already you have exceeded my expectations."

Nicole blushed and looked even closer at the silver arrow. A flutter of wings startled her.

"Larina!" said Nicole.

"I bring unfortunate news from the village, my Alaric," said Larina. "Your grandfather has been killed."

"I know," he said, touching his heart.

Larina landed on his shoulder. She rubbed her little blue head against his cheek.

"I did not think he would survive the attack," Morrel said.

"You are The Alaric now, leader of all."

Just what he needs, thought Nicole. *To be reminded of his crushing responsibilities.*

"Yes," he said. "But look, Larina, we have two of the three shapes already."

"Well done, my Alaric." She bobbed her head.

"It was Nicole. I would not have gotten either alone. She could charm her way into the Forbidden Pond."

The blue jay stared at Nicole with her beady little eyes. "Well done, chosen one," she said.

Nicole grinned.

Larina said, "I hate to disrupt the quest when things are going so well, but I also have more bad news."

"The village!" said Morrel.

"No, it is safe," said Larina. "They plan to stay indoors as much as possible. All but one. An unforeseen complication in the form of a pain-in-the-ass white panther man."

Morrel rolled his eyes.

Larina continued. "Aubin has been behaving strangely since you left. I suspect he is up to something beyond his usual mischief. He continues to move about the village as though there is no danger. He struts about as though he is invincible."

"No doubt," said Morrel. He poured a few drops of water into his hand. Larina perched on his wrist and drank. "You must not endanger yourself out in the open any more, my calia. Go back to the village, and stay there. Keep an eye on Aubin. If he seems about to do something even more foolish than usual, inform my mother. He will obey her direct order. Do not come to me again, though. News can wait."

"Yes, my Alaric," said Larina. "Travel safely. Goodbye, Nicole. Take care of each other."

"Goodbye," called Nicole as the blue jay flew off. "I wish she could have stayed for a while. She must be tired and . . . I kind of miss her company."

"It is best that she be indoors before nightfall," said Morrel.

Nicole nodded. She dropped the silver arrow in her pocket beside the gold half-moon. "So, now what? Do we have any more clues?"

"I do not," said Morrel. "Where would you look?"

"That's hardly a fair question," said Nicole. "I don't even know what's around the next corner. Or *who's* around the next corner. Or *where* the next corner is!"

"True," said Morrel. "But your instincts have been right so far. Pretend we are in your world. If you wanted to find something, where would you go?"

"I don't know. I'd probably ask someone like your grandfather for advice. Are there any other wise panther people?" asked Nicole.

"No," he said. "But there may be others with wisdom."

"Sure," said Nicole. "Do you have any monks from whom people seek the meaning of life?"

Morrel shook his head in puzzlement.

"Okay, nothing so profound," continued Nicole. "Psychologists, advisors, fortune tellers, witches—"

"That's it! Hulda." Morrel's eyes widened with excitement.

"Please don't say she's a witch," said Nicole.

"She has been called that," admitted Morrel.

"Oh, Lord," she moaned.

"She has also been called a wise woman. It depends who is speaking."

"Ah, well then, that's not so different from my world. Do you think she might know something about the third piece?" asked Nicole.

"Hulda knows something about everything. She collects knowledge like The Hoarder collects junk. Whether it will be helpful to us or not, I do not know."

153

They made camp at the base of the mountain. This time Nicole curled up inside Morrel's arms. She wore most of the clothing in her pack since he felt it would not be wise to light a fire. It could draw the dark things. She preferred the feel of his warm breath against her cheek, the heat emanating from his body, and the touch of his soft hair against her skin anyway. The inexplicable erotic feelings she had felt for him earlier now seemed buried below concern, compassion, and admiration. Where at first she had been drawn to his mysterious power, now she was drawn to the perplexed and besieged man below. She enjoyed his company, and she greatly admired his courage and sense of duty. Where once the draw was sexual, she now realized her feelings for him were emotional. She tried to think of him as a friend in need; anything else was self-destructive foolishness.

The dark things seemed far in the past. The last few days since they left the village had been so pleasant. Nicole no longer doubted her value to the quest. Morrel was inexperienced in things that Nicole found second nature. They complimented each other well.

The next day they passed the outskirts of faerieland. A touch of gentle magic floated on the air. Nicole stopped more than once to bury her nose in some exotic blossom. Morrel never urged her to hurry. The scent was both soothing and energizing.

Eventually a simple thatched hut came in view, nestled among a grove of fruit trees.

"That is the home of Hulda," said Morrel.

"Hulda. Got it. Do we call her anything else?" asked Nicole.

"It may not matter," said Morrel. "She does not speak to travelers. She will not open her door or acknowledge our presence. She chooses when and who to interact with."

"What? So what are we doing here?" asked Nicole.

"Do we have anywhere else to go? Besides, I thought my ingenious quest companion might come up with an idea." He smiled.

"Good point about having nowhere else to go, but I'm no Anne Sullivan teaching Helen Keller how to talk to the outside world. If Hulda doesn't want to communicate, I'm not sure what I can do."

An assortment of tree stumps and thick branches were arranged in front of the hut. They had been selected for their unusual features, polished and painted to bring out their odd characteristics. Grotesque faces, twisted animals, and fanciful beings seemed to struggle to free themselves from the wood.

Morrel scratched softly on the door. There was no response. He called. Nicole called. They explained their problem through the door. There was still no response.

"About as cooperative as Queen Melita," said Morrel.

"Perhaps I should play for her," offered Nicole.

"Would not hurt," said Morrel. "Anyone with ears would be charmed by your gift."

Hulda did not respond to the serenade.

"We could build a bonfire from these wood sculptures," said Nicole. "That might bring her running."

"I am shocked you would suggest this," said Morrel.

Nicole giggled. "Just a joke, though they do give me the heebie-jeebies."

"Perhaps a trade," suggested Morrel.

They offered Hulda everything they had left through the door. Still she did not respond.

"Maybe she's not home," said Nicole.

"She is there. I can smell her, and I have heard her. If only Grandfather were alive. He could tell me what to say. They were friends once."

The door flew opened as a woman said, "Alive! What happened to Bethane? He was not ill."

Nicole jumped back, startled by the sudden appearance of the white-haired woman. Hulda stared at her with cold blue eyes.

"The dark things killed him," said Morrel.

"Bah! Nonsense," retorted Hulda. "Nothing could kill Bethane. He was old, but fast and strong and clever."

"It was because of me," said Nicole.

"No. That is not it at all," protested Morrel. "He died protecting Dawn's End from the dark things."

Hulda crossed her arms, waiting.

Morrel continued, "He made me swear an oath to find the three pieces of a key to The Meeting Place and not to turn back to help him. He hoped Nicole and I could push back Nightfall."

Hulda sized each of them up in turn. "Much growth of darkness there has been; much more will be. You do not need me. I can do nothing against this." She shut the door.

"Wait!" shouted Nicole. "We *do* need you. We don't know where to look for the third piece."

"I don't have it," said Hulda from within.

"That's okay, we came for your knowledge," said Nicole.

"What makes you think I can give you any information?" said Hulda through the closed door.

"My Grandfather respected you," said Morrel. "As do I. I seek your advice in his place. Can you give us no direction? If anyone can give us a clue, it is you, the wise woman."

The door flew open again.

"Listen well. I am a busy, impatient woman," she said firmly. "I will say it but once."

The couple nodded.

She chanted:

> "*The piece you seek to fit the key*
>
> *Is always found within.*
>
> *Pierced to be mended, opening all,*
>
> *Allows the light to win.*'

Good fortune and good bye."

The door shut and the lock clicked.

"That can't be all," said Nicole to Morrel.

"It will have to do," said Morrel. "It is only in deference to my grandfather's memory that she spoke to us at all. She does not speak lightly. We must repeat and memorize the poem."

They recited it twice and then looked at each other, expecting some brilliance.

"Well?" said Nicole.

"The meaning eludes me," said Morrel. "What do we do now? There is nowhere else to go."

"Back to the village?"

"No. We know there is nothing there. It may be best if we head to The Meeting Place. Perhaps we will discover something along the way. Perhaps there is a clue there."

"Or someone else may know," said Nicole.

"I do not know who else to ask."

"How about someone at the meeting?"

"I thought you understood. *We* are The Meeting. There is no one else coming," explained Morrel.

"We're on our own?"

"We always have been on our own. Do not look so downcast. We have done well. I am much more hopeful than I was. Have faith. It will work out."

"Okay, Morrel. If you say so. Where is The Meeting Place?"

"I do not know," he shrugged, embarrassed.

"Good grief," said Nicole. "Then how are we supposed to head there?"

"With a guide. Lymn, who lives by the cascades, can bring us. He knows."

They had been traveling for four days when Larina arrived.

"Don't get angry, Alaric" she said. "I am not disobeying. I have an urgent message from your mother. She sent me."

Nicole froze. Had the village been attacked? She thought of Dorinda and the girls who had dressed her.

"What has happened?" demanded Morrel.

"They sent me because I could fly high and find you the quickest," said Larina. "I *can* be of service, you know."

"Yes, Larina. I am aware of that," said Morrel with irritation. "What is the message?"

"It seems your fool cousin is courting danger instead of ladies. Well, both actually."

"Aubin?"

"Who else?" answered Larina. "He bragged that *he* could finish the quest. He said you were too inexperienced with women. He went to the door to fetch another outworld woman. He plans to take her to The Meeting."

Morrel snorted. "How does he plan to do that in so short a time?"

"How do you think?" Larina chuckled. "He is going to dazzle her with his dance, the way he did Nicole."

"He did not!" protested Nicole. They both looked at her. She felt the heat rising in her face.

"My mother will stop him," said Morrel.

"He has already left."

"The fool!" snapped Morrel. "He will frighten the wits out of an outworld woman, just as my grandfather did. He knows nothing about the people there. They will probably attack him. It will be miraculous if he is not killed."

"No doubt," said Nicole.

"Alaric Sabella asks you to bring him back safely," said Larina. "He is the only other male Alaric in the line. His life is precious. He is also valued by many in the village and would be missed. He shares a grief with you since your fathers and grandfather perished together. He did not handle the death of Alaric Bethane well."

"This will take too much time," said Morrel. He paced, his face creased with worry. "How could he do this? Did my mother say I must do this now, or can it wait until after The Meeting?"

"She said to consider Aubin's impulsive nature and decide with your human nature."

Morrel groaned. "Disastrous. I shall have to save his troublesome white skin. Ah, well, we were unsure of our next step. Perhaps this is destiny leading us in a new direction. I will need your help, Nicole."

"Of course."

"We must return to your world," said Morrel. He hesitated. "Will you . . . . "

Nicole stepped up to him and placed her hand around his neck. She looked into the brilliant diamonds within his deep brown eyes. "I will return with you to Dawn's End to complete the quest," she said.

Morrel sighed with relief.

Larina ruffled her feathers and looked away. "I suppose I must return to the village," she said.

"No," said Morrel. "I need your help too. You can help in our search and will attract far less notice than I. You have accompanied me to the outworld before. You will be very useful."

Larina chuckled happily and spun on her branch.

"The fastest way is to the west," said Morrel. "We will meet the stream we passed before at the beginning of our journey in a different spot. There is a boatman who will lend me a craft. We will save time rowing directly downstream, rather than going overland. From our landing spot, it will be a short walk to the door."

Far from the door to Dawn's End, Aubin searched for an isolated earth woman. There was none in the park. He ventured farther, beyond the parkland, along the edge of the city, heading away from the more crowded houses to the rural homes. Peering into yards from the edge of the forest, he came upon Mrs. Brice, hanging out her laundry. She was older and heavier than Nicole, but Aubin was running out of time. As she tucked a loose strand of brown hair behind her ear, she glanced toward the trees. Aubin interpreted this as his cue. He leapt out onto the grass and danced.

Mrs. Brice's eyes widened with shock. When Aubin dropped to his knees in front of her, bared his fangs in a smile, and gazed into her gray eyes with his red irises and white diamond pupils, a scream bubbled up out of her throat like an erupting volcano.

Percy Brice was drinking his second coffee and despondently perusing the Honey Do list his wife had tucked beside his cup, when she tore into the kitchen.

"An animal—in clothes! It threatened me!"

"What?" said Percy, pushing back his chair, the list falling to the floor.

"An animal!" she repeated. "I thought at first it was a man. But it's some kinda freak. It has fangs."

"Where?"

"In the backyard. A beast with clothes. Get up, you idiot." She grabbed his shoulder with both hands and tugged. "Why are you still sitting there? I tell you there's a beast in our backyard, and you sit there asking stupid questions. Get up. Get up! *Get up*!"

"Jesus. All right. It's probably that rogue bear that killed the dog," said Percy rising to his feet.

"With clothes?" snapped his wife. She gestured dramatically. "And it was pure white."

"It must have torn up somebody's clothesline," Percy's forehead wrinkled. "Calm down, will you? I'll get my rifle."

"It had red eyes," said Mrs. Brice, following him into the bedroom.

"Maybe it's rabid or something," said Percy as he unlocked the rifle cabinet. "Stay in the house."

"You don't have to tell me twice." She hugged herself, trembling.

Percy took the bullets from the locked box on the closet shelf and loaded the rifle.

"Be careful, Percy," said his wife as she touched his arm.

"Don't worry, dear." He smiled. "They don't call me 'One Shot' for nothing."

162

Chapter Fourteen—Separate Ways

Nicole and Morrel hiked until the last rays of light dwindled over the horizon, eating from Morrel's supplies as they traveled. They stopped for only one quick rest. Even though Nicole's leg muscles were strengthening and her stamina was increasing, she was exhausted when Morrel finally said they would camp in an abandoned dugout.

"An old miner lived here," said Morrel. "He worked his claim until his final day. It has not been used for a while, but it is a solid structure."

A mildew smell permeated the home, though it did not compare to The Hoarder's storage chambers. Nicole cleaned out the fireplace while Morrel quickly gathered wood. They barricaded the door and lit a roaring fire, planning to keep it going throughout the night. Morrel knew the smoke might attract the dark things, but the temperature was dropping rapidly. A fire in the chimney would also prevent any flying creatures from trying to enter that way. He felt they would be safe in their little fortress. Besides, they could use a hot meal.

Nicole fed more logs to the flames trying not to think about what might be circling above. *What's to stop them from waiting until morning?* she thought. *Won't they just circle the dugout and wait until we try to leave?* She did not voice her fears.

After a wash and meal of hot soup, they turned in. Morrel wrapped his arms protectively around Nicole. She could feel his powerful pectorals against her back. She felt an urge to squirm her buttocks up against him and see how he reacted, but she could hear Larina's little feet hopping about in the dark. "I guess you feel pretty cramped in here," Nicole commented.

"Like I am buried alive," agreed Larina.

"A morbid thought," said Morrel. "Not something we need to think about before sleeping."

Larina snapped, "Panthers might like to sleep in caves like this, but birds do not."

"I am still partly human," said Morrel.

"I apologize, Alaric. This place makes me testy. Perhaps it would be better if I slept outside."

"No," said Nicole. "It wouldn't be better to find you dead in the morning. I'd rather not start my day with a real burial."

Larina gave a begrudging little laugh. "Okay, I'll try to stop fidgeting and relax. I'll imagine I'm sleeping in the lovely brythorn tree behind Alaric Morrel's home, listening to the wind tickle the leaves, and smelling the fresh, green life around me."

"Much better thoughts," said Morrel. "And I shall imagine I am lying in my bed listening to the same wind. You can be lying there with me, Nicole."

Nicole smiled and squeezed his hand as a shiver of desire threaded through her body. She suddenly felt like she would rather be here than anywhere else she had been for a long time. All three adjusted their positions, settling in.

"Morrel," Nicole whispered. "You'll always be partly human, won't you, no matter how often you use the bracelet?"

"Yes, in this life."

"This life?"

"The panther people believe no one really leaves when they die. They are absorbed into the world and born again into their own people."

"I don't think I like that," said Nicole. "That means if your family continues the way it has, you would eventually be reborn as a true panther."

"Yes. Another reason not to use the bracelet lightly. I not only sentence my descendants to a less human life, but myself as well," he said.

"Everyone in Dawn's End believes this?" asked Nicole. "The other families who have worn the bracelet as well?"

"Yes," said Larina. "We do. Sometimes I can almost remember life in a woman's body. It is like an extra shadow. I have odd sensations of hands and fingers, wearing clothes, combing my hair."

"Do you know the same people each time?" asked Nicole.

"I do not know, but I was drawn to the Alaric as soon as I could fly. When I arrived, it was as though he had been waiting for me. The bracelet had somehow connected us. I have always felt that I have known my Alaric at another time. That we were . . . intimate." Larina tucked her head under her wing.

Nicole felt uncomfortable with this turn in the conversation. It was a bit like having someone's first wife in the same bedroom. She drew away from Morrel. He pulled her back into his chest and rubbed his cheek on her hair. Nicole hoped Larina could not see in the low light from the fireplace. He lowered his lips to her ear and whispered, "I have flashes of déjà vu as well, and you, Nicole, are in them. Our paths have crossed before, though always fleetingly. Our destinies are linked, though only for a short time."

165

If he's right, will it always be like this? Nicole wondered. *Will we meet again in the future? Will we ever cross into the other's world for a lifetime?*

They lay silently side by side, warm together against the increasing cold. Nicole wondered if their beliefs about reincarnation were based in reality. Anything seemed possible here. But, while she would return as a human after this lifetime was over, Morrel would not. What would be their destiny then? Suddenly, she blurted aloud, "Even if you were the biggest, blackest, fiercest panther in existence, I would always trust you." She clapped her hand over her own mouth, horrified at her own remarks.

"He had just better not eat blue jays," said Larina, poking out her head.

Nicole giggled, then said, "The first day we met, I hoped that very thing."

Morrel snorted. Larina huffed and then chuckled. Soon, they were all laughing.

"Why did the people choose birds and then panthers?" asked Nicole. "Or did the wizards choose what went on the bracelets?"

"Before Larina's family, there were other animals," said Morrel. "When the wizards come to reforge the bracelets, each family chooses the animal for the next."

"Wizards?"

"I know little about them other than they have been around for as long as we have existed. Perhaps, someday, I can ask the village elders to share what they know."

"I see."

"I cannot imagine why the wizards chose a black leopard for mine."

"I know why," said Larina. "Panthers are creatures of the night. My people hoped that would give you the power to survive when the days lengthened. Also, flying is wonderful, but being small and helpless isn't."

"You have never acted helpless in your life," said Morrel. "Trying to peck out the eye of an armored monster! If you are so small and defenseless, why do you think nothing of rushing in where panther people hesitate?"

"Worm trails," snapped Larina. "I've never seen *you* hesitate. I have no intention of spending my life with my head under my wing."

"You're amazing," said Nicole. "I'm ten times your size, and I've spent the last year hiding from challenges. I wish I had half your spunk and confidence."

"Well, you aren't ducking very well at the moment," said Larina. "In fact, my Alaric will *just* love to hear this, but I may have misjudged you."

Morrel laughed as Nicole thanked Larina. Everyone was relaxed and feeling companionable. Soon, bird, woman, and panther man were asleep. Morrel woke twice to build up the fire when he heard the barricades being tested. Larina stirred. But no entry was gained, and they passed the night safely.

Morning was invisible in their refuge. They sensed daylight by the slight lifting of oppression, rather than by sight. Morrel and Larina said it smelled different. Before smothering what was left of the fire, they ate a warm breakfast cooked over the coals. Morrel removed the barricade. He flung open the door, dagger in hand. Muted sunshine poured in from the gray day. Whatever dark things had tested their fortifications had retreated at dawn.

The three companions hiked to the river. Following the trail alongside the banks, they soon reached the boatman. One large barge, three rowboats, and a small canoe-like craft were moored together.

Morrel shouted, "Josh, are you here?"

A middle-aged man emerged from the nearby shack. He was on the heavy side, but his muscular shoulders and arms showed the strength of a sailor. His hair was pulled back into a scruffy ponytail, accentuating his high cheek bones. His eyes were a bright, clear gray, crinkled at the corners in thick laugh lines.

Probably a real heartbreaker, thought Nicole.

Josh welcomed and hugged Morrel, pounding him on the back. Larina landed on Josh's shoulder and bit his hair.

"Larina," Josh exclaimed, "why are you wasting your time travelling with that young rogue. I've missed you." He scratched her under the chin as she stretched her neck in response.

"I've been accompanying my Alaric, but I haven't forgotten you," she said.

"So, it's *my* Alaric, is it? You break my heart, little one," moaned Josh.

"As soon as we have finished rescuing my Alaric's foolish cousin and returned Nicole to her world, I shall grace you with an extended visit," promised Larina.

Josh stepped up to meet Nicole as Morrel introduced them.

Josh hugged her carefully. "Right, pretty. Could make a new man outta me for sure." He winked at Morrel. "Kinda makes all this meeting stuff bearable, don't she?"

"Without a doubt," said Morrel with a smile. "But I am afraid The Meeting must wait. Aubin has put a twist in our plans."

"What's that bleached-out egotist gone and done now?" Josh crossed his arms and shook his head, his expression sardonic.

Morrel explained. Josh listened attentively, clucking and shaking his head. He welcomed the chance to help by lending them a boat. "Alone in my little water-cutter, you could make it in the blink of an eye. But, with the lovely lady, you will need a rowboat. This is my best. Strong, light, as fast as a rowboat can be."

Morrel thanked him. They embraced once more and then loaded the vessel. There were two sets of oars, but Morrel set up only one. The other he stowed in the base of the craft. Josh waved as they headed out into the stream. Larina flew ahead checking for danger along the banks, a graceful dot of bright blue in a dull sky.

"Sit down in the bottom of the boat, Nicole," said Morrel. "That way you will not break the wind so much."

Nicole wondered how it could make much difference in a rowboat, but obliged. Morrel steered into the current. They quickly picked up speed with the force of the river. Larina returned and perched on the stern. Then Morrel added his own power. The wind whipped back Nicole's hair. She was dumbstruck by the strength and velocity of his strokes. The blades dipped in blurring like a hummingbird's wings. Skimming the surface of the water, the small craft sped smoothly downstream at an alarming pace. The landscape whizzed by. Larina's feathers ruffled, and she gripped tightly to the stern, trying not to be blown off. Eventually, she hopped into the bottom of the boat.

Lunch was consumed on board. Nicole opened Morrel's sling and dug out some of the provisions. She fed Morrel bits of food as he rowed, slackening only slightly. It was close to evening when they reached their landing.

They travelled through the thick forest in which Nicole had been lost. Nicole felt an odd reluctance to return to her world.

"We are almost there," said Morrel.

"Let's go through the door right away," said Nicole. "Then we'll be safe from the dark things during the night."

"Yes," said Morrel. "Both of you do that. You and Larina will be out of danger during the night."

"Aren't you coming?" asked Nicole.

"I cannot stay a full night in your world. My bracelet might be drained by morning. That is why Aubin is in such great danger," he explained.

"Then I'll stay with you," said Nicole.

"No. I will be fine alone."

"But I'll be worried," she protested.

"He will be safer not having to protect us," said Larina.

"Oh. Right," Nicole said.

"Besides, you can search for Aubin much easier without me," Morrel said.

"I guess."

"There is also the problem of time," said Morrel. "You will be quicker without me. Find him, and learn what action he has taken. In the morning, I will let you through, and we will decide what to do."

"Of course. I'm not thinking straight," said Nicole. "Don't worry. I'll find him. He couldn't have gone far. He had to travel overland. Maybe he hasn't even gone through yet."

Larina flew on ahead.

"I wish that were true," said Morrel. "But, more likely, he raced the whole way. You still have no idea how fast my people can travel alone. I suspect his bracelet is already drained."

"That means he's trapped!"

Morrel nodded. "He can be a thorn, but his father and my father were brothers. Once, he was like a brother to me. He can be endearing when he wishes. You were not oblivious to his charms when he danced. I think you liked him in a different way."

"It was like being hypnotized," said Nicole. "But kind of embarrassing. I felt awkward when you wouldn't look at me."

"I know. So did I. There are things about my people you still do not know. We feel sexual arousal, but more intensely and suddenly than you do. It is like a wave of heat. There need not be any emotions attached."

Nicole laughed. "Sounds like a number of guys I've met."

"Oh?" said Morrel. "I also must confess I was jealous of Aubin's skill. I tried so hard to attract you, and, in just a short time, he had you spellbound."

"It was not like you think," said Nicole.

171

"You seemed more drawn to him than to me."

"Not true," said Nicole. "I had to brace myself when you wore your celebration clothes." She ran her hand over his arm. He stopped and faced her. "Very sexy," whispered Nicole. "In fact, I was attracted to you before I even met you."

Morrel studied her face. "Time to leave," he whispered, and then smiled.

"What if the dark things overrun you while we're gone?" said Nicole. "I'll never know for sure why the door wasn't opened for us. I'll be trapped in my world, Larina too."

"I would be happy to know you were safe, at least for as long as the door held," said Morrel.

"But I would never know what happened to you," said Nicole.

"Then we will both have to succeed and survive," said Morrel. He smiled and tentatively put his arm around her in a reassuring hug. Nicole turned her face to his. He hesitated and then gave her a short gentle kiss. His lips were soft and warm, and she wanted more, but he stepped back.

"'If this be magic,'" said Nicole, "'Let it be an art lawful as eating.'"

Nicole pulled him back and softly kissed him again. She sank into Morrel's soft, warm lips as he responded. Then, the kiss became heated. Nicole threaded her fingers into his hair and slid her tongue over his sharp teeth to meet his tongue. He pulled back, startled.

"Go now, Nicole." His voice was husky. "Larina is waiting by the entrance. Walk toward her, and keep walking. I will

172

hold the door until you are both out. When you find Aubin, come and stand by the door. I will sense you are there."

Night had drawn its full curtain while they spoke. Nicole could barely make out the small shape of Larina beyond. Around the bird a haze shimmered. *Odd*, thought Nicole. *For days all I wanted was to go back through this door to home. Now, all I want is to hurry back to Dawn's End.* As Nicole reached Larina, the haze drew into itself into a bright arch.

Chapter Fifteen—Trapped

Nicole halted, the blast of sunlight blinding her. She squeezed her eyes shut until they adjusted. Dew coated the grass. Birds were singing passionately to the eastern sun. Larina led her through the forest. The park was deserted.

It was morning. But what morning? Nicole looked around. Larina landed in a Manitoba maple.

"Stay close to me," said Nicole. "People in my world can be very cruel to birds, even on parkland."

"I know all about that," said Larina. "I can take care of myself. I will be fine as long as I don't eat anything here. It makes me ill."

"Okay. We should split up then," said Nicole. "I'll check my cell phone, if it's still there, and find out what day it is. Then I'll drive to town and see if I can find out anything. You scout out around here. Maybe Aubin is hiding nearby, hoping someone will come through the door. Meet me back here in an hour."

"I don't know hours. I'll watch for you."

Nicole walked briskly down the path as Larina flew out over the park. No one was on the trail, no other cars in the parking lot. She heaved a sigh of relief, reached under the bumper and yanked off the magnetic box. She pried open the gritty cover and took out her backup key.

Inside the vehicle, she checked for her driver's license, ownership, insurance papers, and purse. Nothing had been disturbed. Apprehensively, she inserted the key. The motor roared to life. Nicole quickly checked the car clock. 8:34 a.m. But what day? She flipped open her cell phone. It was

Saturday, a mere day after she had left! Only eleven hours had passed.

Nicole phoned in sick to work. They would not have received her letter yet, and she didn't want them calling her house to see what was wrong.

She dialed a direct line to her co-worker in the back office. "Hello, Helen. It's Nicole. Listen, I'm not coming in today." She hated lying to Helen, so she told a half-truth. "I've picked up something strange, and I just can't shake it. I hope you're not overloaded with work."

"No problem," said Helen. "You just take it easy and get well. Drink Echinacea tea. That always helps me."

Nicole felt a twinge of guilt. "Sure. Thanks. I was just lying here listening to the news, and I couldn't believe how dull it was. How come nothing interesting ever happens here?"

"Well, tune in to KLMK. They had a funny little blurb this morning about some guy out on Highway 64. They're covering it pretty close. It'll give you a chuckle. Seems he caught a Sasquatch. Only he calls it an abominable snowman because it's supposed to be pure white. It's probably an albino bear. What some guys won't say to get on the news, eh?"

"Nutty," agreed Nicole. "Besides, an albino bear would have been interesting enough. Did they say the guy's name?"

"I don't remember," Helen answered. "Go back to bed now, and take it easy. Hey! You've got the next five days off. Good timing. Nah, I guess it's bad timing. No good being sick on your holiday."

"Maybe I'll shake it by tomorrow. Bye."

Nicole dialed KLMK and requested information on the Bigfoot. The DJ told her it was caught by Percy Brice on

175

Highway 64. She hung up and checked the phone book she kept in the car. Percy Brice was listed under RR13. The book gave his house number.

She shut off the engine and walked back to the spot where she remembered entering the park from the forest. It was almost 10:00 a.m. The blue jay appeared a few moments later.

"I know where he is," said Nicole. "Some guy on the highway claims he's caught an abominable snowman. Aubin could easily be mistaken for a yeti. I'm going to drive out and check."

"I haven't seen any signs of him in the park. I'll wait here until you return."

Morning traffic was thinning. Nicole rechecked the house number she had copied from the phone book. Brice lived at 6527. She tried to skim the numbers on the mailboxes. A post-box reading 324 whizzed by. She picked up speed. The lots became more spread out and increasingly rustic.

Nicole knew the house instantly. Even in the middle of a workaday morning, the curious had gathered. A long driveway curved up to a wood frame house, the teal paint peeling away. Two red wagon wheels marked the entrance. On the lawn, a scattering of ceramic ducks and plastic Disney characters weaved around the overgrown flower beds. A chaotic log pile, beside the garage, spilled onto the gravel driveway.

Cars filled the driveway and the sides of the road. Nicole pulled over in front of a mid-sized van. She pushed her bracelet as far up her arm as it would go, covered it with her sleeve and tied her hood over her butchered hair.

Her shoes crunched on the gravel as she walked nonchalantly between the cars and the ditch to Brice's driveway. The babble of excited voices made her cringe. People were gathered around a metal container. It was shaped like a barrel on its side. The front was sealed with a sturdy padlock. The crowd took turns peeping through a grill at the other end.

"Do you think this old bear trap will hold him?" a woman asked. "He looks awfully strong."

"Damn right," answered a man wearing gray Kodiak boots, a plaid shirt, and green work pants. He pushed back his baseball cap, which was crested with a Blue label, and then pulled it forward again. Percy Brice. "The Ministry guy said it'll hold a grizzly. I guess if it'll hold that, it'll hold an abominable snowman."

"I thought they lived in the Himalayas," said a tall man. "I never heard of a yeti in North America before."

"Yeah," said a shorter man. "We're supposed to have Bigfoot in Canada."

"He's white, ain't he?" said Percy. "What else would you call him?"

Everyone nodded, then took more turns peeking through the grill as if to confirm Percy's claims.

"It's too dark in there," complained a young man in jeans. "I'm going to get my flashlight."

"No," ordered Percy. "None of that. It scares him. Then he curls up even worse and hides his face. Probably lives in some dark cave. Probably never saw a flashlight before. I'm guessing he wandered into civilization and is confused and frightened."

"I thought they'd be dirtier," said a woman in a green jogging suit. "His hair looks like it's been groomed."

"My God!" said another woman. "He's got red eyes."

This caused a new flurry of jostling and peering. The man in jeans had retrieved his flashlight from the car and shone it through the opening in spite of Percy's warning.

"Stop that," shouted Aubin. "It hurts my eyes. Take it away!"

Nicole looked around in shock. *How could they do that to a speaking creature? Why were they all so matter-of-fact?*

"Did you hear that roar?" said Percy. "I told you he don't like it. Now, put that flashlight away or you'll have to leave. And don't nobody try to take pictures either. Keep those cell phones away. I don't want your pictures showing up all over the net. He's mine, and I'll decide who gets to photograph him."

"Okay, okay," said the man in jeans. A woman returned her cell phone to her purse.

I don't get it, thought Nicole. *They aren't even impressed that he can speak to them.* She wiggled to the front of the group and looked inside. Aubin had turned his back to the grill.

"Hi, fella," she said. "Don't be scared. No one is going to hurt you."

The others smiled approvingly. Aubin whirled around.

"Nicole! Nicole, get me out of here!" He rushed to the grill. The people jumped back. "Tell them to let me out. None of them speak any sense."

The tall man jerked Nicole away from the cage. "Don't stand so close."

178

"Stay back," said Percy. "He's getting riled up. I don't want him hurting himself."

"Or breaking out," said the woman in green. "He sure can roar."

Roar? thought Nicole. *Of course. They can't understand him. My bracelet is still translating for us.*

"Just one more look," she said, stepping close to the opening. "I won't upset him."

Aubin's red eyes met hers, pleading.

"Shh. Don't make a fuss," she whispered. "They might decide to tranquillize you or make us all leave. And no one knows what you're saying. Understand?"

Aubin nodded. He held up his wrist. The bracelet had altered from gold to a copper brown. The others crowded up, interested in the quiet exchange. Aubin quickly put his arm behind his back.

"I think I'll bring my friend Morrel to see him," said Nicole to the man in jeans.

"Yeah. Bring the whole family. He sure is something."

Nicole gave Aubin a smile and nod. As she turned, he said, "If I do not survive, tell Morrel I am sorry." Nicole nodded, biting her lip.

They couldn't do anything until dark. Unlike in Dawn's End, here, darkness would be their ally. Nicole picked up a chicken salad and a chocolate shake at the Drive Thru, wondering if she would ever be able to indulge again. Then she went to Safeway and restocked her packsack with a mixture of packaged and fresh food. She bought three tetra pack boxes of juice with straws, a travel bottle of shampoo, and a beach towel.

It would be nice to return home for a bath, but her stepmother might show up. She would want to know why Nicole wasn't at work. She stopped at Magic Cuts, inwardly chuckling at the name, and had her butchered hair shaped into a neat style. Then she went to the Canada Games Complex and relaxed in the sauna and shower. It seemed selfish to indulge while both Morrel and Aubin were in danger, but there was nothing she could do right now. She used the time to plan. As she toweled off, she realized her bracelet was now the same color as Aubin's. Neither of them had the power to return to Dawn's End.

At Canadian Tire, she bought a hacksaw, a crowbar, and a penlight on her credit card. She hoped no one she knew would see her. She rooted through Men's Wear for suitable clothing for Morrel. She selected wide, size 12, suede moccasins; sport socks; navy jogging pants; and a long sleeved sweatshirt with a hood and a hand pouch in front. Too bad it wasn't winter. Ski masks were out of season.

She drove back to Brice's house. The crowd had grown. With alarm, Nicole saw a newspaper reporter arrive to document Aubin's capture. Percy bragged that the CKPR TV was coming out tomorrow. He repeated his story for the new crowd.

The beast had come upon Mrs. Brice in the back yard. When Percy saw what had frightened his wife, he decided to catch it alive if he could. He could have brought it down with one shot—that was his nickname, you know, One Shot— but it would be more interesting alive.

Nicole shuddered. She didn't think the people of Dawn's End even knew about rifles.

Percy had previously convinced the Ministry of Natural Resources to set a bear trap up on the crown land behind his property. His dog had been killed the week before, and his screen porch ripped open.

"Think it was the Abominable?" shouted a man.

"No, I saw the tracks. It was a bear. This critter's feet are different."

The crowd seemed disappointed. Percy recaptured their attention with the details of how he had fired his gun beside the snowman a few times to show he meant business and then herded the creature through the bush and into the metal container. He slammed the door shut and yelled for his wife to bring the biggest padlock she could find. It seemed intelligent and might figure out a way to spring the trap. Then, using his ATV, he hauled the trap into their driveway. The Ministry might not like that, but Percy felt the circumstances warranted special consideration.

"Well, we aren't going to press any charges," said a Ministry officer as he approached. "But I am here to claim the trap and its contents."

"No way," said Percy as he crossed his arms. "I caught this animal, and I aim to keep him until I decide where he's going. He was on my land, and I risked my neck to capture him. I just made use of your trap. He didn't climb in there on his own. You can't just take him. This is just one more example of the government ripping off the little man."

The crowd rumbled their approval.

"Look," said the officer. "I don't want any trouble. You best let me take him now, or I'll just have to come back with a couple of police officers."

"Then you damn well do that," said Percy. "This is my land, and I'm telling you to get the hell off. No government Joe boy is going to take what's rightfully mine."

The crowd clapped.

"And you better damned well have the right legal papers if you stick your nose back here again," shouted Percy, encouraged by his audience. "I'll be contacting my own lawyer."

Cheers ensued. The Ministry officer shook his head and retreated. Nicole mingled with the crowd until it thinned. Percy hooked up a hose to the trap and let the water dribble through the grill. Aubin stayed far on the other side. He must have been thirsty, but he knew better than to drink the water. Nicole caught his attention once. She smiled and gave a nod. He nodded back.

"It's getting late folks," said Percy. "I gotta let the creature sleep. Time for everyone to head home."

With a few last peeks, the crowd complied. Nicole melted away with a larger group. As she drove back to the pond, she wondered about Morrel. How had he made out during the night? How strong were the dark things becoming? Was he able to stay close to the door to Dawn's End?

Larina greeted her at the park. "Thank goodness you're finally back. Did you find Aubin?"

"Yes," said Nicole. "Let's get Morrel. I don't think I can free Aubin without his help."

Nicole ran toward the pond; Larina flew ahead. They waited in the forest a short distance from the path where the door had opened. It was a quiet, balmy night. Time passed. An owl hooted. Trees rustled in the wind. Nicole tapped her foot impatiently. *Where was he?* Larina strutted nervously about. Finally, a glow appeared and through it stepped Morrel.

"Have you been waiting?" he asked. His voice sounded tired.

"Yes. What happened?" asked Nicole.

"The dark things are becoming more aggressive," he said. "I don't think the dugout would have been safe last night. I spent most of my time on the run, avoiding them. They are multiplying as well."

"So fast?" said Nicole. "Here. Put these on while we talk." She thrust the clothes at him and turned her back.

"When you returned to your world," asked Morrel, "how many days had passed?"

"Not even a full one. Oh, the time difference you mentioned before. Has it been more than one night for you?"

"Yes," said Morrel. "That is why I could not wait by the door. I had to keep moving and periodically check back. I am dressed. Now, where is Aubin?"

"Put up your hood and tie it," said Nicole. "Just in case someone sees you in the car. I don't know if it would work if we were stopped by the cops. I'll be extra careful driving. We have to drive pretty far. Aubin has been caught and locked in a cage."

"Better caged than dead," said Morrel. "Is he hurt?"

"No, and I don't think it will be difficult to get him out, at least for you. I would take too long. Make too much noise. We'll have to work together. Larina needs to help as well."

They headed for the car. Neither Morrel nor Larina were very happy about getting inside the small Sunfire. Morrel clenched his fists when Nicole started the engine. A buzzer sounded, and he lurched with surprise. She chuckled and strapped Morrel into his seat belt. He sat stiffly erect. Nicole tried not to laugh as she slipped the gear into drive.

She passed Brice's yard, turned in a driveway, then drove past again and parked out of sight from his driveway. There was no one around. Larina flew ahead to check for danger. During the bird's reconnaissance, Nicole explained the situation to Morrel. He selected the crowbar. The hacksaw would be too slow and noisy. One loud snap with the tool and Aubin would be out. Morrel would use the bracelet if necessary. They must work quickly.

Larina returned and gave the all clear. The two passenger doors were left slightly ajar. Larina led Morrel to the cage and then returned to the Sunfire. Nicole scrunched down behind the steering wheel so any passing driver would think the car was empty. Seconds crawled past. She glanced in the direction of the cage. Suddenly, the sky glowed. She sat up, startled. A white face appeared beside the car. She jumped in shock.

"Get in the back," commanded Morrel. Aubin climbed in. Larina fluttered in beside him.

"Slam the door," said Nicole as she started the engine.

"Go!" ordered Morrel. "Hurry!"

Nicole resisted the urge to floor the gas pedal and squeal away. She quietly pulled out on to the highway and surged to a mere five kilometers over the speed limit. "Did anyone hear you?"

"I don't think so," said Morrel.

Nicole said, "There's going to be hell to pay in the morning when Percy finds his Bigfoot missing."

"We didn't take his foot," said Morrel.

Nicole laughed. "A Bigfoot is—I was about to tell you it was a mythical beast."

They both laughed and kept laughing until Aubin and Larina agreed the two of them had lost their senses.

"Nicole." Morrel's voice was suddenly serious. "Can we go faster?"

"I don't want to risk being stopped by the cops," said Nicole. "Aubin has no disguise. I forgot about that. Sorry."

Morrel explained. "I used my bracelet to break the lock. It drained power. I can feel it fading."

"Oh, God." Nicole floored the gas pedal. The car fishtailed.

"Stop!" yelled Morrel.

"It's okay. I'll drive faster. I can handle it."

"No. We'll be quicker on foot."

"You're kidding," said Nicole as she braked.

"Wait by the door."

Before Nicole could reply, they raced into the next driveway and disappeared into the forest behind. She shut the passenger doors and then drove on in silence with Larina. *How fast did they need to be? What if Morrel's bracelet became useless? They would all be trapped here. Unable to eat. Hiding. Who could open the door from the other side? Alaric Sabella and Linnel. Would they be able to get past the increasing dark things? Would they even know Morrel needed them?*

Nicole's hand trembled when she hid the key under the car. The park was empty. She carefully followed Larina through the forest, lighting her way with the flashlight. No one was in sight at the entrance to Dawn's End. She decided that was a good sign. She waited at the door with Larina, jiggling her leg nervously.

"How long does it take the bracelets to return to full power?" Nicole asked.

"It is immediate," answered Larina.

So, where are they? she thought.

Chapter Sixteen—Allies

A few moments later, a glow appeared. Nicole released a tense breath. Morrel stepped through, smiled, and took her hand. Nicole squeezed it with relief. Larina landed on his shoulder. Together, they passed through into Dawn's End.

"I was scared," said Nicole as she threw her arms around Morrel and gave him a fierce hug. Larina fluttered away. It was daylight, murky and overcast, but they could see well enough.

"I like your hair," said Morrel.

Nicole laughed. She looked into his face. They kissed, fervently, nothing held back, and then hugged again.

"Everything is all right now," said Morrel.

"How's Aubin?" she asked.

"Fine. We had a long talk while we waited for you."

"Waited!" said Nicole. "I can't believe you beat me here."

"In your world, we may have arrived only a short time before you," said Morrel. "But, once in Dawn's End, the time changes. We talked and Aubin has seen the error of his behavior."

"A leopard who changed his spots?" asked Nicole.

"Pardon?"

"Nothing," said Nicole. "Silly joke. Go on."

187

"He wants to help us," said Morrel. "He feels responsible, which he is, for the lost time and increased risk. I do not hold it against him. There was much I did not understand."

"You are a wonder, Morrel," said Nicole. "Not many people forgive so readily. Are you sure you trust him?"

"Of course," Morrel looked puzzled. "Two people cannot exist in the same world without trust."

Nicole nodded, silent.

He continued. "Aubin's ambition may have served us a good turn. Before I brought you to Dawn's End, he spoke to Hulda. It seems she actually served him tea."

"Get out!"

"Where do you want me to go?"

"Never mind," Nicole said. "How ever did he manage that?"

"He does have charm," admitted Morrel. "She told him some things we have not learned."

"I'm impressed. Does he know where the third piece of the key is?"

Morrel answered. "No, but he knows of someone who might. High in the mountains lives a talking bruin. He is a descendant of a race who held the bracelets before the bird people. It seems he befriended my grandfather and actually traveled with him on the quest for a while. There is a chance he knows the location of the last piece."

"Do we have time to go to the mountains?" asked Nicole.

"We have to make time, but it is a cold, arduous journey, and I have never been there before. I will be out of my element," admitted Morrel.

"I'm ready if you are," said Nicole.

"There will be three of us," said Morrel. "Aubin will be the guide."

"Four," corrected Larina. "I have been of help, and you are not going to send me away now."

"What's one more?" laughed Nicole.

Morrel smiled. "Aubin!" he shouted. "*We* are ready to travel."

Aubin was subdued and respectful. Grateful to the others, he committed himself to their service. When they reached the river, Aubin put to the second oars with fierce determination. Stroke for stroke, he matched Morrel. Although they were fighting the current, Nicole was amazed at the progress.

The countryside flashed by. Terrain changed from forest, to sparse bush, to rock and back to forest again. The "splat, swish" of the oars beat out a rhythm. No one spoke.

Evening was approaching when the small band reached the boatman's harbor. The panther men jumped out into the water and pulled the rowboat backwards onto the shore. Morrel held Nicole's hand as she wobbled across the stern and hopped to the ground. Aubin went to find Josh.

The husky man welcomed them heartily. He made a reference to saving fools in distress. Aubin took it in stride.

"You plan to stay the night, I hope? Them creepy things have been coming out at night in droves," said Josh. "I wouldn't want you to be out in the open come dark."

"Thank you," said Morrel. "We were counting on your hospitality."

Josh stabled his few farm animals, fed them, and double-barricaded the shed. From inside the house, he shuttered the windows tightly and double-barred the door. Dinner was a casual affair. Josh had only a small table, so everyone ate off carefully balanced tin plates.

"I see you have double doors on the stable," said Nicole. "Have you been bothered by the night things often?"

"Not until the days shortened," said Josh. "It's strange. I've seen a few of them. They look like animals that have been twisted out of shape, puffed up, and then dipped in black paint. They don't move or sound normal. Bold as can be. They make my skin crawl. I don't know where they've come from but they've driven off all the other forest creatures."

"Morrel believes they *are* the normal forest animals, transformed by the abnormal night," explained Nicole.

"That would explain some of it." Turning to Morrel, Josh asked, "What's going on anyway? How did all this start?"

"I do not know why it begins," confessed Morrel. "Nicole and I may learn this when we find the key and reach The Meeting Place. Grandfather said Nightfall alters living things. Somehow the darkness stops them from seeing their true selves. They become enraged, almost diseased. Their physical appearance alters to match the new personality. If the night continues, I suspect everyone, us included, will be transfigured. I feel pity for the night creatures, hideous though they are. Like us, they are victims of something beyond their control."

Nicole had difficulty feeling compassion for the armored beast that had wounded Morrel and trapped her in the tree.

Still, they were living beings who felt pain. She was horrified by the new knowledge that Morrel, Aubin, Larina, and all the villagers would be transformed like Jekyll and Hyde. She wondered if she would be transformed as well.

Thoughtfully, Nicole bit into a delicious stone ground biscuit. This meal was more like what she was used to, two kinds of cooked vegetables—one of which she was sure was turnip, hot pea-like soup, and chunks of cold sausage. Neither of the panther men ate the sausage.

"Do panther people not eat meat?" she asked. "I saw none at the village or on the trail. No poultry either. But there was seafood and fish."

"We feel uncomfortable eating birds and mammals," said Morrel.

"We can't very well ask each animal before we hunt it if it can speak," added Aubin.

Morrel said, "We cannot be sure if any have human ancestry, because of the bracelets. The wizards do not use fish, so they are safe to consume."

"I see," said Nicole, examining her sausage.

"Don't worry, Miss," said Josh. "That's my own farm animals you're eating. None of them ever talked to me. Those two can't eat it because it would shock their systems after being raised without meat. Binds them up something terrible, it does."

Nicole coughed. She bit into her sausage avoiding Aubin's eyes. "Hey," she said. "There must be other talking animals around then."

"Yes," said Aubin.

191

"I'm in Narnia!" she exclaimed.

Aubin looked at Morrel, who shrugged.

"Will we run into any talking animals?" asked Nicole.

"Probably not," said Aubin. "They mostly keep to themselves."

"Why's that?"

"I do not know," he replied.

Morrel spoke up. "I think they feel out of place. Perhaps it pains them to see people like you, the way they could have been. Or to talk to half-men like us and empathize with our fate. Perhaps they simply mistrust us. A few are approachable."

"Larina certainly is," said Nicole.

Josh laughed. "Larina is an unabashed flirt. Almost as bad as Aubin."

He winked at the blue jay who gave a little chuckle.

After the meal, Josh built up the fire. He offered Nicole his rough pallet, but she declined, preferring to cuddle with Morrel on a blanket on the floor. The night passed safely.

As they prepared the rowboat the next morning, Josh offered to go with them. Another fighter might be of aid.

"No doubt you would be invaluable," said Morrel. "But your animals need you. Once we arrived at The Meeting Place, you, Larina and Aubin would have to return alone. None but the couple and The Keeper are allowed inside. Aubin can outrun them. I do not know how Larina survives, but she does. For you, there would be much danger."

"I'd risk it for you, Alaric," replied Josh.

"I know." Morrel clasped the man's shoulder.

"Take care, my friends," said Josh as he hugged each in turn. He stroked Larina's small head. She touched his cheek with her beak. "Come back with the Alaric under more happy circumstances," he added.

They paddled upstream until river travel was no longer feasible. The rough water became wilder. Large boulders protruded. When the river narrowed, channeling the churning water into a turbulent funnel, they decided to travel overland.

They pulled the rowboat far onto the bank and shouldered their belongings. A path wound close to the embankment. Even though Nicole hiked at her quickest pace, they were vulnerably slow.

"Not much farther to safety," promised Morrel. "Up ahead is another panther village."

"Are there Alarics in this village too?"

"No male ones for generations. One young woman, Shandri, keeps a bracelet. Should neither I nor Aubin have children, then the responsibility would fall on her shoulders. Although no one there uses the bracelet, they have intermarried with our village repeatedly, and so their physical features are the same."

"Are your villages often in contact?"

"Yes," said Morrel. "We have friends and relatives in both villages. You will find many good people here. They understand the nature of the quest and will do all they can to help."

"It is unfortunate that we do not have time for a Telling," Aubin added. They celebrate as well as our villages. There are some excellent dancers and speakers."

"And they would, of course, want you to dance," teased Nicole. She could have bitten her tongue the minute she said it, but everyone, including Aubin, laughed good-naturedly.

The village had been built a short distance from the river, on the crest of a hill, surrounded by woods. These homes were constructed with logs and gray rock. The villagers did not have access to a quarry like Morrel's community.

Although lacking the brightness of the quartz structures, Nicole recognized the same clean order. The areas between the buildings were fresh and uncluttered. Every building was in perfect shape. The same town square, with a well off to the side, centralized the village.

Morrel led them to one of the larger structures and scratched at the door. A middle-aged woman answered and ushered them in with a hearty welcome. Inside was the girl, Shandri, whom Morrel had described. She was barely fourteen, with large gray eyes and gray fur, streaked with white. Even at her tender age, she showed a sensual beauty. There was a second middle-aged woman, Shandri's aunt, Olisa. The first was her mother, Dyania. Other family included her uncle, Kiritana, and various cousins. Everyone spoke at once, in a cacophony of excitement.

A boy was sent out with food for Larina, who had had enough of crowded enclosures. The others were fed and fussed over. Morrel explained their plans and the need to hurry. A brood of youngsters and teenagers were sent off in every direction to find suitable clothing for the trip.

A few villagers had climbed the mountains for rare herbs. They explained the routes and how snow fell on the summit in winter. Although it was now spring, the oncoming darkness had caused disorder. White peaks could still be seen from the village.

The villagers understood the clothing Nicole and the Alarics would need. As the apparel accumulated, the travelers searched through for the proper fit. They tied outerwear onto their slung bags and took an extra layer of clothing. Being familiar with northern winters, Nicole encouraged the other two to err on the side of caution.

Dyania gave them a flask of liquid.

"It will ignite wet and frozen wood," she said. "It can make the difference between survival and freezing."

Morrel thought it ridiculous when Nicole insisted they bring soft, down-lined boots that reached their knees and thick socks. He tied the footwear to his pack with a shake of his head. He seldom needed more than bare feet. Aubin stayed out of the argument.

"Surely we will not need all this," said Morrel. "We are not as thin-blooded as you."

"Have you ever traveled in snow before?" said Nicole.

"Well, no, but we have our hair and our metabolism to keep us warm."

"The outworlder is right," said Shandri. "Our climbers speak of cold that we have never experienced in the village. Prepare for the worst, my Alaric, considering how strange the weather is."

Nicole wondered how Larina would react if Shandri was Morrel's mate.

"If you insist," said Morrel.

"I would not have you suffer, most worthy Morrel . . . Alaric Morrel," said Shandri with a little pout.

Aubin rolled his eyes at Nicole.

Once the clothing was selected and the food packed, they were given a sleeping room in the back of the house. There were three separate pallets and a perch for Larina. Shandri set Nicole's things on the pallet by the door, farthest away from the others.

It took longer than usual for Nicole to fall asleep. She wiggled down into the deep folds of her quilts and wrapped her toes in. She missed Morrel's warmth.

The next day, she missed those warm quilts as well. Even with the extra layer of clothing, Nicole's extremities tingled with cold as they hiked.

"I can see my breath," said Aubin. "It steams like a cooking pot."

Nicole smiled. "You *are* new at this."

The trail steeped quickly, zigzagging up the mountain pass. The air was colder with every step. When her feet felt like wooden blocks, she stopped and traded her running shoes for the boots resembling mukluks.

They reached the level where patches of snow dotted the frozen ground. Morrel and Aubin surrendered their feet to boots as well. That night, the men donned their extra clothing. Nicole put on the bulky cape, thumbless mittens, and scarf. It was not enough.

They chanced a fire. The dark things couldn't survive this cold either, could they? They formed a triangle around the campfire, Larina surrounded by their packs on the outer side. Nicole spent a restless night alternating her position. She seared her back against the fire while she froze her front. Then she did the opposite.

They started out the next morning while it was still dark. Morrel and Aubin examined the ice that had formed on each other's beards. They were too cold to sleep anymore, and the daylight was getting dangerously short. The ghostly moon lit their way. Even though they were wearing the outer clothing, the men were astounded at the temperature.

"I bet we ain't seen nothing yet," warned Nicole.

They reached the level where packed snow covered everything. The crust was clean and unbroken. Small whirlwinds danced across the surface, shaping the tiny loose granules into miniature dunes. Their feet broke through the top layers, caving the edges in, leaving behind unrecognizable prints. In places where the snow was shallow, it squeaked underfoot.

Nicole tucked her thumbs into her palms and clenched her fists. She curled and uncurled her toes, urging the circulation. With each step, her feet numbed.

The wind increased, burning their cheeks with the threat of frostbite. They took short, shallow breaths trying to keep the cold from the deepest part of their lungs. Their nostril hairs froze, creating prickles with each intake of air. Nicole warned them that to blow or squeeze their noses would create a risk of a nose bleed. Morrel's frosted face was now as white as his cousin's.

The frigid temperature wore them down. Talking was a strain, so they hiked in silence, each step harder than the last. Nicole fantasized about hot chocolate, blueberry muffins fresh from the oven, and steaming pea soup. It wasn't fair that she had just survived five months of winter and was now back in an arctic world. Her eyes stung. She wiped away the water before it could freeze to her cheek.

"Not far now," encouraged Aubin.

Just as they took heart enough to pick up the pace, Larina landed on the ground in front of them. She staggered a couple of steps, flapped her wings spastically, and then fell over. "Alaric," she croaked.

Morrel snatched her up. He fumbled with his jacket and placed Larina next to his skin. "I am sorry, little one. I should have realized. Can you breathe in there?" They crowded around.

"I will be fine now," she whispered weakly.

"Poor Larina," cried Nicole. "She didn't have any extra clothing. In our world, birds eat continually on days like this to maintain their body temperature. They huddle together in piles to stop from freezing. We have to feed her and check for frostbite. She could have hypothermia."

"What's that?" said Aubin.

"The cooling of the core of her body, so dangerous it can kill. We have to get hot liquid into her."

"Then we will," said Morrel. "Aubin, the first cave we find will be our camp for the night. It is almost dark, so we must hurry."

Chapter Seventeen—Land of the Snow Queen

Aubin found the perfect location. He left the three of them inside and braved the cold again to find fuel. They heated a broth over the flames and fed it to Larina pinch by pinch. Nicole felt ashamed she had not anticipated the danger Larina had faced.

When Larina had recovered slightly, Nicole coaxed her into eating bits of dried fruit from Morrel's supply. She was determined *this* bird was going to survive. Slowly, the blue jay's circulation returned to normal.

"Next time you are in trouble, tell us before it becomes near fatal," Morrel scolded. "I would never have forgiven myself if you had frozen to death."

"I will, Alaric. Perhaps I should travel inside your cloak while we are in these mountains, if Nicole doesn't mind."

"Larina!" exclaimed Nicole. "I am not that green-eyed. I care about you, too."

Aubin said, "Your eyes are blue."

"'Green-eyed' means jealous," explained Nicole.

"I see," said Aubin. "Well, there is no reason for Larina to be cold or for you to be green-eyed. I would not mind a little extra body heat next to my chest, if she will accept white instead of black."

"I would be honored, Alaric Aubin."

Aubin smiled. It was the first time she had addressed him by his title.

As Morrel checked the cave, he disturbed a roost of bats. They squeaked and flapped chaotically around their heads. Aubin unsheathed his dagger and stabbed. One fell dead at his feet.

"Don't," said Nicole. "They won't harm you."

The others looked at her in surprise.

"They are dark things of the night," protested Aubin.

"No more than Morrel is," argued Nicole. "Unless they are vampire bats, which this one certainly doesn't seem to be. He looks like the Big Brown Bat from home. They aren't dangerous unless they're rabid."

"Rabid?" asked Morrel.

Nicole explained what rabies was. Aubin confessed that they did not have rabies in Dawn's End, but he still mistrusted bats.

"It flies like Larina and has fur like me," said Aubin. "What kind of creature is that?"

"You talk like me and have fur like a panther," countered Nicole. "What kind of creature are you?"

"Good point," said Morrel.

"Don't you have bats in your village?" asked Nicole.

"I do not think so."

"Jeez, they're all over at home," said Nicole. "When I was little, I was terrified of bats. My grandfather was alive then, my mother's father, and whenever we visited his house in the country, I was frightened by the bats."

"No wonder," said Aubin, as he flicked the dead creature against the wall with his dagger.

"Grandpa and I sat on the back porch and watched the stars come out and the fire flies blink past. We looked for the Big Dipper, that's a constellation, and waited for shooting stars. It was magic in the dark, good magic, until I spotted a bat. Then, I would run shrieking into the house."

"Understandable."

"Grandpa decided I should face my fear. He caught a bat when it was sleeping inside the shed, stuck to the wall like a splat of mud. He put it in a jar with holes in the lid and gave it to me. I wouldn't even touch the glass. He said wherever I went I would have to bring that jar. No one was allowed to free it but me. I didn't have to free it either, if I didn't want to. In a day or two, it would die of thirst. Then, I could throw it away.

"That sounded just fine to me. One less bat. I did what I was told, although I hated picking up the jar. Grandpa pointed out features about the little guy and explained how they can consume 3,000 insects in a single night. I looked at it more and more. I noticed its tiny fingers and bright, brown eyes. It seemed so small and helpless in the jar. I knew it would die just because I was afraid of it. I envisioned its withered body rotting and knew I couldn't have that on my conscience."

"I should hope not," said Larina.

"I begged Grandpa to take it out into the woods and let it go. He wouldn't change his mind. 'It lives in the shed,' he said, 'with his friends and his family.' I cried and cried, but he wouldn't back down.

"That night, when we sat on the step, another bat flew by. I wondered if it knew the bat in the jar and missed him. I reached over and unscrewed the lid. The bat crawled over the top and fell onto the step. I felt terrible. But, then, he flew away. I stayed on the step and watched the bats until bedtime."

"Good for you," said Larina.

"All the times I watched bats, they never hurt me. Once, one even banged into me when I was chasing fireflies. Grandpa said I changed direction too fast and confused it. It didn't bother me to be near them ever again. I'd forgotten all about that until now."

"Your grandfather was a wise man," said Morrel.

"I won't kill any more," said Aubin. "But I shall move *very* slowly."

The icy walls absorbed the heat from the fire and gave nothing back. The travelers slept fitfully. They woke often to jog on the spot and rub their bodies. By breakfast, they were more tired than rested.

"I want to go on ahead to find the bruin," said Aubin. "I can do it faster alone. I will return and guide you straight there. That way, Nicole will not have to search in the cold."

This plan saved time. Aubin also was warmer when he used his intrinsic speed. He returned, ravenous from the exertion. While he ate, he explained the location. By nightfall, they should reach their goal.

They headed out. Nicole felt doubtful when dusk came, but soon after Aubin called, "There it is. On the left. There won't be a fire. The bruin doesn't cook his food, but the cave is snugger than the bat cave."

The bruin had used branches and small rocks to plug the drafts in his den. A large boulder partially blocking the entrance was an effective windbreak. The travelers squeezed through the opening and into the dark interior.

The bruin was waiting. He was old, his brown fur matted and scruffy, with a thin patch on one shoulder. He stood slowly to greet them. His voice rumbled loudly, "Welcome, keepers of the bracelets. Welcome to my humble home."

Nicole stumbled back. He was taller than Morrel, and, even in age, his powerful bulk intimidated her. They had said they wouldn't run into any talking animals. They didn't say they were planning on meeting with one.

Aubin gently nudged her forward. They sat in a circle as the bruin settled back comfortably.

"Alaric Aubin did not explain your visit," he growled. "While you eat, explain what you seek."

He laid dried berries on a rock. Morrel added food from his pack. "We would like to share with you as well, great bruin, in gratitude for your hospitality."

Nicole gratefully nibbled on Morrel's provisions, taking a withered, dirty berry whenever the bear looked in her direction.

"We seek knowledge, great bruin," said Morrel. "You have traveled with my grandfather, Alaric Bethane. I am on the same quest and need information."

The bear stared at Nicole for uncomfortable moment. "But why not ask Alaric Bethane?"

"He has been killed by the dark things," said Morrel.

The bear absorbed this quietly. "A loss for all," he said. "A good man and a good friend."

"Yes," said Morrel.

"I will help any way I can," said the bruin.

"Nicole and I have found the first two pieces of the key but are unable to find the third. Hulda recited a poem to us. Perhaps you can explain its significance."

"I will try."

"She said:

The piece you seek to fit the key

Is always found within.

Pierced to be mended, opening all,

Allows the light to win.'"

The bruin nodded. "Your grandfather spoke often with Hulda, before she became an old recluse like me. I am distressed to say, I do not know the poem and can only guess at the meaning."

"Any hint at all," said Morrel.

"None, unfortunately. Alaric Bethane traveled with a panther woman. When they reached The Meeting Place, I left. They no longer needed my protection. It is a sanctuary, safe from the dark things, unless the night gains total control. Although we saw each other again, we never spoke of The Meeting. It was not for me to know."

The listeners leaned back, discouraged. They ate silently, lost in their thoughts.

Finally, Nicole gathered up her courage and spoke. "Alaric Bethane died before he could explain much of The Meeting. There is a lot I don't understand."

"I will tell you what I know. What is the question?"

"I know that The Meeting stops the progression of the darkness," said Nicole. "The use of the bracelet affects the user, whose race gradually takes on the characteristics of the animal on the band. But how did all this start?"

"I *can* answer that," said the bruin. "It is an ancient story of ambition and power gone astray.

"Long ago, the wizards who forged your bracelets combined their powers. Their desire to improve the world drove them to tamper with things best left untouched. They wanted to make Dawn's Land into a perfect paradise. Instead of teaching the people to live with the elements, as I do here, they sought to change them. They proclaimed that no one else would ever die in a blizzard."

"What's a blizzard?" asked Aubin.

"A storm of snow. In those days, our world had very different weather. The wizards sought to drive winter into the highest peaks, giving the land eternal warmth. In this, they were successful. They combined their magic into an enormous diamond. It was made to absorb the cold and turned black when this was accomplished.

"Unfortunately, the diamond's power was uncontrollable. It not only absorbed what the wizard's desired, but seeking its own natural balance, soaked up the sunshine as well. The wizards tried in vain to break the spell. They even tried to smash the crystal, but nothing could stop it. Dawn's End was on its way to destruction."

"My heavens," said Nicole.

Aubin shook his head in dismay. Morrel silently stroked Larina's wings.

The bruin continued. "A temporary solution was found. The wizards forged magical bracelets and embedded them with slivers left over from the original cutting of the diamond."

Nicole looked at her wrist. "The stone in the panther's eye."

The bruin nodded.

"Wait," she said. She dug below her outer clothes, unzipped her pocket, and took out the gold spiral. "In the middle of the engraved sun is a tiny black stone. Do you think it is from the same diamond?"

"Yes."

Nicole passed around the spiral for examination as the bruin continued.

"The Meeting was all that could combat the black diamond. Whenever The Meeting is held, the large diamond fades to gray, and the smaller diamonds darken. The day returns to normal. The more successful The Meeting, the paler the crystal becomes. Alaric Bethane achieved only a very slight difference in the color of the stone. That is why Alaric Morrel must take on the quest so soon after."

The bruin continued, "Even though they devoted their lives to seeking a solution, and trained many others, the wizards could not undo the damage. Many wizards only come out of seclusion to gather new apprentices or to reforge the bracelets."

"How do they know when it is time?" asked Nicole.

"When the wearer does not have enough blood of his original people, the bracelet will not obey his commands," answered the bruin.

Nicole realized the wizards were no more foolish than most scientists from her society. Had not Einstein invented atomic power in hopes of making a better world? The best laid plans. At least the wizards were still searching for a permanent solution. In the meantime, she would help Morrel put Dawn's End back in balance.

They spent the night with the bruin. His body heat in the small enclosure provided them with warmth. The smell of penned animal did not appeal to Nicole, but she tried to be a gracious guest. It was with relief that she thanked the bruin the next morning and stepped out into the fresh air.

The sky faded to white, pressing down with gathering snow clouds. Aubin was depressed, his idea of visiting the bruin not proving fruitful. He had contributed nothing of value to the quest. Nicole watched with apprehension as the first flakes fell.

Morrel and Aubin were charmed by the beauty of falling snow. Larina peeked out from Morrel's collar to watch the falling feather-like grace of the snowflakes. The landscape was frosted like icing sugar. Trees seemed to cherish their burdens of snow.

As the day progressed, the ground cover deepened. Walking was a struggle. They took turns breaking the trail, the followers treading in the leader's footprints. The snow continued to thicken. Crystals united into oversized flakes. Wind blew aggressively into their faces. They blinked repeatedly and wiped their eyebrows and lashes. The white fury blinded them.

The third time they lost sight of each other and wasted time reuniting, Nicole called a halt. "*This* is a blizzard," she shouted. "We must connect ourselves together. Does anyone have a rope?"

"I do," said Aubin.

"Great. We must all hold on to it to prevent becoming separated. We must get to shelter and wait for the storm to break."

"What if it never does?" asked Morrel. "Dawn's End is rapidly sliding into chaos. This blizzard may not stop until it covers our entire world. We must keep going."

"You don't understand," shouted Nicole. "People die in this kind of weather. They wander around, getting nowhere, until they collapse in the snow and freeze to death. What happened to Larina was a warning."

"She's right," said Aubin. "We must take shelter. At least to rest and eat. If the storm keeps up, we can start fresh in the morning."

This was easier said than done. They staggered forward until Nicole stumbled to her knees, exhausted.

"We must get her to safety," shouted Morrel. "I am not sure how much longer I can last either. This wind and cold are wearing me down. One of us must race on ahead to find shelter."

"I will, my cousin," said Aubin. "Stay with Nicole."

The Alarics hugged clumsily, and then Aubin left with Larina. Morrel hooked his arm under Nicole as they stumbled on.

"He'll burn himself out," said Nicole.

"Do not worry. He will not take too much risk with Larina with him. They will reach warmth before us, rest for a bit, and then come back. He will be back before you know it."

209

"He won't be able to find us," said Nicole. She stumbled again. "We have to keep moving. If we stop, we'll fall asleep and never wake up."

"All right. Straight ahead," commanded Morrel. "We will meet Aubin coming back. He has a good sense of direction. He will find us."

But Morrel was mistaken. They trudged on until Nicole sobbed soundlessly with cold and fatigue. Morrel pulled her on, forcing her to keep moving, like a zombie, devoid of feeling and will. Alone, she would have given up. When he stumbled, she found the strength to encourage him to stand. On and on, a white nightmare, into the land of Anderson's Snow Queen, where feeling was dead.

Nicole was barely aware of Morrel yelling. *What is he saying? Why are we stopping?*

They had stumbled upon a small den. Morrel entered first, dragging her behind. Huddled together, at last they were out of the wind and blinding whiteness, Nicole's last thought before losing consciousness was of Aubin. He would never find them now. He would die in the snow searching in vain, and little helpless Larina would die with him.

Chapter Eighteen—Divided We Fall

Nicole dreamed an evil wizard smashed his enchanted mirror into billions of tiny shards and sent them out on the icy wind. A splinter pierced Nicole's eye, and another pierced her heart. Now, Nicole could only see the ugliness of the world. She could feel nothing. As the Snow Queen bore down on her in her icy sledge, Nicole surrendered to the cold. Morrel searched for her, calling her name, but Nicole sat on the floor of the Snow Queen's palace trying to spell eternity with shards of ice and ignored his shouts.

While Nicole slept deeply, Morrel woke repeatedly and reopened the entrance. Finally, he scrambled outside, first tying one end of the rope to entrance as a guide back. It was a good thing Nicole had shown him that trick.

Morrel broke off a long branch and brought it into the den. Whenever the snow packed the opening, he poked the stick through. This ensured a fresh air supply without much loss of heat. The warm air from their bodies melted a thin layer of snow which refroze, like a quinzhee. They were protected from the worst of the cold and the wind. When the howl of the blizzard ceased and the air hole revealed light, Morrel tried to wake Nicole.

But Nicole was dreaming. *This is your last chance*, said Morrel in her dream from the ice palace gate. *Come with me now, or remain frozen forever.*

Nicole reached for his hand, but it was too far away. Her legs would not move. Her feet were frozen to the floor.

"Wait," she called. "I don't want to stay here. I don't want to be like this. Wait."

"Wake up, Nicole," Morrel shouted. He shook her and pinched her face.

"Ow," said Nicole. "I felt that."

"You were shouting in your sleep. We have to get up now anyway," said Morrel. "The night and the blizzard have both ended. Have something to eat, and then we must go."

Nicole flexed her arms and legs, stamping and rubbing.

"Are you all right?" he asked.

"Yes," she said. She gripped the sides of his hood and pulled him to her. "We could have died yesterday," she said. "And I've barely kissed you. If you knew the yearnings I had, you would blush—can you blush? Never mind. If we get through this, I'm going to find out."

She kissed him fiercely. Morrel was startled at first, but then he responded. Nicole kissed his cold nose and frosty beard. She kissed each wet eyebrow and his forehead and then his lips again. Morrel gave a low rumble, and then he pulled away.

"We have to go," he said, his voice strained.

Nicole nodded. They dug and pushed until they tunneled through the drift. They wormed their way to the surface and emerged upon a winter wonderland.

"How could something so brutal create such beauty?" gasped Morrel.

The entire mountain was encased in white. Sticky snow clung to the landscape, even to the underside of the branches, painting them a brilliant ivory.

"Be careful," said Nicole. "The cold can be seductive."

The sun struggled through the clouds, reflected everywhere in a blinding dazzle.

"Wrap your scarf closely around your eyes," recommended Nicole. "It might help to reduce some of the glare. We have to be careful of snow blindness."

"I am glad I found a Northern woman to be my quest companion," said Morrel.

"I know you're going to think I'm losing my mind, but I'm glad you found me too. I haven't felt this alive in a long time."

"That is because of our close brush with death yesterday," he responded.

"I'm sure that's part of it, but not the whole," said Nicole. She wished they had time to talk, for her to sort out her feelings, but this was not the right place, and Aubin was still out there somewhere, with tiny Larina cuddled against his heart.

They gobbled food from their packs and then headed down the mountain, Morrel choosing their direction based on the position of the feeble sun. Trails were obliterated, and landmarks obscured by snowdrifts. Neither of them mentioned Aubin.

Will we even notice his body? wondered Nicole. *Or will we walk right past it, buried in snow, without even realizing he's there?*

Morrel stopped beside a small coniferous tree. He sank in a white cascade. Only his shoulders and chest remained in view. It was actually a much larger tree buried in the snow. The air space between the branches collapsed from his weight. Nicole helped him struggle out. They avoided walking close to trees after that.

Even though Nicole had difficulty keeping pace, they reached the panther village near day's end. Morrel was rushing, anxious for news of Aubin.

Shandri answered the door. She gripped Morrel by the arm and rushed him to the fire, barely aware of Nicole tramping behind.

"Aubin?" asked Morrel. "Is he here?"

"No, my Alaric," said Shandri. "You are the first to return." She continued to brush snow from his clothes as she spoke.

"Give Nicole hot liquid. I must search for him."

"No!" chorused both the panther girl and the woman. Shandri glanced at Nicole with irritation and continued, "You must regain your strength. You will be of no use dead."

"But—"

"She's right," said Nicole. "Sit down, Morrel."

Shandri pursed her lips at Nicole's familiarity.

Dyania brought two bowls of soup and hurried back to the kitchen. Kiritana went to gather blankets and fresh clothing. Morrel gulped down the hot soup and then stood. He gathered up his belongings. Shandri hurried outside and looked toward the mountain. The storm clouds had regrouped. The peaks were once again assaulted by blizzard.

"It is no use, Alaric Morrel," said Shandri as he stood in the doorway. "You must wait until the storm clears."

"I should have gone right away," he said.

"No, my Alaric. You would have been caught in it," purred Shandri as she led him back inside and shut the door. She helped him off with his coat. She rubbed his back soothingly and lowered him into the chair. Nicole sipped her soup trying not to grit her teeth. Shandri pulled off Morrel's mukluks and lifted his feet onto a stool. She massaged the bottom of his feet. Nicole's stomach knotted. She was relieved when Dyania requested Shandri's help in the kitchen.

They spent the night by a roaring fire. Nicole was glad this village enjoyed indoor cooking. When Shandri set out two pallets separated by a heavy table, Nicole gave her a cold look. The teenager wished Alaric Morrel a good sleep and left reluctantly.

"Help me move the table," said Morrel. "We are not going to sleep apart."

"Good," said Nicole. "She isn't exactly subtle, is she?"

Morrel smiled crookedly, but didn't answer as they slid the pallets together. They kissed, but softly this time. They held each other tightly, glad to be alive. But they were unable to lose themselves in the joy of their togetherness, knowing Aubin and Larina might no longer be with them. Morrel nuzzled her throat, and Nicole felt goose bumps rise on her flesh.

"You are cold," he said, wrapping the blankets around her.

"No," said Nicole. "Those aren't that kind of goose bump."

When morning came, the mountain looked clearer. Morrel prepared to find Aubin. Alone, he would move much more quickly.

Shandri brought food and a hot drink in a leak-proof pouch. She frowned as Nicole helped her mother fold the quilts and roll up the pallets. She turned away as Morrel kissed Nicole goodbye.

"Take care," whispered Nicole. "Come back to me."

"I will."

Nicole watched Morrel speed away. He leaped, rather than ran, his strides long and fluid. He was gone from sight in seconds.

"Too bad you couldn't keep up with him," said Shandri.

"Shandri, go do the washing up," said Dyania. "Relax by the fire, Nicole."

Nicole waited, adding wood to the flames whenever the room chilled. Shandri emerged from the kitchen. She sat by her.

"My mother says I have been rude," she announced. "I apologize if this is so."

"I am sure it wasn't intentional," said Nicole. "You are probably worried for Larina and Aubin."

Shandri bent her head. "I have behaved badly."

"Is it Morrel?" asked Nicole. "You have feelings for him, don't you?"

The girl nodded. "Foolish, I know. He sees me as a child, and he is so far above me."

"You are very young still," said Nicole, "but you are an Alaric too, aren't you?"

"Yes," said Shandri. "But not a 'rare woman from the outworld.'"

"Ahh," said Nicole. "The Meeting."

Shandri picked at her skirt. "Alaric Bethane chose a panther woman. I could fill in for you if you changed your mind."

Nicole laughed. "You're too late with that offer, Shandri. Besides, Alaric Bethane had limited success. I want to help Morrel succeed completely."

"But, if—"

A scratch at the door interrupted them. Nicole leapt up, and then checked herself, realizing it was too soon for Morrel to have returned. Shandri answered as Nicole returned to the fire. "It's you!" Shandri cried, throwing herself upon the person.

Nicole raced to the door, unsure what to expect. Both panther men grinned broadly over Shandri's shoulder. Aubin was clutching Morrel tightly by the waist.

"How did you find him so fast?" shouted Nicole. She threw herself into Morrel's arms as he passed Shandri to Aubin. They hugged fiercely.

Shandri released Aubin and went into the house.

"No hug for me?" teased Aubin.

Nicole laughed and hugged him as well. Larina protested and wiggled out from under his clothes.

"Larina!" cried Nicole. "You're all safe. I'm so relieved."

"If you'll let us in," piped Larina, "we can be warm as well."

The panther men laughed, stamping the snow from their boots as they entered. They warmed their hands over the fire. Dyania recruited Shandri to the kitchen again.

"Aubin, where were you?" Nicole asked.

"I found shelter, as I promised. But when I returned, you were gone," he explained. "I circled, to cross your path, but no luck. I thought you might have been turned around, so I headed back toward the bruin's cave. I was getting worn out. When I did not find any trace of you, I spent the night with the bruin."

As he spoke, Nicole rested her hand on Morrel's arm.

"Come morning," said Aubin, "I found you had spent the night in a tunnel. Your trail headed down the mountain. Unfortunately, the blizzard started again, so Larina and I took shelter in the same den. It wasn't as bad as the other storm, but since I knew you two were well on your way to safety and the shelter had kept you from freezing, we stayed put. This morning, I met my ebony cousin here heading back while I was heading down."

"We were worried," said Nicole. "I am so relieved that you are both all right."

"We, too, spent a fretful night with the bruin. We did not know you had found a safe shelter. You were right about us staying together," acknowledged Aubin. "From now on, we'd better keep each other in sight."

They all agreed.

"I've been thinking," said Nicole. "Come morning, I think we should go to The Meeting place."

"But we haven't found the third piece," said Morrel.

"We have no more clues. Time is running out," said Nicole. "We can't keep wandering about aimlessly until we're killed."

"That's true," said Aubin. "The sun sets earlier and earlier."

"In six or seven days, it will set at noon," agreed Morrel. "Perhaps there will be a clue at The Meeting Place. It is not as though we have any other options."

"I have a feeling about this," said Nicole. "I think we should put our faith in what we've accomplished so far. Trust me on this, Morrel."

Morrel raised his eyebrows. "I trust you."

Nicole smiled.

"We should leave as soon as Aubin is rested then," he said.

Kiritana and Dyania topped up their supplies. Shandri did not see them off.

Nicole was surprised at her energy. She should have felt worn thin by the last days, but her pace was her fastest yet. It was much easier traveling on dry land. They ate cold provisions as they hiked. As dusk descended, Morrel called a halt.

"I know of no shelter close by," he said. "Do you, Aubin?"

The white panther man shook his head.

"Then we will have to camp in the open. No fire."

Nicole consumed her fresh food from Safeway. She laid out the oiled cape and curled up with Morrel. As the night progressed, Nicole's teeth chattered. She shook continually with the cold.

"You will not sleep like this," whispered Morrel. "Aubin?"

"Yes."

"Come over here and help keep Nicole warm," ordered Morrel.

"With pleasure," Aubin purred.

"Remember," Morrel warned, "I am on the other side."

"And I'm watching too," stated Larina as she snuggled up to Aubin.

"Right."

Aubin pressed his back against Nicole's. The added body heat eased the chill in her chest and arms, but her feet were still freezing. Perhaps she had a touch of frostbite. Finally, she fell into a shivery sleep.

"Danger!" shrieked Larina.

"Nicole," Morrel hissed in her ear. She woke, alarmed by his tone. "Do not move."

Nicole was still, conscious of the cold space behind her. Where was Aubin? Tensely, she waited for Morrel to explain. There was a scuffling sound, like hundreds of little feet. She whimpered. Something touched her leg. Something small and sharp pierced the fabric. She opened her mouth to scream, but Morrel clamped his hand over it. More movements. She suppressed a struggle and pressed her lips together. Morrel released her mouth. He slashed quickly with his arm. He was using his claws. What were those horrid things crawling on them? Why wouldn't he let her move?

The scurrying increased. Nicole shivered. A small raspy sound surrounded them. Morrel slashed at something near her face. She felt a splash of wet on her cheek and a horrible smell filled the air. Bile rose in her throat. The creatures were all over them, more coming.

A clap sounded to her right, another and then another. The slithery animals scrambled off. The clapping continued, fading away. The creatures followed and finally disappeared.

Nicole let out a pent-up breath, and then stiffened at her own noise.

"It is all right," Morrel whispered into her ear. "Aubin has drawn them away. Be very quiet."

She whispered back. "What are they?"

"Night lizards," said Morrel. "They are attracted by rhythmic noise. En masse they build themselves into a frenzy and attack the source of the noise. It usually takes more than chattering teeth to arouse them. They were larger than usual, too."

"Chattering teeth! Did I draw them to us?"

"It is not your fault. I felt the cold as well. We must keep warm and quiet until morning. It should not be long now."

"What about Aubin?" said Nicole. "The lizards can't catch him, can then?"

"I think not, unless he is surrounded."

"He's risking his life for us. No, for me. You could just run away."

"Shh," said Morrel. "He needs to do this. He will no longer feel so indebted to us. Now lie quietly. I do not want stragglers to hear us."

Dawn seemed a long time in coming. Nicole's jaw ached from clenching her teeth. When feeble sunlight struggled over the horizon, they resumed hiking.

"It would be foolish to wait for Aubin," said Morrel. "We may criss-cross one another's paths like we did in the mountain. Our goal is his goal. We must go on."

"What if he comes back to look for us and we aren't here?" asked Nicole.

"What if he does not? Besides, he is a good tracker."

"I will search for him," said Larina, "and bring you news."

"Fly safely, my calia," said Morrel.

Chapter Nineteen—Death in the Dark

As Morrel and Nicole hiked, they heard the sound of rapids and a waterfall in the distance. They spoke little. Nicole remembered the last time they had hiked together, singing "There's a Hole in my Bucket." Now, they had a hole in their hearts named Aubin.

They stopped to eat in a small clearing.

Larina arrived as they were finishing up. "I found him," she said flatly. Nicole's heart skipped a beat. "He's alive, but the lizards surrounded and trapped him." Nicole groaned and buried her face in Morrel's chest.

"He must have fought like a crazed being," said Larina. "The bodies of the disgusting varmints were scattered for strides. He lost a lot of hair and blood from the looks of it, but he made it to the panther village. He was badly wounded, but I think he will mend. He is strong. The villagers were determinedly nursing him. Shandri is running the show. There is a string of young women competing to have their turn."

"Oh, good," sighed Nicole, with a small smile.

"I'm sure he will make good use of the scars during the next Telling," said Larina.

"He has earned the right," said Morrel. "It took courage to face those creatures alone and not bolt until we were safe."

"Yes," agreed Larina. "That's a pleasant surprise, Alaric Aubin putting others first. Dawn's End is topsy-turvy. I can't imagine what is going to happen next."

In spite of Aubin's injuries and the absence of the third piece of the key, the travelers' spirits rose. They had survived a night in the open. Nicole had never felt more confident, alive and connected to others. In this world of magic and mayhem, anything was possible.

When they stopped for a midday rest, Morrel stunned them with a pronouncement. "I want Larina to return to the village and stay there."

"What?" squawked the blue jay.

"When Aubin was with us, he could look out for you in my stead. Grandfather warned me about dividing myself between Nicole and another. I cannot protect you both. We are close to the cascades now. Soon, Lymn will guide us to The Meeting Place, and you will have to leave anyway."

Larina responded, "So, I will leave when you go to The Meeting Place."

"No, you will leave now," said Morrel. "Bring news to my mother. She will be worried about how we fared against the lizards. In spite of Aubin's bravery, no one knows if we are safe."

"I will tell her and then return," said Larina.

"No. We will have to spend another night in the open. I want you home safe."

"I was in no danger last night, and my warning helped Aubin," said Larina. "This is not the time for me to be faint-hearted."

"No one would ever think you were faint-hearted. Please," said Morrel. "I want no more bloodshed. Nicole and I have to stay. You do not."

"You're wrong, my Alaric," insisted Larina. "Did not the great bruin stay with your grandfather until he reached the meeting place?"

"You compare yourself to him?" Morrel smiled.

"Just because I am little does not mean we are any different. Please, do not make me leave," she said. "You may force me to disobey for the first time."

Morrel shook his head and looked at Nicole for help. Nicole shrugged and bit into a dried apricot.

"Very well," said Morrel. "I hope I do not regret this."

"I hope you have no further need of my help," said Larina. "But I will rest easier once I know you have safely reached your destination."

They walked until the daylight weakened.

"The water sounds louder," said Nicole.

"We are close," agreed Morrel. "We will reach Lymn early tomorrow. This is a good place to camp for the night. We will keep the river at our backs. After last night, we have no choice but to risk a campfire. At least this open space makes it difficult for someone to sneak up on us."

Nicole swallowed and tried not to envision that. After a hot meal, she laid the oiled cape out and curled up with Morrel. She shivered.

"Cold?" asked Morrel.

Nicole nodded. *And also scared,* she thought. She rearranged and tucked her clothes for maximum warmth. She wrapped the edges of the large cloak up and around herself and

Morrel, tucking them under her chest. They were like little sausages in a dough blanket.

"You have to keep warm, too, Morrel. I can't have you getting sick either," she said. "Then what would I do?"

Morrel answered her literally. "Do not bother asking Lymn for help. He is not much of a healer, nor generous with his time. I am hoping he will accept a small bag of precious stones given to me by Kiritana in exchange for guiding us to The Meeting Place."

"I'd have to care for you here! What an awful thought," said Nicole. "We'd run out of food. Ugh! I don't even want to think about it. One night here is creepy enough."

"It would not be as desperate as that," he consoled her. "You could send Larina to the panther village for help. Also, there is a healer named Asa nearby. You take the fork up ahead to the right instead of to the left. Larina could bring her back in no time. So, go to sleep, and stop worrying. Nothing bad will happen."

Soon, they were all asleep. As night passed and the cold deepened, Nicole wrapped herself deeper into Morrel's warmth, drifting into sweet dreams

 One by one, yellow eyes appeared in the forest around them. Unblinking, oozing eyes circled the sleeping couple, watching, preparing.

Morrel shifted uneasily. Nicole entwined her legs with Morrel's, slid her hand along his chest, and then hooked it around his neck. As if waiting for this signal, the dark things surged forward. Larina screeched a warning.

Morrel snapped awake. Still half asleep, Nicole wrapped tightly around him, hampering his movement. Howls and shrieks rent the night. Nicole woke.

The first shape hurled itself upon the prone couple. Morrel barely had time to roll onto Nicole as the leathery, black figure lunged. Fangs entered Morrel's shoulder as Nicole shuddered underneath. The deformed cronies joined the attack.

Larina flew at the beasts, flapping, scratching, and pecking. The defenders were hampered by the pitch darkness. The night creatures did not care where their strikes landed, as long as they drew blood. They gouged and tore indiscriminately, indifferent to whether their comrades were harmed.

Wrapping his right hand over his left wrist, Morrel summoned the bracelet's power. His body hardened and increased in strength and resilience as a brilliant light infused the darkness. Two beasts, one clinging to his leg and one to his shoulder, shattered, muscle, bone, blood, and tissue exploding into shrapnel. This seemed only to infuriate the rest even more.

Morrel roared as half a dozen demonic beings clawed and chomped his flesh. Filled with ferocious strength, he hurled them from his back and legs and stood protectively over Nicole. Nicole unsheathed her knife and sat up. Only coals glowed from the fire. The creatures had been driven back to the edge of the clearing. Larina's angry screeches mingled with hideous screams. Nicole tossed a log on the fire. It did not catch.

Morrel's eyes gleamed like a night cat's. He leapt among the creatures, cutting and thrusting with his dagger. Their lust for blood increased, causing them to tear into each other. Nicole stood, her back to the shouldering flame, knife slashing at every approaching sound. She stabbed and swung the blade, her pulse pounding in her ears. She could see neither Morrel nor Larina. A dark shape advanced. She screamed and lunged.

"Stop! It is me, Morrel. It is over."

Nicole stood, unable to relax the dagger in her fist. She trembled from head to foot, her heart pounded fiercely. "Where are they?"

"Dead," he replied

"All of them?" she whispered.

"All," he confirmed.

"Oh, Morrel. Come close to the fire." She poked at the log, threw on kindling, and coaxed the flames to surge. "Let me see you."

"I must sit," he said. "I have lost much blood."

 Gagging in horror, Nicole pressed on the two worst wounds, side by side on his back, trying to stop the bleeding. "Larina!" she shouted. "Morrel is hurt. Larina."

Larina gave no response.

Nicole pulled off his jacket and shirt, pushed up the legs of his breeches and washed the wounds with drinking water, trying not to touch the open cuts with her germ filled hands. Morrel swayed limply. Nicole feared he would faint and fall. After spreading out her cloak, she sat him down. Using all the supplies she could find in both their bags, she bandaged him, covered him with her own jacket, and laid him back on her cloak to rest. She built the fire us as high as she could.

"Rest until dawn, my darling," she said. "I'll keep watch."

She sat beside him, Morrel between her and the fire. She drew her dagger and faced the woods. *I'm not much of an obstacle if any more come,* she thought. *But I'll take a few with me before I let them get to Morrel.* The night was silent. *Where is Larina? Is she hurt as well? Why didn't she answer?*

Morrel's breathing was ragged. He tossed and turned until dawn.

Nicole checked his face in the feeble light. It was soaked with sweat. His forehead was burning with fever. He moaned, pushed off her jacket, and tried to rise.

"No," she said. "Sit down, Morrel. Drink some of this water, and rest. I'm going to look around."

He gulped the water and then sank back on the cloak. Nicole lit the end of a stick and checked the area. She poked each bloody beast with the little flame. She wanted to vomit, but she had to be sure they were all dead. What if one suddenly sprung up and attacked? She'd watched too many horror movies to feel safe.

The creatures were soot-colored, a mixture of scale and claw, fang and horn. Two resembled mutated hawks, three giant Komodo dragons, and two metamorphosed rams. Two were in such small bits from the bracelet that she could not tell what they were. They stank, an odor that was a mixture of slaughter house and damp mold. Stepping carefully between their bodies, Nicole counted nine.

Is that all? she thought. *It seemed like a thousand.*

Three were as large as the Alaric. Without using the power of the bracelet, he would not have survived.

A splash of blue caught her eye. Near the woods lay a lump of amethyst feathers stained with red.

Larina! Oh, no! Nicole raced to the small body.

"Larina! Can you hear me?" She knelt by the bird and touched her with the tip of her finger. There was no heartbeat. The body was cold.

Nicole's tears flowed as she carried her broken friend toward the campfire. Morrel was watching. He sat up slowly and held out his hands. Nicole laid the little bird on them. Larina's feet stuck stiffly into the air.

Morrel stroked her small neck with his finger. "Larina. Fiercest fighter." His voice choked. "You should have gone home," he whispered. "I should have ordered you."

"That would have broken her heart," said Nicole as she wiped her cheeks. "I don't think she would have obeyed anyway."

"My brave calia, my friend, you were to be my companion for life, my advisor." He took a deep breath. "Now, I will be alone."

Nicole stroked his hair in comfort. "You're not alone, Morrel."

"I will miss her so," he said. "Her stubbornness, her truthfulness, and her love." Lifting her to his cheek, he rubbed Larina's soft head, oblivious to the streak of blood she left behind. "Bring more wood, Nicole. This will be her funeral pyre."

Nicole collected dry wood. She piled it on until the flames leapt skyward. Morrel stumbled to his feet and tenderly laid Larina in the blaze.

"Now the night creatures cannot get her," he whispered. "More fuel, Nicole." She piled on another armful of wood. "Goodbye, Larina, descendant of the bird people, keeper of the band, advisor to the Alaric. Until we meet again." He threw back his head and half roared, half yowled.

Nicole felt a shiver of grief and fury. Then, Morrel slumped against her. She eased him to the ground. The wood blackened and twisted, collapsing on the bird. Nicole held Morrel until the fire died down.

He spoke with difficulty. "We cannot stay here. If more creatures of the dark come, I cannot protect either of us. I don't have the strength to fight or summon the power of the bracelet."

"You can hardly stand," said Nicole.

"You must go back to the panther village for help. If you push hard, you may make it before nightfall. You can return with my friends by midday tomorrow. Leave me a stockpile of wood." He wiped the sweat from his face. "Do you remember how to get there? I am ashamed to leave you so unprotected. After all my assurances. I have failed you, Nicole."

"Stop talking like that. You're feverish and wounded," said Nicole. "I can't leave you alone for two days and a night. No, I am not going back to the village." She gathered up their things. "We will go on together, to the healer's place. You said she wasn't far."

"If she is still there," said Morrel. "She lives alone. I do not know if the night creatures have threatened her cabin. I do not know if she is even alive."

"We'll know when we get there. Either way, at least we'll be indoors. I can take care of you then. Come on," urged Nicole.

They moved slowly, Morrel leaning on Nicole. As the day progressed, she ceased watching for attackers. Instead, she concentrated on helping Morrel move as painlessly as possible. He grew heavier and heavier upon her shoulder until he finally sank to his knees.

"I can walk no further," he whispered. "Go on, Nicole. I have been poisoned. There must have been venom in the bites. Asa's cabin is not far. I will rest and wait here for her. Go."

As Nicole protested, Morrel slid to the ground, unconscious. She shouted and shook him to no avail. He was far too heavy to carry. His forehead was burning hot.

What should I do? she thought. *I can't wait for him to wake. That might not be for days. Or never, if he doesn't get medical aid. We can't stay here. We won't survive another night. I'll have to hide him and go on alone.*

She dragged Morrel, under the arms, as gently as she could, off the trail. She was puffing and sweating when they reached a cluster of rocks. She spread the oiled cape out, laid Morrel on top, and covered him with loose clothing. She set their packs on either side. Then she laid leafy branches over the top. She put his hand on his dagger hilt, hoping he would not stab himself in delirium. Should danger approach, he might wake enough to use it. She suspected it was a futile gesture. His breathing was shallow, and his color gray.

She tried to hide the drag marks as best she could. She hoped the wild things would not smell his blood. She looked around one last time, then broke into a jog.

Her heart pounded in her ears, but, whenever she slowed, the image of Morrel being torn to shreds where he lay, drove her on. Time coldly trickled its hourglass sand.

I'm taking too long, she thought. She blinked away the tears. She was too slow. *You're not going to make a living playing the flute.* Her father's voice haunted her. *You need to be able to take care of yourself, and you'll never succeed with these foolish dreams.*

She pushed on, pushing down the pain in her side and her legs. Morrel needed her to be strong. Morrel, who had protected her, over and over. Who had faith in her when she did not have it in herself. Who had shown her it was okay to trust again. He had promised to keep her safe and was dying in an attempt to keep that promise. He said he had failed and, maybe, technically, he had. But she knew trust was about more than keeping the letter of your word. Trust was about intention, determination, devotion, and love. She knew she loved this half-man, half-panther more than she had ever loved anyone. She hoped she would have the chance to tell him.

A hazy figure appeared ahead on the path. Nicole sprang off the trail and crouched, trying to quiet her raspy breathing. The shape did not move while she drew her dagger. It was dead center; she could never sneak past. The silence of the forest pressed down, waiting. *I'm going to have to fight it. Do it! Go!* She took a deep breath and stepped back on to the path.

As she approached, the figure took shape. It was a fallen tree, the gnarled roots resembling a man. Nicole swore and picked up the pace. In any other circumstance she would have thought it was funny, but, now, it meant lost time, time leaving Morrel in danger. She slapped aside an overhanging branch as she ran.

On and on, she trudged until her legs began to feel like rubber. When she turned a bend, the path opened into a clearing. Over a small hill, stood the cabin. Nicole's eyes filled with tears of relief. She wiped them away and picked up her pace.

Herbs were hanging to dry from the eaves. Surrounding the hut was a tidy garden. A thin, wispy woman bent, examined the plants.

"Asa!" shouted Nicole. The woman turned. She frowned at Nicole's appearance. Nicole hurried forward. "My name is Nicole Newman. I'm travelling with Alaric Morrel to The Meeting."

Asa smiled, glancing past her.

"He isn't with me," explained Nicole. "He has been badly injured by the dark creatures. I had to leave him behind when he lost consciousness. Please, can you help?"

"Of course," answered Asa. "I'll get my things."

The healer returned quickly with a small bundle. She put her fingers to her mouth and whistled. A mare trotted out from behind the cabin.

"We will ride." She jumped onto the horse's back and helped Nicole up. "Then we will use a travois for Morrel. Which direction?"

"That way. We came from the village of the panther people."

With every passing second, Nicole's anxiety grew. She dreaded what they might find. The mare was steady, but they could not go faster than a trot on the tight path.

When they arrived at Morrel's hideaway, Nicole flung herself from the horse and raced to the rocks. Nothing was disturbed. She burst into tears and fell to her knees. She had expected to find him torn to bits by scavengers.

Asa patted her on the shoulder and took charge. Nicole followed her commands as they chopped and tied the long branches. They made two parallel poles one and half times the length of the patient. From her bundle, Asa drew a heavy material, already laced. They knotted the poles on either side and laid Morrel inside the travois.

The slow journey back was agonizing. Morrel groaned when the cot jostled. Nicole kept expecting something to leap on him from the woods. Night was snaking its ashen tendrils when they arrived at Asa's home. They unhooked the travois from the horse and dragged it into the house.

The interior was homely and organized. Labeled jars and jugs filled the shelves. The room smelled green and spicy. Asa left to stable the mare while Nicole removed Morrel's dirty clothes. Blood had seeped through the bandages.

Asa returned. She gave Nicole a wash cloth, towel, pitcher of cool water, and a ewer. Nicole washed Morrel first and then wiped the blood and grime from her own face and hands while Asa prepared her property for the night.

"I'll treat his wounds now," said the healer when she was finished. "Please build up the fire. Get the water in the kettle to boil. I want to sterilize my needles."

Nicole smiled. "I wasn't sure if Dawn's End knew about germs. I thought the medical treatment might be primitive. I come from the world on the other side of the door."

"I know your world," said Asa as she raised an eyebrow. "You confuse simplicity with backwardness. We live with all the necessities of life. Many, such as the panther people, have rich cultures. We believe that the energy expended to acquire and care for material things interferes with the true enjoyment of life. I have everything I want in my little hut."

"I'm sorry. I didn't mean to be condescending."

"I understand," said Asa. "When I am finished sterilizing my tools, would you prepare a soup as I close Morrel's cuts?"

The housework helped to distract Nicole from the distress of hearing Asa clean, disinfect, stitch, and freshly bandage Morrel who had begun to moan. Twice she helped the healer shift his position. A pain seized her stomach when he opened his eyes and loudly cried out. He fainted again and mercifully remained unconscious throughout the rest of Asa's ministrations.

During the night, the two women took turns bathing his hot forehead with cool water and administering spoons of medication whenever Morrel woke enough to swallow.

By morning, his fever was broken. Nicole slowly fed him an ominous-smelling broth the healer said was fortifying. Afterward, he slept comfortably.

Nicole drew Asa aside. "The night grows rapidly," she said.

Asa nodded.

Nicole continued, "But Morrel is not fit to travel. I'm going on to the cascades. When Lymn has shown me the way to The Meeting Place, I will return for Morrel. If you're sure he is no longer in danger, and if he is well enough to be moved, I would like to leave tomorrow morning. Will you care for him while I am gone?"

"Of course," replied Asa.

"Please don't say anything to him," said Nicole. "I want him to concentrate on getting better. He may attempt something foolish if he thinks I am in danger."

Asa nodded thoughtfully.

Chapter Twenty—Fork in the Path

The morning was misty and eerily quiet as Nicole prepared to leave. She wondered what kind of creatures might be using the fog as cover.

"Take the mare," said Asa. "You will be less vulnerable on horseback. The dark things will attack during the daylight if they catch you alone and on foot."

"No, thanks," said Nicole. "I don't know how to handle a horse. I'd probably just draw their attention."

Asa shook her head. "Smokeweed is a dependable mount. She's steady and sensible, with more intelligence than a lot of people."

"I want her here for you," said Nicole. "If something happens, if I don't come back, or you need help for whatever reason, I want you to have the horse. Morrel is very vulnerable right now. I honestly will manage on foot. I've never been in better shape."

"All right, but I insist you take my crossbow. The special pulleys make it easy to pull and quick to load. Nothing will get close if you aim carefully. It is very deadly. If they attack in a group, it's best to run for it."

"Thanks. I'll take that. How does it work?"

Asa demonstrated. Nicole hit a small target six out of ten times. Not great odds, but better than nothing. Her first defense would be to run, if possible.

Asa explained the route to the cascades. Nicole left with a few basic supplies and Morrel's bag of jewels.

The morning was damp and chilly. Plants were dying, yellowed, and brittle from cold and lack of sunlight. It seemed more like autumn than spring. Brown leaves curled on the branches and crunched underfoot. But, unlike in autumn, the plants were not in seed. Growth had withered in its infancy.

Traveling at a steady pace, Nicole reached a small footbridge spanning the river. Asa said there was another crossing half a day further along the stream. Nicole preferred to risk the bridge than take a longer time to reach Lymn.

The footbridge was weathered gray, the wood rotten in spots, leaving jagged holes large enough to trap her leg. She glanced through to the raging swirl below. *I don't want to fall into that*, she thought. *I'd better spread my weight as much as I can and move carefully, like I'm walking on thin ice.*

She crossed slowly, trying not to look past the boards to the water below. The wood protested her weight with creaks and groans, splinters cracking as she stepped. She did a small hop of joy when she reached the other side just in time to see one rope snap and several boards fall into the ravine. *That's going to be a whole lot harder on the way back*, she thought.

Nicole headed down the path. At the fork in the road, she turned left and searched for the cave. Asa, who had helped Lymn in the past, had described his location in detail. Futilely, Nicole hunted for an entrance with a pink bush on the left and a pile of stones, shaped like a bear on the right.

"Lymn," she called. "Are you here?"

There was no response. Nicole climbed over a rock ledge. With relief, she spotted it. The bush was withered and brown, but the stones remained. She approached. A suede tarp hung over an opening. Eagerly, she hurried inside.

"How dare ya enter my home without welcome!" yelled a voice from the interior. "Get out!"

"Lymn?"

"Didn't ya hear me? Get out." He snarled.

"Please, listen," pleaded Nicole. "I called, and no one answered, so I thought the cave was empty."

"So ya walked right in and made yerself ta home. I don't know ya, and I don't wanta know ya. Now fer the last time, get out b'fore I sic ma dog on ya."

Nicole drew out her dagger. "Sic your dog on me, and be prepared to bury him."

"Feisty bitch, ain't ya?" He chuckled as he pushed back a wooden barrier and entered. He was a stocky man, with rugged features, a crooked nose, and scruffy brown hair.

"Stop wasting my time with your peevishness and listen," she snapped. "I am traveling with Alaric Morrel. He has been severely wounded."

"Ya came to the wrong place," he said with a wave of his hand. "Go see that skinny healer, Asa."

"He's with her now. I want your help to guide me to The Meeting Place."

Lymn laughed. "Ya can't go there alone. Guardians won't let ya in."

"I've brought a bag of gems from the panther village. I'll pay you to guide me. Now, are you interested or not? I'm in a hurry."

"So ya said, so ya said," answered Lymn. "Toss that bag over here, and lemme have a look see."

Nicole complied. Lymn lit a small liquid fuel lamp. He undid the drawstring and emptied the stones into the palm of his hand. "Pretty," he snorted. "But ain't gonna do me much good if I can't spend 'em. The black things been creeping around more often. Trying to get past my barricades at night. The damned dog lies in a corner and whines."

"So you're going to give up," said Nicole. "Let them grow until they're strong enough to get you no matter where you hide."

"What're you talking about?" said Lymn.

"If you don't guide me to The Meeting Place so Morrel and I can complete the quest, Nightfall is going to continue to grow along with the dark things. Dawn's End, and everybody in it, will be destroyed."

"Superstitious rot." He crossed his arms. "It's just a spell of bad weather."

"If you don't believe what is happening all around you, then you're nothing but a fool," snapped Nicole.

"I ain't gonna help no mouthy bitch for a bag of rocks. I said get out, and I still mean it." He tossed the bag by Nicole's feet. The tawny dog trotted over and sniffed it.

"Larina is dead, killed by those monsters," stated Nicole. "Alaric Bethane as well. Alaric Aubin is wounded. Alaric Morrel is wounded. Who's going to hold this world together when the last brave soul is gone? You and your cringing dog? You think you can survive what they couldn't? I hope your fortifications are strong and you have enough food here to last the rest of your life."

"Lies," muttered Lymn. He snapped his fingers, and the dog went to him. Lymn scratched the dog's ears.

"When the panther villages fall and faerieland is destroyed, you'll be alone, holed up in this little space," said Nicole. "Even Queen Melita knows she can't fight them. Dawn's End will be in total darkness. But it won't matter. Everyone will be dead or transformed."

Lymn huffed, but his brows were furrowed with worry.

Nicole continued, "See this bracelet. Why do you think they were made? Where do you think the panther people came from? It's all connected, and like it or not, you're in it, too. And you've just refused to let me take our last chance." She picked up the stones and turned to go.

"Wait."

Nicole stopped. She refused to turn back. She had nothing left to say.

"You tellin' the truth about Alaric Bethane? He's a livin' legend."

"He's not living anymore. Dark flying things killed him."

"Damn," said Lymn. "I ain't no panther man. If them things can kill Alarics . . . . "

"Can you make it back by dark if we leave now?" asked Nicole.

"Ya. But I don't think you can make it back to Asa's."

"Let me worry about that."

"Ya got anything else to give me?"

"The stones aren't enough!"

"Don't want the stones," said Lymn. "If my days are numbered, I want something more comforting than rocks."

"I have a flute, a musical wind instrument, but it is at Asa's cabin."

"Naw," said Lymn. "I want ya to take my dog."

"What?"

"Them black things scare him. If they get in here, they'll tear him up. Don't want that to be my last sight. He'll be safe at The Meeting Place."

"I think I've misjudged you, Lymn," her voice softened.

"Is it a deal?" he demanded.

"If it is what you really want," agreed Nicole. "But reconsider. Even The Meeting Place will fall if Morrel and I are late. Wouldn't you rather your dog was here with you than with strangers? I think he would prefer it."

Lymn crouched and hugged his dog to him. He rubbed his neck and back. "All right. I'll take the stones. I'm counting on you to make sure they'll be of use to me someday. Now, we better get moving."

They headed off, the dog running ahead and waiting, running ahead and waiting. *At least he can give us warning*, thought Nicole. They met a fork in the road. Lymn stopped.

"This way's The Meeting Place. That way's to the bridge ya crossed."

"I didn't cross there. I crossed further back at the wooden footbridge."

"You *are* a crazy woman! Ya coulda fell to yer death."

242

"I'll take the other one back."

Lymn nodded. He pointed out trail marks whenever paths merged. He explained the landmarks at each path so that she would remember the way. Finally, they halted.

"This is the last fork before The Meeting Place. Straight ahead and ya'd be there in no time."

"Is there a building?" she asked.

"Yup, and a keeper guarding it. Only the chosen couple will get inside."

When they separated on the return trip, Lymn wished her well. Nicole broke into a jog. Night was falling as when she sighted Asa's house. She heard a grunt to her right. She ran, preparing the crossbow as she went. *They aren't going to get me when I've gone this far! s*he thought.

She reached the step and pounded on the door shouting for entrance. She whirled, ready to shoot anything that had followed. There was nothing there. Asa opened the door, and she stumbled inside.

Morrel was propped up on elbow, looking anxious. She hurried over and felt his forehead; it was cool, and the color in his face looked almost normal. He took her hand and frowned.

"You took a terrible chance," he said. "Asa wouldn't answer my questions, but when I asked for my pack and found the stones gone, I figured it out."

"I'm sorry I worried you," she said, kissing his forehead.

"If you had been killed," Morrel stopped, looking down at her hand in his.

"Oh, Morrel," said Nicole as she knelt by the bed. "I had to do this."

He nodded. "I am tired," he said.

"Lay down. Sleep."

"Stay with me," he said. "I've been too worried to sleep. Talk with me for a while."

"I don't have any more cormorant stories." She pulled a stool up beside the bed.

"You never cease to surprise me," he whispered. "Far beyond my expectations."

Nicole smiled and kissed his hand. "No one is more surprised than me. I haven't felt this alive in a long time."

"What happened to you, Nicole? Why did you turn away from life?"

"I don't know. I was a happy child. I felt loved and safe." She hesitated. "When Mom died, things changed. Then, the man I loved lied to me. Cheated on me. Broke my heart. It was just too much after the way Dad had changed. I guess I gave up on men."

"How did your father change?"

"At first, my Dad was angry all the time. He scared me. Then, he spent more and more time at work. I was always with babysitters, and later I spent a lot of time alone. When Dad met my stepmother, I thought things would get better. He did stop being angry, but he became more driven, like he had to prove something to her."

"How did your mother die?"

"In a car accident. She was killed by teenager speeding in his souped-up car."

Morrel pulled her to him. She rested her head lightly on his cheek, careful of all the bandages. Soon he was asleep.

The next day, Nicole helped Asa in the garden. They stayed fairly close to the house. The sky was overcast, and the air smelled dank.

Nicole ate lunch with Asa and then brought some soup and bread to Morrel. Asa had done wonders with his recovery. The fever had not returned.

"That was good," said Morrel as he passed her the empty bowl. "I'd appreciate more, if you have it. Asa is a good cook."

"I made it," said Nicole. "I learned to cook quite young."

"Beautiful, brave, and a good cook," said Morrel. "You are a rare woman."

Nicole laughed. Morrel studied her face.

"What?" she asked.

"Nothing," he said.

"No, what?" she insisted.

"I was wondering why you never met someone else after your fiancé."

Nicole stood and picked up the bowl.

"Do not be angry," said Morrel.

"I'm not. There's just a lot I haven't thought about lately." She smiled. "I've been kind of busy."

"When you go home, Nicole, bring some of Dawn's End with you. Do you know what I mean?"

"Yeah. I think I do." She nodded.

"How far to The Meeting Place?" asked Morrel.

"Less than a day."

"Good, we will go tomorrow," he announced.

"You can't be serious," said Nicole. "You'll start bleeding."

"We will go slowly. I am feeling stronger every minute. I suspect, when I used the bracelet, it kept me from bleeding to death. With Asa's excellent care, I should be able to handle a stroll."

"What about the dark things?" asked Nicole. "We'll be targets."

"Perhaps we could borrow Smokeweed and send him back when we get there," replied Morrel.

"I know Asa would lend him, but won't the riding hurt you, too?"

"Maybe you are right. We should wait another day." Morrel sighed and readjusted the quilt. "I hate being a patient."

"Well, you are," said Nicole. "So just relax and cooperate, and you'll heal faster. Put some trust in your healer and your nurse."

"Trust," said Morrel. "We cannot survive without it, can we, Nicole?"

"No," said Nicole. "It's scary, trusting again. But it's a lot less lonely."

246

Asa insisted that Morrel take at least two more days for recovery. Nicole told him not to argue with the doctor's orders. She did allow him to walk about the hut and sit on the front step. Besides, for all they knew, the Keeper of The Meeting Place might refuse them admittance without the third piece.

"You may be right," said Morrel. "Without the complete Key to Light, we may not be accepted."

"The Key to Light," said Nicole. "I never heard you call it that before."

"It has many names. The Key to Balance. The Key to Harmony. The Key to Self. I do not know which one is correct."

"Maybe they all are," said Nicole. "I wonder how Aubin is doing. He's probably up and about by now."

"I hope so," said Morrel. "I am anxious to see him. I think we can be good friends again."

"Why did you pull away from each other?"

"Misunderstandings. Aubin feeling second-best because I was older and chosen. He could have been the one just as easily, but, after the decision was made, he grew resentful. I think they did not choose him because he was unpredictable. I have always been rather steady." He shrugged.

"I think he's over it now."

"Yes," said Morrel. "It will be much better. I should have tried to reach him before we grew so far apart. It is as much my fault as his."

"It's hard to talk about things like that," said Nicole.

"But harder when you do not," he said.

Nicole nodded. "I need to have a long talk with my father when I get home."

"And start opening yourself up to other people, including men."

"Morrel, I can't talk to you about that."

"I envy whoever he will be," said Morrel. "I am as jealous as Aubin when I think of you with someone else, but it has to be."

"Does it? Couldn't I stay here?" she asked.

"No," said Morrel. "I'm not sure your people can survive here for long. I don't know how the food will affect you. I know you've eaten in our world, but we don't know the long-term effects of this world on you. Also, there is the time difference. I don't know if you will age the same as the rest of us."

"Asa's no different than me. Or Chas."

"They are. They were born here. We can't stay in your world because the food makes us ill. I think we each belong in our own worlds. You have to return home. But we will have The Meeting together first. Then, you must go."

"I won't be happy there," said Nicole.

"If you choose to be miserable and isolated again, you are right," said Morrel. "You will not be happy. You have so much to offer Nicole. I know it. You just need to know it. Do not be afraid to let it out. Look what you have accomplished here by trusting and by taking risks."

Nicole nodded. "I'll think about it," she said. "But first we'd better concentrate on making it to The Meeting Place tomorrow."

"Yes," he agreed. "We should sleep now. It will be a slow journey."

Morrel made better time than they anticipated. He used a crutch, but he kept a steady pace. Asa had stocked their food supply and given Morrel a packet of medication with powder from the Lilyvern to encourage his healing. They reached the last fork before midday meal.

Nicole fingered the two pieces of the key in her pocket and considered. *The keeper can't turn us back now. We've done our best. Look at what has already been sacrificed. At least, he'll have to let Morrel heal for a while before sending us away. He'd better provide some clues of his own if he expects us to know where to continue the search. I have to think positively. We're almost there. Soon we'll know if the price we've paid is for an empty package.*

Chapter Twenty-one—The Meeting

The Meeting Place was a stone structure of singular beauty in shades of pink and cream marble with a heavy beam roof. The door was of thick metal, embossed with a rising sun. It stood firm and solid, and resonated with a gentle glow. It was an island of peace in a turbulent forest. There was a subtle vibration of energy emitting from the place. Nicole knew the dark things would never gain admittance until the whole of Dawn's End had fallen.

The door was barred and locked. Morrel scratched on it, and then Nicole knocked.

"What should we do?" she said.

"Use your key," answered a thin voice. "If you have one."

The speaker stepped around the side of the building. He wore a milky white robe tied with a black sash and black short boots. His long, bedraggled beard was white, and his face lined. He smiled. "I am the Keeper of The Meeting Place. Reveal your bracelet, Alaric."

Morrel lifted his arm. The Keeper nodded.

"I am Alaric Morrel. This is my companion, Nicole Newman. She is from the outworld."

"Yes," said the old man. "You have been injured." He took a small vial containing purple fluid. "Two drops a day," he said as he passed it to Morrel. "The oil of the Lilyvern is more powerful than the powder."

"He has medication from Asa," said Nicole, concerned about mixing or overdosing on drugs.

"This will not harm him. It will erase all poison from his body. He does not need to use anymore of Asa's, although hers is a worthy substance."

The Keeper took a silver object from his pocket and inserted it in the door. The lock clicked. Nicole smiled at Morrel.

"Now your key," said the old man.

Nicole's smile faded. "I . . . . We only have two pieces," she said.

"Yet you came. Why?"

"We did not know where else to go," she said. "We thought it might be enough. Please. We've gone through so much to get here."

The Keeper held out his hand. Nicole unzipped her jacket pocket and took out the silver arrow and the gold half-moon. The Keeper took the arrow, inserted it in the lock, and turned it. The door clicked again and swung open. He handed the arrow back to Nicole.

Nicole helped Morrel in through the door. She turned to speak to the Keeper, but no one was there. "He's gone! I have a million questions."

"No matter," said Morrel. "We are inside. I am very tired."

The panther man slept on the twin chaise-lounge in the entrance room. He took two drops of the purple fluid. While Nicole explored, he melted into the furniture's unyielding surface like a relaxed cat

The floor plan resembled that of Morrel's house back in his village but on a larger scale. Everything was designed for a couple. Detailed paintings and wall hangings filled the rooms, romantic compositions of flowers, clouds, waterfalls, and animals. The sleeping room delighted Nicole. In contrast with the stark chamber in Morrel's home, the room was decorated in the Alaric colors, white and gold, with accents of black. It vibrated health and strength, with an undercurrent of sensuality. The double pallet was smothered in satiny quilts. Outside, an overhanging tree tattooed a rhythm of shade and light on the translucent ceiling.

Nicole pampered Morrel for the rest of the day. After a good night's sleep, she confronted him. "So, now what? We made it to The Meeting Place. I don't see an agenda. We're missing the third piece of the key, and we don't know what it's for anyway. What's the game plan here?"

"I'm not sure," admitted Morrel. "Grandfather just gave me hints. He said each couple had to design The Meeting according to their own needs."

"Okay. Here ye. Here ye. I hereby call this meeting to order," said Nicole. "First on the agenda, kisses."

She laughed and grabbed Morrel. He responded without hesitation. Nicole felt like a cactus finally reaching the rainy season. She drank up his kisses like water.

"How are you feeling, Morrel?" she asked.

"Mmm," he growled, biting her shoulder.

Nicole laughed. "You mustn't overdo it. Nobody heals that fast."

"A panther body aided by healers and wizards does. Come here."

He kissed her again, sending shocks of desire deep into her belly. Nicole ran her hands down his back, over the bandages. She felt him flinch and pulled away.

"Uh-uh," she said. "You're not as tough as you think you are."

Morrel smiled. "Guess not."

They spent the day inside. Morrel found a popular panther game containing circles and squares on a spiral board and taught it to Nicole. They played six times, Nicole winning only the last match.

"I think you let me win that," she pouted playfully. "Out of pity."

"Who me? Why would I ever pity a clever lady like you?"

At the sound of a scratch at the door, they exchanged glances. Nicole fetched their daggers. She flung open the door. On the step sat a bundle of food. No one was in sight.

"Must have been the Keeper," said Morrel as he unpacked the food.

"Social, isn't he?" commented Nicole.

"Well, now you have a chance to show off that great cooking skill you bragged about," he said.

"So. You're a chauvinist. I knew it all along," said Nicole.

Morrel laughed. "You cook today, and, if we live to see the end of it, I'll cook tomorrow."

Nicole gave his shoulder a small punch.

"Ohh," he moaned. "Hitting a wounded man."

"Why, Morrel," said Nicole. "I think I've been good for you. You're developing a sense of humor."

"You have been very good for me," he said, pulling her into a kiss.

That night, Nicole dreamed of Morrel. His wounds were healed. He waited for her under the quilts. She crawled in beside him and realized they were both naked.

Nicole was nervous. How did panther people make love? A woman from her world might be too tame, disappointing, but Morrel's eyes shone with joy. He ran his fingertips along her throat. She arched her neck as he bent to kiss it. His rich lips trailed across her cheek. She shivered. His strong hand stroked her breast. A wave of heat rolled down her spine as she ran her hands down his chest. She looked into his face and jerked back. It was Randy wearing a smirk.

Nicole woke feeling edgy. She climbed off the pallet and went to make breakfast. Morrel woke a little later, took his medication and joined her.

"I need a bath," she said. "They have a pump in the bathroom, but how do you heat the water? There's no fireplace."

"I don't know," said Morrel.

Nicole poured a little water from the bucket in the sink to prime the mechanism. On the third pump, steaming water gushed out. It smelled like minerals.

"Morrel!" she squealed. "It's hot." He came to the door. "How is that possible?" she asked.

"Hot springs," he said. "We have one a couple days' walk from my village. They have piped the water right into the house. Very clever."

"You bet," said Nicole. "I'm going to have a long soak. Look, there's liquid soap I think I can use for my hair. This is going to feel so good."

When she had finished, Morrel wanted a turn.

"Are you sure?" she asked. "You don't want to risk infection."

"Only two cuts are not healed shut," said Morrel. "One on my back and one on my thigh."

"You're kidding! That's incredible," said Nicole.

While Morrel splashed about, she found a set of drawings in a box on the shelf. The first was of a panther man and woman. The man, who was young in the picture, reminded Nicole of Alaric Bethane.

The next picture was of a panther man and a human woman. There were more pictures, each panther man looking more human as she dug down.

Morrel passed by on the way to the bedroom. He was wrapped in a large towel.

Then, the men in the pictures changed. They were bare-chested and had wings. They were the bird people. Nicole was fascinated. Further back, the pictures faded and yellowed, and were of bear people. These drawings were of all the couples who had met here to push back the night. If they succeeded, would the next picture be of Nicole and Morrel?

"Morrel," she shouted. "Look what I've found." He gave a muffled response. Nicole burst into the bedroom. Morrel was standing there, in his breeches, trying to bandage his back.

"Here, let me help," she said. She set the box down and wound the bandage around his chest and back. He smelled good, clean, and masculine. When she tied off the bandage, Morrel took her arm.

"Nicole, I want to tell you something."

"Wait, I want to show you these pictures," she said.

"No. Listen. This is hard for me. I want to take you back to your world."

"I know you will, when the quest is finished."

"No," he said. "Now. I have failed. We have just enough time to get you to safety before the night wins. I promised I would take you home, and I will. I have all my strength back."

Nicole looked into his sad eyes. "I don't want to go," she said.

"You have to."

"No," she said. "I want to stay here with you."

"You do not understand. It is the end of all."

"I do understand," she said. "I don't care."

"Nicole," he whispered, drawing her close. "Nicole. You cannot ask this of me. I have seen too many of those I love die. I cannot watch another."

"Do you love me, Morrel?"

He put his hand under her chin and looked into her eyes. "That is not for me to say. It would only bring us pain," he said.

"Then, don't say it. Show me how you feel," said Nicole.

Morrel groaned and pulled her to the pallet. They tumbled into the quilts, kissing, stroking, touching. Nicole suddenly stiffened.

"What?" he asked.

"Is there enough human in the panther people to impregnate a woman?" she asked.

"I don't know. Why?"

"I don't have any contraceptives," she said.

"What is that?"

Nicole explained. Morrel was dumbfounded. Panther women knew exactly when they were "in heat" and when they were not.

"It doesn't matter," said Nicole as she ran her fingers through his glossy black hair. "There's probably no risk."

Morrel pulled away. "This is not the kind of risk I wanted you to start taking," he said. He voice was strained.

"Morrel," she whispered.

He groaned and kissed her neck. He ran his rough cat-like tongue up into her ear. "Sweet, Nicole. I want you more than anything," he said. "I love you." Then, he left, the door clicking softly behind him.

"Morrel? Morrel? Damn it."

Outside, Dawn's End stirred. Pale green shoots poked up by the dead plants. Sap pulsed through the trees.

In a stench-filled den, a dark creature moaned. Crazed eyes rolled back in its head. The night beast fell over, thrashing. Skin tightened and cracked. Its features changed slowly. It moaned in pain. Black pus oozed from the animal's pores as its body shrank. Fangs and claws retreated to normal size. Armor flaked off it as its sides heaved with exertion.

It staggered to its feet, shook. Clear, brown eyes shone from a bewildered face. The animal wrinkled its nose at the strange smell. It lumbered off in search of a new den, pausing to sniff at an interesting, pale green plant.

Morrel sat cross-legged in the meditation room. Nicole looked in once. He sat as still as a statue of stone. She did not know what to say.

Evening enfolded Dawn's End in a peaceful cloak. The animal glanced at the sable sky as hoary stars appeared. The air was cool and fresh. The animal breathed deeply and then waddled through the undergrowth. Night felt different.

Inside the Meeting Place, Nicole prepared a meal. For the first time in her life, she had trusted someone enough to give herself completely, and he turned her down.

Why? she wondered. *I know he wanted me. I guess the risk of pregnancy meant as much to him as to me. Come to think of it, it wouldn't be fair for him to never know if I had conceived a child, if he had a baby in my world. But I think there's*

258

something else. I just can't put my finger on it. It can't be
because I'm human.

She ate alone and then knocked on the meditation room door.

"There's food on the table if you want it," she said. "I'm going to bed."

She pulled the pallets apart, thinking of Shandri as she did. A small metal object fell out from under the pallet. Nicole picked it up. She gasped and then ran into the kitchen. Morrel was eating.

"Look!" She placed the gold half-moon on the table in front of him.

Morrel picked it up, his eyes widening.

"I'll get the other two pieces," said Nicole. She ran for her jacket. Morrel handed her back the piece when she returned. She laid the two gold half-moons and silver arrow on the table like pieces of a puzzle.

"It is the opposite of the other," said Morrel.

Nicole examined the back of the silver arrow and then snapped one of the gold shapes onto it. Laughing, she snapped the second in place.

"One side has a moon, and one has a star," she said.

"The spiral's spin in opposite directions," said Morrel. "What is it?"

Nicole stared at the shape and then nodded. "Yin and yang. It's a symbol from Oriental philosophy, from my world, held together by the silver arrow."

"But what does it mean?"

"Positive and negative. Male and female. Yield and push. Dark and light." They looked at each other. "Dark and light, day and night, balance, and harmony. That's it."

They scrambled to the door and raced outside.

"It's dark," moaned Nicole.

"No," said Morrel. "It's late. It should be dark. But listen. I've been feeling something, but I thought it was my imagination. Things are changing. For the better, I mean."

The trees swayed as a breeze passed. A night bird called.

"Listen. Smell," said Morrel as he inhaled deeply.

"Fresh," said Nicole. "Like spring. There are birds too. Well, how about that?"

They joined hands and sat down on the front step. They stayed in the gentle night until dawn came, early as it should.

Chapter Twenty-two—In the Light

Nicole and Morrel watched the sun rise over a healing land. They smiled as morning birds fluttered about and a small furry creature scuttled threw the grass. Then, they went indoors and collapsed on the pallets. As much from relief as from tiredness, they slept for more than half the day.

"Get up!" coaxed Morrel. "I want you to see Dawn's End as it was meant to be."

Nicole moaned and rubbed her eyes.

"Get washed and comb your hair," he ordered. "It looks like a prickle bush."

"Well, excuse me," said Nicole as she stood.

Morrel had breakfast on the table when Nicole finished grooming. She ate quickly, anxious to be out in the sunshine.

They spent the rest of the day watching buds unfurl and grass literally grow beneath their feet. They wandered the blossoming fields. White, brown, gray, and yellow birds fluttered about singing songs of courtship. Soft mammals with soft eyes and tickly whiskers peered out at them. Wild flowers burst forth in abundance.

"How could this happen so fast?" said Nicole.

"Magic!" shouted Morrel. "Beautiful, wonderful, magic."

He swung her around and kissed her. They pulled slowly apart, studying each other's faces.

"We have to talk," said Nicole.

"I know. We have to talk about The Meeting and Dawn's End and your fiancé and the key and us. It is all webbed together."

They sat on the grass. Nicole traced the petals of a small pink flower with her finger. She would start with the less painful questions. "Why was the third piece of the key under the pallet?"

"It was between us," said Morrel.

"Okay. Between us."

"No," said Morrel. "The final key to the completion of balance was *between* us."

Nicole frowned. "Are all the answers this enigmatic?"

"Probably," said Morrel. "I figured out a few yesterday, but I may never understand it all."

"Fair enough. It comes back to 'why me?' though. I still don't understand that."

"You were withdrawn, isolated deliberately from emotion, afraid to trust or to take risks, turning into a man-hater, when you started the quest."

"Uh-huh."

"Would you say you were still like that yesterday?" asked Morrel.

"No. I was the opposite." Nicole nodded. "I see. The opposite."

"Now you have seen both sides," said Morrel. "Now you can make balanced choices. I think, because I'm not human, you were able to half-convince yourself this wasn't real. That let

262

you open up, the way you wouldn't with a man in your world."

"I still have moments when I think I'm dreaming," said Nicole. "But I see what you mean. A panther man was able to get under my radar. What about you? How did you change?"

"I have always prided myself on my self-control. I was almost arrogant about it. I can see why Aubin was sickened by me. Yet, underneath, I had all the passions of a panther. I needed to see those passions, recognize them, and accept them. That's where you came in. I guess an outworlder was able to get 'under my radar' too."

"I see."

"Lord, Nicole. I have wanted you since the first day I saw you. I have been suppressing it, distracting myself. Then, last night, when I recognized that I could have you and that you wanted me, that you could be the greatest passion of my life, I realized that was the panther way. Not to think past the moment. Suddenly, I felt completely human. I could not do that to you. The pregnancy thing, that was just a reminder that being intimate with you would have hurt you in the long run. I realized I loved you more than that. Too much to bring you harm."

"You wanted our love to be more than physical, so it wasn't," said Nicole. "That's pretty ironic. But, also, amazingly wonderful."

"Thank you, Nicole," he said. "I have tried so hard to cling to that which is human in me, to not give in to my base instincts."

"I think you overestimate the human male, darling."

"I care for you, Nicole, deeply. I would never want to hurt you."

"Now that we have that out of the way, I need you to realize something. I *want* to be intimate with you, whatever the risks. You taught me to take risks, remember. You can't tell me not to when I could finally get something I want for myself."

"What happens tomorrow?"

"Tomorrow?"

"When I bring you back to your world."

"Not tomorrow."

"Yes. You cannot stay here any longer. It is dangerous. We don't know what living here will do to you. Should you start to sicken, I may not be able to get you back. The door is not always available."

Nicole swore. "I finally find someone I could love and trust, and I have to leave."

"There are others worthy of love, others who would be good for you."

"But I want to be with you."

"That, too, was part of your quest," he said, "to open yourself up to someone when it was risky. To know how it felt. To care for the safety of others—people you didn't know—more than your own. Now, you need to take what you have learned back to your real life."

Nicole tugged at a patch of grass.

"Now, you are ready to take a risk with someone again." He raised his hand as Nicole opened her mouth to speak. "Someone human, I mean."

"Do you think I'm just going to bounce from your arms into some other guy's?"

"I think you are ready to give love a chance. A real chance." He smiled. "But perhaps you should forgo the bouncing."

Nicole snorted. "All right. If I say I will try, someday, will you stop talking about it?"

"Yes."

That night, Nicole played the flute for Morrel. They looked at the pictures of previous couples, Nicole noticing sadness in the many of the women's eyes. They sang "A Hole in My Bucket" until they dissolved into laughter. Morrel recited some of his favorite poems. Nicole told him faerie tales from her childhood. She stopped part way through Anderson's *Snow Queen* and started to sniffle.

"What is it?" said Morrel.

"Shandri loves you, you know."

"What?" said Morrel, bewildered by her train of thought.

"She does. She's still too young, of course, but you should be aware of it."

"I don't want to think of anyone else," said Morrel.

"Double standard," said Nicole. She gave a half-laugh. "Can we spend one more day here? Please?"

"Then we have to go, straight to the door."

"Okay."

"No arguing then, promise?"

"I promise."

"Nicole, will you be my betrothed? Just for one day. I am sure the bonds will not count once you return to your own world. But, for one day, I want you to be mine. Only and all mine. I love you."

"Are you asking me to marry you?"

"Something like that," he replied.

"I guess this will be our honeymoon then," she said.

"Is that a yes?"

"Yes. But how? Don't we need a minister or someone?"

"No. It is not necessary. You just repeat what I say."

"All right."

They faced each other, holding hands.

"Nicole, I choose you as my mate, my companion, and my wife for the rest of this existence." He smiled. "Now you."

"Morrel, I choose you as my mate, my companion, and my husband for the rest of this existence."

"Now, we kiss," said Morrel.

"Oh, I like this part," replied Nicole as she reached up to meet his lips with her own. A sweet, yearning flooded through her body.

"That's it," said Morrel.

"Really? Can I add something?" she asked.

Morrel nodded.

"I love you, Morrel, now and forever. No matter where I go, you will always be part of my heart. You don't have to repeat that."

Morrel smiled. "I love you, Nicole, now and forever. No matter where you go, you will always be part of my heart."

He swayed a little as he ended this.

"You're still not one-hundred-percent well," exclaimed Nicole. "You need to rest for a while. Back to bed, sweetheart."

"Mmm," said Morrel.

"Not yet," chided Nicole.

The next morning, Nicole went for a walk before Morrel woke. He had breakfast ready when she returned.

"Let's have a picnic," she said.

"What's that?"

"Go for a walk. Lay out a blanket and eat."

Morrel laughed. "After all the meals we have eaten outdoors?"

"But it's different now," protested Nicole. "Spring is in the air. I want to watch the green things grow."

"All right."

Nicole insisted on preparing the food alone. She rolled up a thin quilt and took some items from her pack. They walked to the river and watched the otters playing. Then they headed for the clearing behind The Meeting Place and laid out the blanket near the well. They stretched out on their backs and watched the wispy clouds weave across a robin's egg sky. Nicole wriggled over and rested her head on Morrel's massive shoulder.

"No bandage?" she said.

"Completely healed."

"Amazing." She kissed his ear then traced it with her tongue. Morrel did not move. She blew into it.

"I don't think you should do that," said Morrel, sitting up.

Nicole grabbed his shoulder and pushed him back. She climbed on to his chest. "I disagree."

"Nicole," he said. "This is cruel."

"No, it's foreplay." She kissed him, exploring his sharp teeth with her tongue. He sat up, flinging her to the edge of the blanket. "I went to see the Keeper today," she said as he bent to gather up their things. "He gave me something to prevent an accidental pregnancy." Morrel straightened slowly. He looked into her eyes.

"Are you sure?" he said. "I still have to bring you back tomorrow."

"I'm sure. I want you, Morrel. I want just this one day to feel that total surrender to the man I love. Completely. We will never have another chance. There are no guarantees. What if this is my only chance to feel like this? At the very least, I want to have this memory until I am an old, forgetful crone."

"Will it not make it harder to say goodbye?" asked Morrel.

"It can't get any harder."

Morrel gave a deep groan and gathered her into his arms. He bit her softly under the edge of her jaw and then ran his rough tongue down her throat to the top of her shirt. Nicole ran her fingers through his hair, pulling him close.

They undressed each other, slowly, with wonder. Nicole kissed each scar. With sweet gentleness, they formed and reformed into each other. Nicole burned for him, and he fed her fire until she blazed up in an explosion of pleasure and happiness. Then, they continued, this time quick and wild, Nicole's sounds matching Morrel's growls and final roar of ecstasy.

Afterwards, they cuddled, damp and sticky, Morrel's head resting on her stomach.

"We need a bath," said Nicole.

"That will take too long," moaned Morrel. "I am starving. We can wash by the well."

He drew up a bucket and set it on the stones. Nicole fetched two pieces of soap and towels from the building.

"We could go inside and use the tub," she said.

"Whatsa matter? Soft?" said Morrel.

"Why Morrel, I've totally corrupted you. You're teasing and speaking slang. You've lost all your dignity."

Morrel grinned and took soap. He dipped it into the bucket. "Wash first. Then we'll rinse." His grin widened.

Nicole dipped her soap and covered her arm with suds.

"Not like that," said Morrel. "You wash me, and I'll wash you."

Nicole smiled and accommodated him. Morrel soaped his hands and slid them over her, producing shivers of delight. Nicole responded in kind. Soon, they were lathered from head to foot, each bubble a testament to arousal. Morrel pressed her bottom up against the well and growled gently into her ear. Nicole wrapped a leg around his back. He pushed forward. She pulled him into her. Washing was postponed while fresh desires were satisfied. They slid over each other like otters. The soap dried to a crust on their skins.

It took two buckets of water to rinse Nicole clean. She squealed from the cold and danced about. With a gleam of sweet vengeance, she rinsed Morrel. His hairy body clung to the soap, while she repeatedly scrubbed and doused him with the chilled water. He clamped his teeth and looked her straight in the eye, steadfast after the first gasp of shock.

Toweled dry, they dressed quickly. Nicole, like Morrel, kept her feet bare. The new grass was pleasantly alive underfoot. She felt anchored.

The next morning came all too soon. Nicole almost resented the short night. Morrel laid out a new route.

"The journey back will be much quicker," Morrel explained. "I do not want to be slowed by grateful friends."

"I understand," said Nicole. "But I have to confess, I wouldn't mind stalling. When I went to the keeper, he reminded me that life is a journey, not a destination. A cliché, I know, but one with wisdom I had forgotten. It was by our journey that I fell in love with you, Morrel. Although I am so grateful that we made it to The Meeting on time, what I learned about myself on the way here was as important. But I don't really understand what you learned."

"I have always been afraid to surrender to my emotions. Afraid that the beast would take over and that I would deliberately, in anger, or accidentally, in lust, harm someone greatly. By the well, with you, I learned I could surrender to love and lose myself in another without becoming dangerous. I never wanted anyone as much as I wanted you, but I didn't have to struggle with being gentle. I was afraid a human woman would be so fragile that I would break her, but I didn't even think about it when we made love. Everything just unfolded as it should."

"You would never hurt me, Morrel. I know that."

Morrel squeezed her hand. They cleaned up The Meeting Place and put the third piece of the key under the pallet.

"I don't know what else to do with it," said Morrel.

They stepped out into the morning sun. Nicole locked the door with the silver arrow. The Keeper appeared as they stepped away from the door.

"Dark Morrel and light Nicole," he said, "I come to thank you."

They nodded holding hands. "Thank you," said Nicole.

The Keeper smiled. "You have met the quest like no other before you. You both placed yourselves in danger repeatedly for the sake of others.

"Morrel has suffered severe physical injury. He has lost his grandfather and his calia. He risked more to save his cousin, one he had grown away from, and in doing so gathered him back into the side of light. He resisted animal urges in favor of true love.

"Nicole has grown immeasurably, spiritually and emotionally. She has come out of her own darkness, bringing light to everyone who has met her in Dawn's End, by her presence and by her acts of courage and sacrifice.

271

"Now, you both prepare to sacrifice the personal joy you have found on your quest. I bow to your enlightenment."

Nicole and Morrel smiled awkwardly, not knowing how to respond.

"You have already seen the proper balance of night and day return to our land," said the Keeper. "You have watched the plants renew and the animals freed of the dark burdens. This will last a long, long time because you have exceeded our expectations. The black crystal has paled to pure clarity. Dawn's End will live in balance for many generations.

"Go in peace, Alaric Morrel of the Stone and Esteemed Nicole Newman of the Stone. Know that your love and sacrifice has brought salvation to you both and to an entire world."

He bowed again and then left. The return journey began amid the songs of mating birds.

Chapter Twenty-three—New Journeys

"Are you sure a few more days in Dawn's End would be risky?" asked Nicole as they hiked across country.

"I don't know the long-term effect of our food and air upon your body," said Morrel. "Besides, the door does not remain stationary. It may move at any time. Then, we would have to search for it, and you might come out on the opposite side of your world. Or it may disappear completely for many years."

"Could that have happened when you were in my world?" said Nicole.

"Probably not," he said. "It tends to stay for at least a few seasons in the same spot. But I do not wish to take any unnecessary risks now that the quest is complete."

"What if something delays us, like Gaul and his brothers?" asked Nicole.

"I will not allow that to happen. If I have to, I will call upon the power of the stone. I am learning to use the bracelet with more control. Nothing can stop us."

"I hate the idea of you using it again," said Nicole. "You've used it too many times already."

"I will not be rash."

That night, they built a large, cozy fire at their campsite. Morrel explained they would be in no danger from the dark. Any natural animal would stay away, and there had been no sign of remaining dark creatures. They curled up together under the large cloak.

Nicole dreamed of a child with curly brown hair. He took Nicole's hand and said, "Mommy." She awoke with a memory of large, trusting eyes. Morrel was watching her.

"It is a foreshadowing of a possible future," he said. "If you bring what you have learned in Dawn's End into your own world, you could be happy. You would be a wonderful mother."

"Without you?" said Nicole.

"I will be with you in every good dream," said Morrel. "But you must choose to live a full life this time. A life with an entrusting heart. You must open your own doors."

"I don't want to be without you," said Nicole.

Morrel smiled. "The Esteemed Nicole Newman of the Stone. Charmer of faerie queens. Out-bargainer of The Hoarder. Solver of riddles. Lone traveler through dangerous country. Companion of panther men." He squeezed her hand. "Do not lose sight of your true courage. Do not slip back into the woman I called."

She hugged him tightly. "You, too, Morrel. I suspect you aren't as tough about all this as you pretend."

They reached the door at midday.

"You'll have to take it off," said Nicole, holding out the arm with her bracelet.

Morrel shook his head. "There are too many bracelets, used lightly," he said. "I, too, visited once with the wizard. I want you to keep the bracelet. It will be safe from abuse with you. Only a chosen few will know where it is gone in case it is needed again."

"Thank you," said Nicole, as she ran her fingers over the panther's outline. "It will lose its power in a few hours, I suppose."

"Yes. No one can use it in your world."

Nicole touched the black crystal. "Could I have used it when we were under attack to fight the dark things?"

"I never wanted to leave you scarred in any way," said Morrel. "You carry too many scars already."

"I didn't know how to work it. What do you have to do?" she asked.

"Concentrate. Visualize what you want to happen."

Nicole touched her lip, remembering her father. "Would it have affected any children I might have?"

"Yes. Each time the effect would intensify. Once, it might be as subtle as darker hair or slightly extra speed when running. Repeatedly, the effects would be more noticeable. Undesirable."

Nicole nodded. "So, when you open this door for me, that'll happen to you again."

"This will be the last time," said Morrel.

"You said it left you drained when I came through the first time. Will you be all right?"

"Do not worry," he answered. "It was because I had to hold it for so long. I have become an expert at handling the disorientation. Now, you must stop stalling. It is time to go."

Nicole's eyes stung as she looked into his somber face. She would never see it again, only in dreams. Even there, it might fade in time. She threw herself into his arms and kissed him fiercely. They clung together. Slowly, Morrel loosened her grip.

"Good-bye, Nicole. Sweet dreams."

She shook her head, unable to speak.

"Go home," he said, "but make it a home of warmth this time."

Nicole sniffed and nodded. "I love you," she whispered.

Morrel ran his hand through his hair and looked into the sunny sky, trying to control his emotions. While he was distracted, Nicole stepped back into the haze, turned and placed her right hand over her bracelet and closed her eyes in concentration.

"Nicole, no!" cried Morrel.

The haze drew itself into a bright arch. Nicole smiled through the tears. She turned and walked quickly under. The world spun. Before she collapsed face down in the grass, she heard Morrel's voice. "I love you, too." She dreamed of the dark man.

Queen Melita greeted Morrel respectfully. "We apologize for our behavior before, Alaric Morrel. We do not know what came over us to be so possessive of an object of the big people. Truly, we are not usually so grasping."

"I suspect the darkness was touching you as well," said Morrel. "No offense is taken. Many in this land were not themselves when the crystal darkened."

"That must be it," said the faerie queen. "We are relieved it has been stopped. We already feel more ourselves. Rest assured, we will care for it dutifully and return it to your people when next it is needed."

Morrel returned to The Hoarder's cave. The hunched old man refused to see him. Morrel left the silver arrow at the entrance of the cavern in which they'd met with Nicole.

He gave Aubin the vial from the wizard, which still held a few drops of healing enhancer. A bevy of panther ladies pampered and fussed over the white panther man.

"What can I do?" laughed Aubin. "They enjoy helping me. I cannot deny them their pleasure." He winked.

"I am relieved to see you back to your old self," said Morrel.

"My old, old self," said Aubin. "The one who was your faithful and trusted cousin."

"Of course," said Morrel. "And, when you are well enough, we shall fish again together, like we did when we were younger."

"I look forward to it," said Aubin.

Later, Morrel sat in his meditation room. Peace of mind seemed elusive. Someone scratched at the door. He sighed and bade them enter.

"I hate to disturb you," said his mother. "But a traveler named Lymn has left something for you. He insisted I give it to you right away. He said he got it from The Hoarder."

277

Alaric Sabella left the small black bundle in the doorway of the meditation room. Morrel stared at it for a long time before standing.

He unwrapped the bundle as gently as a father undressing his newborn. There, on the black cloth, was a swirl of flame and earth. Morrel gathered a cluster and trailed its softness across his lips. They tingled at the touch. The long, auburn hair still smelled like Nicole.

Nicole woke in the damp grass, her face smudged. Her clothes were wet and wrinkled. She pulled herself onto her knees and looked around. Mist rose from the pond while the birds glided over the placid surface. Patches of morning fog played hide-and-seek through the woods and marsh plants.

Did I dream it all? she thought. *Am I nothing but a silly grown-up Alice in Wonderland?*

She brushed off her clothes and saw the bracelet. She smiled.

She walked to the parking lot, passing no one. Her car was still there. She retrieved her key and once again checked for her personal things. She drove home feeling as though she'd spent the night on an airplane and was suffering from jet lag.

Her letterbox was stuffed with envelopes and flyers. She checked the date on the television. It was Thursday morning, five days since she had returned to help rescue Aubin. She sorted through the mail. It was all bills and junk.

She telephoned the book store manager and apologized for quitting on such short notice. "I've been going through a lot lately," she said.

"Why didn't you talk to me about it? I didn't realize you were having difficulties. We could have tweaked your schedule to give you what you needed," he said.

"I don't know," she said. "I'm not very good about talking things out. But I'm going to change. I need to get more involved in things I care about. I'll need to keep my job after all."

"Good for you," he said. "You're one of my best employees."

"Thank you. That's decent of you," said Nicole. "You could actually help me with my first idea."

Together, Nicole and her manager devised a plan whereby customers could, by paying a little extra on their bills, sponsor bright, new books to be sent to reservations in the far north. Nicole found a fly-in fishing company that was willing to ship boxes when space was available. The bookstore received numerous drawings and thank you notes from children and teachers.

A friend of her stepmother, Gloria, was retiring from teaching. She asked Nicole if any of the northern schools could use her materials. Nicole called the principal of one of the schools and asked. After picking through the materials and shipping north what would be of use, she realized there must be a couple dozen teachers retiring each year. She approached the teachers' federations and asked if they would send a newsletter on her behalf asking for their teaching materials. Most teachers were thrilled to be rid of the boxes and shelves of posters, guidebooks, children's books, and activities. Nicole sent more materials north and then arranged a giant yard sale the first weekend after school began, attracting new and young teachers who took most of the remaining items. She used the money to buy science equipment for reservation schools.

Over the summer, Nicole volunteered in a senior citizen's home, sometimes taking the elders on simple outings, other times reading to them or helping them complete routine tasks. She discovered one man in his seventies, Carl, was not only sound of mind but bored and lonely. He had lost two legs to severe diabetes and was in fragile health but yearned to be of service. By contacting a local literacy group and providing an introduction, Nicole arranged for a recent immigrant to partner with Carl who helped him improve his English speaking and writing skills. It was delightful to watch improvement in both his progress and Carl's sense of worth.

In spite of this, Nicole felt disconnected. Her relationship with her father and stepmother remained courteous but distant. She tried talking to her father about her feelings after her mother's death and the way they had grown apart afterward. He seemed bewildered and uncomfortable. She realized he would have to figure it out for himself.

She had no interest in dating. The bracelet never left her wrist. She felt as though she was waiting for something, but unable to say what.

While biking one autumn day, she spotted a tall, dark, broad-shouldered man ahead on the path, and her heart leapt in her chest. When he stepped aside to allow her to pass, she stared longingly into his face. That evening, she cried herself to sleep. Yes, Morrel had taught her to trust again, but he had also stolen her heart. There was also another complication, one she had not thought possible. There was only one solution.

She slept with one hand over the bracelet, dreaming of him and Dawn's End, calling his name and visualizing his face. When she woke, she experienced a bizarre moment when she expected him to be standing there. Her next day off, she drove to the pond and picked her way through the path to where she thought the door had been. The leaves had fallen from the trees and crackled underfoot. When a blue jay flew by, she shouted out "Larina!" before she remembered the little calia was dead. Despondent, she turned to go. A light flashed behind her, and she whirled back, her heart fluttering wildly.

There stood Shandri, or a more mature version of her at least. Nicole remembered that the months in her world would be years in Dawn's End. Shandri was a full grown woman and very pregnant.

"Hello, Nicole," she said. "I felt your call last night. I imagine you were trying to contact Morrel, but he would have been blocking you. You must have also been thinking of me. I have wanted to contact you for a while, to get you up to date."

"Oh," said Nicole. "I can see that there have been big changes for you."

Shandri rubbed her large belly and smiled. "Yes, we are growing our own little Alaric."

Tears stung Nicole's eyes. "Congratulations. I wish only the best for you and Morrel."

"Morrel?" Shandri replied. "Oh, no. I am mated with Aubin."

"Aubin!"

"Yes, I know it seems hard to believe that he would settle for one woman, but he has changed since you last saw him. He is happier, less driven, and content. This will be our second child."

"Oh," Nicole sighed with relief. "I am afraid to ask . . . . "

"What of Morrel?"

Nicole nodded, biting her lip.

"He was already mated and unavailable to me."

Nicole turned her head away, quickly brushing the tears off that spilled onto her cheeks. "Who is she?" she whispered. "Do I know her?"

"Very well, I would hope," replied Shandri. "He told us all the two of you had completed the mating ritual at The Meeting."

"Oh! But I thought he would find another after I left," said Nicole.

Shandri shook her head. "He will never find another. You live in his heart, and there is no room for anyone but you." She smiled. "That is why I responded to your summons. I need to know why you called."

"I still love him!" blurted Nicole. "I will always love him. I don't want to live without him. No matter what I do, I can't fill the void. I want to go back."

"There may be risks," said Shandri. "We have never had anyone from your world stay very long."

"I drank the water and ate the food," countered Nicole, "and I was fine. I really don't think I am in danger. I'm willing to risk it."

"But I do not believe Morrel is," said Shandri.

"It's *my* life, *my* choice," insisted Nicole.

Shandri nodded. "So it is. Are you ready to leave now?"

"Yes!" said Nicole. "No . . . wait. I can't just disappear. My parents and the police would look for me."

"Then, I will be back soon," said Shandri. "Make your preparations."

"Do you mean it?" cried Nicole. "You'll come back for me."

"As long as the door is still here," said Shandri. "I had a little difficulty opening it. I think it is fading."

"No! Damn!" said Nicole. "I'll be back in a couple of hours."

"I will try my best," said Shandri.

Nicole wrote a letter to her parents saying she had been accepted to work in Africa. There had been a last minute cancellation, and she must fill in immediately or her chance would be gone. She would be going where there was no telephone or email and did not know when she would ever be able to contact them. She told them she loved them and not to worry. She packed two suitcases of things she might want or need in Dawn's End and took a cab to the park.

Fortunately, no one saw her enter the trail and later head off into the woods carrying two suitcases and a packsack. She waited in the same spot Shandri had entered. Two hours passed, then three, and then four. She consumed a lunch she had brought in preparation. Time passed, the park darkened, and Nicole began to despair. *What if the door had moved somewhere else? Or disappeared? How would she know? How long could she sit here before she ran out of food?* She had brought a parka, mittens, and a wool hat in case she had to stay all night. There was heavy frost most mornings. She should have brought more food; she only had two more meals. She decided to eat only once a day.

When darkness came, Nicole wished she was able to light a fire. However, so close to the edge of the park, she might attract unwanted attention. She pulled on an extra pair of socks and her winter clothing. She cut boughs of evergreens to spread on the cold earth, also piling some over her body for warmth. Soon, she could see her breath crystallizing in the air.

"She'll come for me," Nicole whispered to herself. "She has to."

Eventually, she dozed off, one hand clasped over the wrist where she wore the panther bracelet below layers of clothing. She dreamed of Morrel, his sweet smile, his warmth, and his passion.

"Nicole," his voice was husky with emotion, warm against her cheek. She sighed. "Nicole!" Her eyes snapped open. His deep brown eyes met hers. He was down on one knee beside her.

"It's much nicer on the other side of the door," said Morrel.

With a squeal, Nicole sat up and threw her arms around him, knocking him off balance and pulling him down on top of her.

"You might want to wait for that until we're some place warmer," he said, laughing as she covered his face in kisses.

" *You* came for me!" she exclaimed.

284

"Shandri told me everything," he said. "Are you sure you want to do this?"

"More sure of this than of anything in my life."

"But I'm not. What if you become ill? I don't know what effect the water and food will have on you over time."

"Oh, Morrel, honey, if you only knew what has been done to the water and food in my world, you would be more worried about me staying here."

Morrel frowned.

Nicole squeezed his arm. "Didn't Shandri tell you that I'm not happy? Is that how you want me to spend the rest of my life?"

"No, of course not."

"I brought a few things," she said, pointing to her packsack and suitcases.

"A few?" Morrel smiled.

"Well, I'm assuming this is a one-way trip," said Nicole as she shrugged on her pack sack and reached for a suitcase.

"Oh, and I'm bringing something else as well. Shandri and I have something in common." She rubbed her hand over her belly and grinned.

Morrel's mouth dropped open in shock. "But, the wizards . . . ."

"Apparently, they don't know as much about human contraceptives as they think," she said. "How do you feel about this?"

Morrel threw back his head and gave a roar that caused every animal within hearing to scurry for cover. It made the hair on Nicole's neck stand at attention.

"So, is that a good thing then?" she asked.

He laughed, deep and booming, then picked up a suitcase in one hand and held hers in the other. They took two steps forward as a light blazed around them.

~The End~

Other Adult Books by Bonnie Ferrante

Poisoned - Dawn's End Book 2

Outworld Apocalypse - Dawn's End Book 3

Bouquet - Short Stories with a Buddhist Scent

Inhale - Short Story Collection

Terror at White Otter Castle - young adult novella

My Ass - play on words humor

Learn more about Bonnie and her books online at
BonnieFerrante.ca

Check out her author page on Amazon or Goodreads.

Follow (@Bonnie Ferrante on Twitter.

Connect on Linkedin, or Pinterest.

Follow her Facebook pages:

Bonnie Ferrante - Author

Bonnie Ferrante - Books for Children

www.ingramcontent.com/pod-product-compliance
Lightning Source LLC
Chambersburg PA
CBHW060542180626
46817CB00002B/696